Stories on the Four Winds

Stories on the Four Winds

Ngā Hau e Whā

EDITED BY BRIAN BARGH AND ROBYN BARGH

First published in 2016 by Huia Publishers
39 Pipitea Street, PO Box 12280
Wellington, Aotearoa New Zealand
www.huia.co.nz

ISBN 978-1-77550-306-4

Copyright © The Authors 2016

The authors have asserted their rights to be identified as the author
of their respective works.

Cover images:
Ceramic swan © Gilmanshin/Shutterstock.com
Compass © Huia Publishers
Te Rauparaha and Te Rangikoaea © Andrew Burdan
Palm tree © Chuck Wagner/Shutterstock.com
Man and child with tricycle © Dubova/Shutterstock.com
Bicycle © pzAxe/Shutterstock.com
Child with moko © Soldiers Rd Portraits
Young woman © Soldiers Rd Portraits
Picture frames © 501room/Shutterstock.com
Wall and back cover image © Robert Kneschke/Shutterstock.com

This book is copyright. Apart from fair dealing for the purpose of private study, research, criticism or review, as permitted under the Copyright Act, no part may be reproduced by any process without the prior permission of the publisher.

Printed in China by Wai Man Bookbinding Ltd

A catalogue record for this book is available from the National Library of New Zealand.

The assistance of the Māori Literature Trust is gratefully acknowledged

CONTENTS

Introduction		vii
Briar Grace-Smith	*A Small Light*	1
Terence Rissetto	*Delirium Tremors*	9
Albert Wendt	*Fast*	19
Paula Morris	*Three Princesses*	49
Alice Tawhai	*Killing Ginger*	61
James George	*Moontide*	73
Jacquie McRae	*Time*	93
Eru J Hart	*May Board*	105
Helen Waaka	*The Apology*	119
Patricia Grace	*Hey Dude*	131
Toni Pivac	*The Tree House*	139
K-t Harrison	*That Last Summer*	155
Anya Ngawhare	*Byron and the Bastard Blues*	167
Renée	*This Day Was Different*	183
Albert Wendt	*Neighbours*	193
Ann French	*Pointing the Bone*	211
Tina Makereti	*Frau Amsel's Cupboard*	227
Piripi Evans	*Late Antiquity*	241
Mark Sweet	*Trust*	261
Terence Rissetto	*Morningslide for Life*	269
The Authors		283

Introduction

Life is full of surprises. After twenty-five years of publishing, we asked the best of our storytellers to give us something that would surprise us and you, the reader. This collection is the result of our invitation. These are stories told with humility, humour and a good dose of irreverence – for the whānau, the Church, the authorities and contemporary obsessions with self-image. They are stories that weave values of manaakitanga and utu. And above all, these are stories of aroha – for whānau and 'āiga, for those who have passed on to the spiritual world of our ancestors, for the nostalgia of old age, and of the gritty reality of aroha mixed up with violence and social injustice.

Huia Publishers continues to be a proud discoverer of new writing talent in New Zealand; many of the authors in this collection began their publishing with us and have become established literary identities.

BRIAN BARGH AND ROBYN BARGH

A Small Light

BRIAR GRACE-SMITH

None of them had expected Toi to be any good as a weaver, because, like his body, his fingers were short and square. But sensing the need for this man to hold onto something with long roots, the women had one day introduced Toi to a stand of flax.

There were many things Toi liked about flax, starting with the way it made him feel when he was cocooned inside its cool cathedral of leaves, listening to the hollow clatter they made in the wind. And the press and slide of the mussel shell against the dull underbelly of the leaf, forcing the greenness to fall away and reveal the silken wefts inside. Then, at the end of the day, when the women had gone home, Toi liked to stand with his bare feet flat against the wooden floor and breathe in the bittersweet smell that the flax left behind.

But while the women were impressed to meet a man who loved flax as much as Toi did, they believed that his desire to weave was transitional. Each morning when he turned up at the space, they would look up from whatever they might be weaving, their mouths slightly open in surprise. Then after a second or two of taking him in, the snap, crackle and flick of flax would continue. Not one of them imagined that in two years, Toi's wedge-shaped fingers would be outtwisting, outbending and outknotting all of theirs.

But now here he was, Toi. Circled by loud, laughing women weavers, in a room earthy with the smell of muka, weaving a kākahu made from feathers of the purest black.

Before Toi's fingers found the rhythm that came with making patterns – the over one, under one weave of taki tahi; the over two, under two weave of taki rua; the stairways of poutama and the canine peaks of niho taniwha – he had been a person who didn't take the time to remember the past, or plan the future.

Before the time of patterns, Toi had been all about what was happening now.

This didn't mean he'd had a past that he wished to forget, but instead one that he'd never belonged to, full of people who looked better, spoke better and who sat more comfortably with each other than they did with him.

And so, at a very early age, Toi decided that instead of engaging in life, he'd tread lightly along the top of it and not let it catch him.

If Toi looked backwards to his past, he saw a never-ending blackness. Once inside of it, he could make out the thin, luminous line that was the curve of his mother's back. As he walked towards her he found himself growing smaller and smaller, until he was his five-year-old self again.

Toi buried his face in the material of his mother's shirt. It smelt of washing powder. He put his ear to the ground and heard the mumbled

A Small Light

voices of his sisters and brothers and the mosquito-like whine of his father's trout fishing line as it sliced through the air, cutting into the shine of the lake. But none of these pictures, sounds or smells stayed around long enough to take real form.

Since Toi was a man who had no real past, he understood that it was dangerous to think about the future. The ground he stood on was a thin biscuit of washing powder. If he craned his neck suddenly to look ahead, it would crumble, turning into an avalanche of whiteness that would slide down the bank and into the lake, taking him with it. The lake would finish him off, drowning him in a churning whirlpool of foam. Scared of what was both behind and in front, Toi had learnt to make his present-day self become nearly invisible. So, even though he was a solid man, people looked right through him.

But today, as he carefully twisted and half-twisted aho around whenu and secured black feathers onto the growing kākahu, he saw his past begin to thicken and grow, and he didn't flinch.

Toi had met Ru in the same way, in the same place, at the same time, that he met all the women he slept with – at the nightclub that stood on the hill beside the lake, at midnight. The club was dimly lit, but every time the door to the Ladies squeaked open, a blade of light would shoot across the space, slicing through whatever lay in its path. This included Ru's head of bright hair. So when Toi looked up, his eyes were stung by the flash of her. An hour later Ru appeared at his side. She pulled at his shirt like a child and said, 'I want to go now.'

And in the early hours of the morning, as Ru skipped and tiptoed along the Rotorua footpaths beside him, her hair caught the beams emanating from streetlamps and cars. A few small insects fluttered around its glow.

When they got back to the unit, Toi turned on the light and immediately felt ashamed of its plainness. The brick walls were the same dirty cream colour as the roof, and the carpet was thin and grey. The only decoration in the place was a calendar. It hung limply from a nail by the fridge. The man from the dairy had given it to him. Inside it were images and information about the things you could buy from the man's shop. January was ice cream, February was peanut butter and March was all about Milo.

Ru looked around the room and made a clicking sound with her tongue. Then, reaching up with her leg, she turned off the light switch with her toe.

Everything went black.

That's when Toi saw who this young woman really was. While Toi was strong and heavy, Ru was as small and delicate as a bird. Every part of her looked as if it had been carefully sculpted out of polymer clay, using dentist's tools. The spirals of a moko kauae lightly dusted her chin, and Toi imagined they must've been painted on using brushes made out of spider webs. Much later, when they were in his bed, Toi could feel the slender frame of her skeleton beneath him and was scared that the weight of him might snap her.

He had woken late that morning to a sweep of cold air across his face and found her gone. The window had been opened just wide enough for someone with a body as slim as Ru's to slip through. Standing outside with a mug of tea, he saw the wet prints of small feet on the driveway, and there was a violet scarf stuffed into the letterbox. Looking out onto the lake, he thought he saw a figure skipping across its steamy surface, but then it disappeared and he wasn't sure if it was real. People were always seeing things on that lake that weren't really there.

A Small Light

Toi decided to keep the scarf. He hung it in his wardrobe. It caught his eye every time he looked for a shirt.

Something in Toi changed after he met Ru. His job in the Warehouse office where he had spent years counting, adding up and ordering plastic toys, outdoor equipment, kitchenware and shovels, had once been enough for him, but now it seemed pointless. He used to look forward to his Friday nights, but now the nightclub where he went to get drunk, pick up women and joke with other men reminded him of the bottom of his rubbish bin. It was damp, smelt sour and was alive with wilted and unwanted things.

Toi was sitting on his doorstep one morning thinking about all of this when he heard a loud shriek of laughter. The squeal was joined by another squeal and then a snort. A river of chuckling followed.

Over the road, Toi saw seven pairs of legs walking down the narrow footpath. The bodies and heads attached to the legs were obscured by bunches and bunches of trembling flax leaves. Toi couldn't help himself. He followed the seven pairs of legs and eight bunches of flax and the river of chuckles, to the weaving space. At the door the women put down their flax, narrowed their eyes at Toi and placed their hands on their hips.

'Why are you following us? they asked him. Toi shrugged, which made one of them guffaw for some reason.

'Better watch out, we're all on the lookout for new husbands, us,' said one.

'I need a bloke like you to mow my lawns, and can you cook and clean and paint my house as well?' said another.

'Sounds like we're going to have to share you, one day each,' said the tallest of the seven, who always had the last word.

Toi wasn't scared by their carry on. Instead of running he looked at his feet for one thoughtful moment, then followed the women inside.

They told him he should give the first basket he wove to someone he was grateful to. Toi had placed the bright green kono on the surface of the lake and watched as the current took it away.

'Thank you and goodbye, Ru,' he said.

But it wasn't until he started weaving the kākahu that he realised Ru was someone he didn't want to forget – and nor would he, for just a year later Toi came home to find his sister standing in the kitchen with a bellowing baby in her arms.

'I came to borrow your weed eater, and a girl turned up holding a kid. Oh my god, Toi! Did you sleep with her? Anyway she told me she couldn't look after your baby any more. Toi, why don't you wear protection? Why don't you take some responsibility for your actions? Why don't you just … I mean, you know what's gonna happen, don't you? You'll be done for maintenance and Mum and Dad will end up with this angry baby and they're old, Toi. Old, old, old! Don't look at me like that! I can't help you. I'm not the maternal type. Besides, I'm leaving. Moving to Dubai for work.'

Toi pulled back the blanket and looked at the baby in his sister's arms. She had big black eyes and a wide mouth. Her hands were clenched fists and her legs already looked solid enough to hold the weight of her body. He imagined how hard it would be for this loud giant of a baby to grow up in a house full of tiny-boned, bright-haired people like Ru. She was a squawking, shining cuckoo who had been placed in the wrong nest, and he knew just how that felt. The difference between the baby and him was that she wasn't scared to let people know she was angry.

Toi took the child and held her close. After a moment she stopped crying and burrowed her wet face into his chest. His sister put her hand to her mouth and gasped. 'Well, would you look at that? She knows who her papa is.' It was the first time he'd clung to someone for more than a heartbeat, and he knew in that moment he was never letting this child go.

While all around him the weavers talked and laughed, flax rustled and his sure-footed child laughed, screamed and stomped, Toi sat back in his chair and took in the half-finished kākahu.

Reaching into his bag, he pulled out Ru's violet scarf. He placed one of its tassels in the middle of the sea of black feathers of the cloak and secured it tightly.

There it sat, a small light flickering.

Below this halfway mark of his life, Toi saw the trembling threads of his future. They fell in a delicate veil waiting for his thick-fingered self to turn them into something beautiful.

Delirium Tremors

TERENCE RISSETTO

Our hospital is situated on top of a hill, nestled in the bend of the river, its grounds and views making it prime real estate for modern would-be developers. The main buildings, including high walls and four watchtowers, were built in the early 1900s as a prison but never used as one. Due to supply and demand at the time, the latent prison was turned into a mental asylum instead, one institution substituted for another.

Practically the only difference, though, is that in the asylum, patient behaviour is managed by legal drugs, whereas prisons are managed by illegal drugs. The asylum buildings have all the rudiments for incarceration, including reinforced floors and walls, bars on the windows, secure cell blocks, enclosed exercise yards and a farm run by the inmates. Most of the staff here don't wear the white uniforms of other hospitals, so there is no obvious delineation between staff and patient. The hospital administration needn't have worried. When I first applied to work here it seemed that to be employed as staff, you had to either drink heavily or be called Pita. I fell into both categories. The only way to differentiate between Pitas was to attach an appropriate characteristic, for example, Pita piano, Pita hair-do, Pita knitting, Pita poof and so on. I was just Pita. To my face, anyway.

I have fitted into hospital life like a prison glove on a recidivist, so much so that on my first day I showered a patient against his will and found out later he was the ward charge nurse. That didn't go down particularly well at the time, but earned me a lot of drinks in the retelling.

In my flimsy defence, it wasn't entirely my fault. I'd grabbed him and he'd said imperviously, 'Do you know who I am?' So I figured if he didn't know who he was, then he must be a patient. His name was Greg the Egg, and we've had a running feud ever since. Greg doesn't drink but I do. Unfortunately.

Like today, for instance. After a late night and early morning I had a blinding hangover and needed a drink badly, or my name wasn't Pita. I'd survived the morning showers, feeding, toileting and clean up and was on my way to the mess hall to line the stomach with some breakfast at least. It was a beautiful morning, and even the male peacocks seemed happy, resplendent in their outlaid shimmering rainbow finery. God knows why the English thought peacocks roaming freely had a calming effect on patients already suffering from hallucinations. Being pōrangi and coming face to face with their unworldly psychedelia and nocturnal cries for help would turn even the most ardent bipolar into a paranoid schizophrenic. But that wasn't any of my concern. I had other things on my mind.

'Hoi. You! Stop!'

The sudden demand spliced through the crisp air in five directions and splattered against the fragility of my hangover. I kept walking.

'Stop! Halt! About face and come here, soldier! Now!'

I heard a heavy scrambling scrape of hobnails and felt a hand on my shoulder. Turning slowly, I found myself staring into the cold blue eyes of Dolph Lundgren from *Universal Soldier*. This person with the hand was younger, dressed in army fatigues, beret and epaulettes. As tall as me, only bigger. Much, much bigger.

'What's your name, soldier?' he bellowed into my twitching face.

I was definitely not in the mood.

'Jack Nohi. What's yours, superboy?'

'Adrian. Call me Sir.'

I saw Adrian was cradling an ominous-looking black object in the crook of his right arm. As you'd expect from a soldier armed to his yellowing teeth: a toy truck.

'I'm a private,' he said proudly.

'Excellent,' I said, nodding my head. 'Let's keep it that way.'

'Are you a truck driver?' he asked, suddenly obsequious.

'No,' was the short answer.

'Do you drive a truck?' he persisted, patting his toy fondly on the head.

'No,' I answered, even shorter than before, and turned to walk away towards the mess hall.

'You're really big and strong,' he gushed, rubbing my biceps. 'Are you in the army?'

'No. Bugger off.'

He stepped in front of me and held up his truck.

'Do you like my truck? I saved up and bought it myself.'

'Really? Yes. It suits you.'

I put my arm up to push him aside and he grabbed my forearm to take a closer look at my watch.

'I like your watch!' he enthused.

Without warning he started gnawing at the watch face and band, slobbering over my wrist.

'What the hell?'

I hit him with a hanged man's reflex: closed fist hammered behind the left ear and a kick to his well-worn privates. He screamed in agony, bending in half and dropping the truck beside him. Given his size, I kneed him in the nose, just in case, and just hard enough to draw blood as he fell. Noticing the people around me, I grabbed his arm.

'Are you all right?' I asked, in a loud voice. 'You tripped over your truck.'

I helped him to his feet and bent his little finger back, feeling him wince with the pain.

'Piss off,' I whispered into his ear before saying loudly, 'better go and see the doctor.'

Adrian stumbled off, clinging to his truck with his non-wounded hand.

'You shouldn't have done that, Pita,' said a voice matter-of-factly.

I looked around and saw Little Ronnie, graduate of the Children's Cottages. On rubbish duty. He posed mid-cigarette amongst the litter like a smoking Zen master gnome caught short in a crazy wavy raked garden of attrition. My head felt the same way. Lucky that I liked Ronnie.

'It was self-defence, bro. Did you see what he tried to do? Do you think he'll tell the Matron?'

'No. Nothing like that. But you made a big mistake there.'

He shook his head sympathetically.

'I had to, bro. He's a big boy and could have done a lot of damage,' I said.

'No, you got it wrong. He likes his pain. A couple of years ago he got picked up by a truck driver who beat him up and then bummed him. The truck driver had a big watch on, like yours. He's been going around ever since asking every guy he meets if he's a truck driver. He's in love with him. No one's ever given him a hiding before. He'll think you're the truck driver and the more pain you give, the more he'll like you.'

'Thanks Ronnie, I needed that,' I said, patting his bald head like Benny Hill on fast-forward.

I walked into the mess room and there she was. Cathy, the flame of my oily life. Slow motion. Queasy. I wanted to throw up. She was so beautiful. I collected the hospital breakfast and sat down with her. My hands started to tremble. We talked and talked until I noticed that the room had gone quiet and a shadow had fallen across the table. I looked up and saw a minotaurised replica of Popeye, sans horns, hat and pipe, stalking purposefully over towards me. Nobby.

Nobby will do anything for a cigarette. There was one conspicuously tucked behind his left ear.

'Patients aren't supposed to come in here, Nobby,' I admonished him, glancing up deadpan into his eyes.

Nobby chewed his cud nervously. He knew me from working on his ward a few times.

'Ah, um, Pita, um Pita, I've ggggot a ppppresent for you.'

'A present, Nobby? Who from?' I enquired, eyes full of hidden meaning, my fingers steepled in front of me.

He handed over an unidentifiable object, wrapped neatly in a pair of men's jocks. My head was throbbing and the eggs in my stomach were starting to get restless.

'Who's it from, Nobby?' I encouraged him sweetly. The room had gone even quieter.

'HHHHe said, um, he said yyyyou'd know,' Nobby replied, trembling through a mouth uncluttered with teeth and filled with trepidation.

'Oh,' Cathy sighed. 'Isn't that nice. What a beautiful boy. What a nice boy.'

I opened the pants cautiously, to reveal a recently spruced-up toy truck. Nobby immediately decamped, scattering for the door like a bird with three broken wings. I threw the truck after him, managing to bounce it off the back of his head and into the face of a male nurse who was just about to walk into the hall. Greg the Egg. Perfect. Or not.

Greg cursed in heartfelt passion and made a petulant beeline towards us.

'Pita, you prick! How dare you do that to me.'

He grabbed my arm and pulled me to my feet like a recalcitrant patient.

'Come with me now to the Matron's office.'

The sudden upward movement and my bilious head managed to stir the poached, scrambled, and fried eggs composting in my stomach into violent action. I vomited over him, barely managing to pull the neck of his freshly washed white jersey out far enough to allow most of it to splatter over and down his shirt without damaging anyone else. A five-pointer without trying. A clean kill with minimum collateral damage. No wonder he hated me.

I wiped my mouth on his look of horror and quickly turned to leave.

'Thanks for that, Greg. I feel much better now. I'll leave it with you, then? Better get back to the ward.'

I grabbed Cathy's arm and we went out into the sunshine again. At least my head had cleared.

'What just happened?' she asked in disbelief, turning to face me, away from the noise and bedlam inside.

'Oh, just Greg living up to his name. You okay?' I asked, deflection being the better part of valour.

She hugged me warmly. 'It's about time you asked. Coming down to the Skinny Dog at lunchtime for a drink with me?'

I knew I was. It was the same dog that had bitten me last night after late shift. I walked her to the admissions ward door, where she kissed me on the cheek and went in after unlocking the door, waving to me through the window.

My own ward was a short walk further on down past the morgue and the nearby surgery unit, opposite the Children's Cottages. It was pleasant in the sun. Birds were singing, lawns were being mowed.

As I unlocked the ward door, a small sound distracted my attention and I felt an indistinct movement nuzzling my left foot. Looking down I saw a toy truck. A slightly bent toy truck with a slightly bent quivering toy truck owner lurking behind the tremens of a nearby bush. I also saw red.

'*Mothertrucker*! Bugger off, Adrian!'

The scream echoed and threw itself back at me several times before finally dying down. The acoustics were very impressive. I briefly enjoyed the silence until I heard loud guffaws and laughter coming from the vicinity of the Children's Cottages.

It was Ronnie and Nobby, pointing and laughing in my direction while simulating various unexpurgated truck and trailer copulations. Dolph the Adrian had long since vacated the area, stampeding the preening peacocks in his haste.

For good measure, I gave Ronnie and Nobby a flurry of two-handed one- and two-finger salutes in a scattergun profusion, a drunk juggler throwing his toys in the air and the knives after them. It had the desired effect. I could see a look of alarm on Ronnie's face. He pointed urgently behind me before sprinting off, with Nobby wobbling close behind him.

Too late, I felt a large hairy hand on my shoulder and remembered that I had left the ward open while trading insults with the boys. My ward was maximum security, full of the criminally insane and sundry unmanageable violent offenders from the justice system. There were no second chances in this place. I could smell horrendous breath with a hint of bourbon, vomit, stale cigarettes and cheap cologne.

Turning quickly, I grabbed the hand and twisted it up behind its owner's back, putting my arm around a fat-arse neck and squeezing a barely existent Adam's apple. You don't work in a men's ward for violent offenders and not know how to defend yourself at any moment. Faint heart never won a fair lady.

'Pita!'

Greg stepped towards me, superciliously dressed in a freshly laundered patient shirt. Snotty little prick. He should have helped me. My hangover was back, breaking chunky masses of loosening brainfreeze from my forehead. I needed a drink. Badly.

'Pita!' he urged.

I snarled back.

'What the hell do you want, Greg? Can't you see I'm slightly busy here?' I said, emphasising the words with a vicious twist of hand neck, and being rewarded by a strangled gasp of pain.

'Pita, please let the Matron go. She only wants to talk to you.'

Fast

ALBERT WENDT

… And it is blinding morning, laced with the unpleasant odour of winter mud, bursting through the gap under your bedroom curtains and flowing over your duvet and up over your chest and into your nostrils and eyes. You remember, you push your legs out of bed, your feet find the floor and you re-hitch your 'ie lavalava round your waist and start rushing for the bathroom. Shit, shit, shit, you're going to be late for your 9.30 am lecture, again! No time to shave or have breakfast. Final week of lectures and then finals, and hopefully the completion of your MA and your graduation and getting a teaching job. You have to be at Professor Thalmer's last class of the year because he is going to tell the class what is in your final exams on The New Zealand and Pacific Novel.

All your family have left already: your father to his chef's job at the Battersea on Ponsonby Road, your mother to the Williamson Avenue

Foodtown and your sister and brother to Auckland University of Technology, where she is completing a BA in film studies and he is studying for a diploma in nursing. You fling your backpack into the back seat of your 1996 Honda Civic, which your parents bought for you two years before as a reward for completing your BA – you are the first in your 'āiga to graduate from university. You slide into the driver's seat, start the car and head for university, which, if the traffic is light, is only ten minutes away.

Once you're into Grafton Road and turning into the Owen G Glenn Building and parking, you know you'll only be fifteen minutes late.

Through the narrow glass partition in the back door, you look into the small brilliantly lit lecture theatre. Professor Thalmer is down in the front behind the desk, his purple-rimmed glasses glinting, and behind him on the screen is a PowerPoint slide of a list of items. You count the students quickly. You're the only one absent out of the fourteen. And Graeme, your ally, is there.

You pull back the door quietly; your heart is thumping like thunder and you hope beyond hope no one, especially Professor Thalmer, is noticing your entry. You start towards the empty seat beside Graeme.

'So, my handsome Samoan Viking, I'm so glad you're able to be with us today.' Professor Thalmer catches you on your third slow step. Excruciating embarrassment: your ears hot, your heart thumping, your throat parched dry.

'Hi, Jonas,' Graeme whispers. On his retirement as a highly successful architect, Graeme decided to pursue the love of his life: poetry and the literature of his country. Balding, with long straggly wisps of white hair and a few days' growth of white stubble, paunchy, always dressed in black polo necks, navy blue corduroys and thick-soled suede boots – he claims he'd been a beatnik. He is by far the oldest in your class and the one Professor Thalmer is most *careful* of.

Using his prepared PowerPoint presentation, Professor Thalmer takes you quickly through a summary of all the topics and the novelists you've covered this semester. You've spent four years with him, from Stage One New Zealand Literature through his second-year course on the New Zealand/Pacific Short Story to his third-year paper, 'Post-colonialism and Pacific Literature', and now The New Zealand and Pacific Novel. Because New Zealand and Pacific literature is your passion, you've studied hard, doing far more than the required reading and research and writing and handing in your assignments on time, and he's given you an A-minus average for each course, your best grade in all your studies. Yet you've never felt he respects your intelligence and ability; you've suspected that he's unconsciously assumed that being a Pacific Islander, a Samoan – at least he knew that! – English is your second language, and because of that you're struggling to cope with the literature of that language. So you can never break that A-minus barrier. (It is a joke among PI university students that all PI students start with C.) So it's strange, bloody strange, that you continue to hold some admiration and respect for him. Or is it out of the fear that if you don't pander to your lecturers' tight-arsed egos they won't give you good grades?

'... So, I'm now going to go through the exam questions – oops! Sorry!' Professor Thalmer's eyes shine with fake horror. There's a scatter of student laughter. Graeme doesn't laugh. Professor Thalmer sniggers and corrects himself. 'Sorry, I'm going to talk about the topic areas I'll be giving you exam questions on. If you're shrewd, you can just get the last three years' exam papers and all the questions will be there!' You and Graeme don't join the laughter of your classmates.

'God, he loves himself!' you hear Graeme whisper. 'We're going to need a strong cuppa coffee after this corny shit!'

Looking straight at Professor Thalmer, you reply to Graeme, 'Shit, yeah!' Over the past three years, Graeme has been the only other student who has been in all your Professor Thalmer classes, and you usually have coffee or lunch together at least once a week. As a superannuitant, Graeme can simply audit his courses and does not have to do the assignments or sit the exams, but he always does, and insists his lecturers award him grades for them. When he doesn't like the grades or disagrees with his lecturers' remarks on his essays, he challenges them. Graeme doesn't take notes at lectures but recalls everything almost verbatim, and when he makes a presentation, he doesn't refer to notes or a prepared text, yet he is always absolutely fluent and delivers without faltering. Name any poet he admires and he can quote verse after verse from their work. Photographic memory? You've wondered but have never asked him.

All your sessions in this class are student seminars, each presenter talking about the topic for at least twenty minutes and then leading a class discussion for the rest of the session. At the start of the course, Professor Thalmer got you to choose your seminar topics, and then set a date for each seminar. Graeme chose to give the third seminar, on the intriguing topic 'Courage and Architecture in James George's Novels'. As usual, it was flawless in delivery and innovative and original in analysing the novels, complex and sophisticated in the way he wove in the latest theoretical readings while simultaneously undermining them with a mesmerising sense of irony and fun, which, you sensed,

Professor Thalmer didn't appreciate because it was aimed at *his* style of lecturing and reading. And as usual Graeme conducted the class discussion with verve and tolerance and insight, getting every student to participate fully and with enjoyment. He also used it to murder the theoretical jargon that Professor Thalmer and his pet students are fond of using.

'Well, Jonas,' Graeme says as you leave the lecture theatre, 'we've survived another semester of the great Professor Thalmer.'

'He's not *that* bad,' you try to say.

'Contrary to the Kiwi stereotype of you being violent and mean, you Samoans are too generous, Jonas,' Graeme says, chortling.

'Thank you for *your* generosity,' you say. Graeme guffaws and punches you lightly on the arm.

Graeme needs a left knee replacement, and he refuses to use a walking stick or crutches, so you have to walk at his hobbling pace to the Student Union building. Once you jokingly suggested he should get one of those fancy motorised wheelchairs that go faster than Superman, and he'd laughed and said those were for 'the lazy Kiwi middle class, who are too cowardly to face the cleansing pain of worn out joints and souls'! That comment still puzzles you.

Since your first coffee together, Graeme has insisted that he pay. 'You're a bloody poor student, Jonas,' he'd reasoned. 'And I know you Samoans are big on reciprocity, so I'm reciprocating you, Jonas, for your generosity towards egotistical pricks like Thalmer and your kindness towards old bastards like me. Is that fair enough?'

You take the lift up to the restaurant.

The café is fairly full but there is an empty table near the front windows. Graeme joins the short line at the counter while you hurry over and take the table that looks down at the courtyard four stories beneath you. Your legs grow goose pimples and nausea nibbles at the tip of your tongue. Heights have always frightened you. You look away from the drop, and sit down with your back to it.

'What's the matter? You look as pale as a Pālagi,' Graeme says when he sits down opposite you.

'So you know what the Samoan is for Pākehā?' You try distracting him.

'Too right, mate, I have a good teacher of Samoan!'

'Your teacher is shit-scared of heights,' you admit.

'Just like Melissa,' Graeme says. Melissa is his wife, his third one, and at least fifteen years younger than him. 'I designed and built at least six of Auckland's highest buildings and she's absolutely refused, even at their official openings, to go above the third floor. And would you believe it? She's the bravest person I know, afraid of nothing, except heights of course.'

You first met Melissa at their home, in St Mary's Bay right at the water's edge and looking across the harbour and up at the Bridge, at their oldest grandson's twenty-first birthday. (You hadn't wanted to go, but Graeme had insisted over three lunches that his 'bloody wasteful mokopuna need to meet someone who's focused and bloody hard-working. Besides, I need an intelligent drinking mate'.)

You don't know much about art, but you recognised a Hotere and a Pule as Graeme took you into the spacious sitting room. You'd expected a large, palatial home with a swimming pool, and it *is* large, three split levels large, with lots of rooms and equipped, furnished and carpeted lavishly, and there is a swimming pool, but as Graeme said it was 'a very messy, shambolic reflection of me and my beautiful Melissa.'

You'd expected it to be a lavish, expensive party with lots of wild students and their wild friends and raucous music and dancing fuelled by unlimited alcohol and food such as caviar and champagne and whatever else rich people's parties are supposed to have, but you counted only about fifty guests, including Graeme's two daughters from his first two marriages and their husbands, his son with Melissa and his wife, his four grandchildren, other relatives and Ralph's, the birthday boy's, friends. You've grown up with Pālagi but you've never felt fully comfortable at their functions, but after Graeme introduced you to Melissa and some of his family, and he put a glass of champagne in your hand and said 'Ia Manuia! and you drank with him, and his grandchildren immediately drew you into their celebrating circle, you slid right into their family and into the party. You'd expected Graeme to be in control of that gathering, like your father would have been, but you soon observed he wasn't. Melissa, a tall, stately woman with short-cropped silver hair and wearing what appeared to be a Pacific-blue puletasi with light frangipani motifs on the front and black pearl earrings, was in charge, in a quiet, almost unnoticeable way. You recalled Graeme telling you that Melissa had been a VSA volunteer in Samoa, years before.

Over dinner – after Melissa introduced Ralph and you all toasted him and he spoke and thanked his parents and grandparents and then blew out the twenty-one candles – Melissa brought her food and sat down beside you at a table by the swimming pool. 'I expected someone older,' she told you. 'Graeme finds all young people, including his mokopuna, *difficult*, so when he came home and told me he'd found a good classmate, I assumed it would be someone older than "young people".' She laughed softly. 'You must also be exceptionally bright and able, because he can't tolerate "unbright" people who believe they're brighter than they are! And best of all, he's so chuffed you're the first Samoan friend he's made, without my help.' She went on to talk about her VSA year in Samoa and 'her Samoan 'āiga', which now had a branch in Auckland and which she maintained close ties with. Since that party, you've lunched with her and Graeme many times.

The waiter brings Graeme's double-strength latte and piece of carrot cake with a dollop of cream, and your flat white, mince pie and mixed salad. Two Samoan students you know wave at you; you wave back and hope they don't come over – they don't. Three of your MA class smile and head towards you, but when they see Graeme they veer off to another table.

'Do I have a bad smell?' Graeme asks. You pretend you don't know what he's referring to. 'Are they scared that my making *their* Professor Thalmer look like an amateur will jeopardise their grades?' You don't understand that. 'That because I'm belittling Thalmer's ego he'll take it out on the whole class?' he explains.

'I guess so,' you reply.

'Then how come you don't mind being seen with me?'

'Cos, no matter what, I'll get another A-minus, as always.' You both laugh.

He spears his carrot cake, digs out a hunk of it and shoves it into his mouth. 'You know what we should revive?' he asks through his bulging mouth.

'Yeah, cannibalism!'

His eyes bulge with mirth and he can't swallow his large mouthful of cake. You hope he doesn't choke as he laughs, bits of food flying out of his mouth. 'That's good, yeah, fucking cannibalism so we can gobble up second-raters like our Professor Thalmer!' You're no longer self-conscious about laughing with abandonment in that public place.

A short while later, after Graeme dries his tears of mirth and wipes his face and clothes clean of food, he asks, unexpectedly, 'What are you going to do with your MA?'

You shrug your shoulders. 'Teach at high school,' you reply. High school: that's what your careers advisers and your teachers told you best suited your abilities, strengths, interests and grades. Because of that, your parents have supported that too. So you've never seen yourself doing anything else.

'Are you interested in doing a PhD?' he asks.

'You must be joking! With only an A-minus average, the department won't let me do a PhD.'

'Have you actually talked to the head of department about it? Even Thalmer?'

You shake your head, and say, 'You know Thalmer gave me the A-minuses.'

'Okay, so just tell him how you feel about that; just let him have it.'

'That would shut the door completely,' you say, but you feel encouraged.

'Are you bloody sick of hearing the self-righteous confessions of old fogeys?' he asks, from under his closely cropped white eyebrows. You can almost hear him chuckling.

'Not as long as it is a captivating, inspired, meaningful unpacking of that old bugger's story.' You imitate Professor Thalmer's tone.

He guffaws. 'Throughout my childhood and early life you know what my teachers and parents and everyone else, including my classmates, came to believe? That I was a mental retard: mentally handicapped was the uncool vocab of that time. In a literate culture if you can't read or write properly, you're fucked. They knew nothing about dyslexia in those terrible days. I couldn't read, and they equated that with retard intelligence. So they "promoted" me from class to class to get rid of me. And as I suffered my bloody parents' abusive treatment, I believed I deserved it. At the age of sixteen they took me out of school – I wanted out too – and apprenticed me to a butcher, a friend of my father's.' Graeme went on to explain that he was so ashamed of himself he even believed that his obsession with drawing – he drew on everything and all the time – was another feature of his retardation. At the butcher's, because he didn't have to know how to read and write properly, he learned by doing whatever the butcher showed him, and found his body, his eye, his memory absorbing everything with faultless accuracy, but again he was too unsure to reveal that to anyone. And he continued to draw with an obsessive compulsion, finding he was drawing everything he was doing at the butcher's, right down to the minute details of the various parts of the slaughtered beasts, and learning the names of all those parts. 'Is your dad a kind and generous man towards you?' Graeme suddenly asks. He waits for you to decide.

'My father is tired and stressed most of the time: the result of working too hard to pay for us to get a good education and never have to do what he and our mother do,' you confess. 'It is also not the Samoan thing for a man to show affection for his loved ones, publicly.'

'And your mother?' He pursues you, and you don't understand why.

You nod repeatedly, annoyed. 'She's a bit overboard with the public display of parental love.'

'Well, mine simply saw me as a burden, a lifelong burden, and a public stigma, evidence that their genes might not be *normal*.

Fast

So when I got my first pay packet they arranged for me to board at a male boarding house mainly for sickness beneficiaries,' he continues. You can feel the bitterness in his voice. 'At first I felt utterly abandoned, but ...' – his eyes light up with a piercing brilliance – 'a few weeks later, alone in my spacious room away from every element of my dreadful serfdom, I suddenly felt *released*. I had a sanctuary in which I could do what I liked and not be judged useless, a nong, a halfwit, a moron, an idiot, a dummy, a mental retard, and now "an intellectually challenged person".' He pauses, breathing deeply, elated. 'And at work, that kind and generous butcher Fred Calhoun found my stack of drawings behind the freezer and, instead of berating me for wasting my time and his, simply went through them, studying each one slowly. Yeah, Jonas, he didn't need to tell me how he was feeling, no. I could feel it, observe it in his manner, hear it in his silence. And for a moment I couldn't believe it. He was, so he told me a few minutes later, amazed. And what was I doing there instead of developing my talent?' Graeme lowers his head and gazes into his coffee. He goes on to say that Fred gave him time off work to attend the art classes one of his friends was teaching at a nearby polytech. In those days it didn't matter how talented you were; you had to write essays and sit written exams. Failing those meant the end of your studies. So he started printing the words he wanted to learn into his drawings and memorising them visually. He would take his textbooks and course hand-outs home and pay one of the beneficiaries to read them aloud to him. He would memorise those, or at least those sections he had to know to pass. And as he did that he was composing his essays in his mind and then, after he was satisfied with them, laboriously writing them down. 'Melissa reminded me years later that I was doing what you Samoans did before the introduction of written language: memorise everything, catch reality in your memory, translate it into oral language – poetry, oratory, song, music; carve it out of your environment, out of the spirits in the wood, the clay ... Fuck, I'm sounding like all our over-literate academics, tied to the technology and limitations of writing and written language, eh?' He gazes across at you, unsure of your reaction.

'What happened to Fred Calhoun?' you hear yourself asking, and wonder why.

He hesitates, surprised. 'I worked for him for another five years, until I'd completed my diploma in art and my confidence in myself was strong and I knew that I wanted to study architecture.' He stops and looks as if he's forgotten what he's been talking about. 'Bloody Alzheimer's!'

'Fred Calhoun?' you remind him.

He smiles, relieved, and says, 'He and his doting wife Jill and their two kids became my 'āiga – right word?' You nod. 'Yeah, they saved me, Jonas. I never lived with them, but their home was always open to me, and when I established mine, it was open to them. Whatever success I made was theirs. They were my special guests at all my graduations, parties, openings, birthdays, everything, Jonas. I made sure they needed for nothing. In their retirement, I designed and built them their dream home at their favourite summer beach, Whangamatā, and filled it with a selection of those drawings I'd done when I'd been his apprentice. And when Fred died of prostate cancer twenty or so years ago, Jill and I carried out his last wishes: that he be cremated and his ashes scattered at our favourite fishing spot in Whangamatā Bay.' He pauses again, looking inwards, and then ends his narration. 'Jill died two years later and we buried her beside her parents in Taihape – her last wish.'

The café is now crowded, and many people are looking for seats. You and Graeme ignore them as you sit in that special healing quiet that eventuates when a confessor has been relieved of his burden, his story, by the listener, who, in this case, will continue to try and unpack the full implications of his wise confessor's tale, at least until their next lunch together.

'For many years I regretted that they didn't know anything about dyslexia then; maybe they wouldn't have treated me so unkindly. But, Jonas, don't you think that's what turned me into whatever I am today?'

'Shit, yes!' You hear yourself celebrating his triumph over circumstances and ignorance.

'I like that, Jonas, I like that you agree with me!'

That afternoon, just before you go into your class, Shakespeare in Film, your cell phone rings. 'Hi, Jonas!' It's Donna (Samoan name Matagi, which she doesn't like), and you're immediately wary because she's been pressurising you, mainly over the phone and through common friends, to restart a three-month relationship you'd had the previous year. After four years of revelling in a rollicking social life, she is still trying to finish a BA in journalism. 'How was your Poly lit class this morning?' she asks. You've never liked the way she exaggerates the way she talks, like a stereotypical Poly student, and you resent the way she always seems to know what you're doing.

'Fine, great.' You replicate her jovial tone. 'Gotta go into my Bill Shakespeare class now.'

'Awesome. I *love* Shakespeare films, man, I really do! By the way, who was that old Pālagi dude you were lunching with today? Your prof or something?'

'Naw, he's just a classmate.'

Staccato laughter, and then she says, 'Where's he bin all these years instead of getting a degree?'

Now you have to work hard at suppressing your rising contempt. 'Donna, the old guy's a retired architect who's keeping his mind alive studying literature.'

'Our other Poly friends tell me he's bloody rich and famous …'

'Fā, Matagi, gotta go to class!' you interrupt her, and switch off your phone.

It's your turn to cook at home, so after your Shakespeare class you stop at the supermarket where your mother works, and she helps you get the supplies you need.

'Who's that wealthy Pālagi businessman in your class? Ben told us last night that you spend a lot of time with him,' she says in Samoan. Again you have to stop yourself from being angry openly. The whole fucking Samoan community must know about it! 'Ben says he looks as ancient as Moses!' She laughs.

You try to smile. 'Yes, e makuā pei o Moses but e kelē aku aga kupe,' you say in the usual mixture of Samoan and English that is your language at home. 'Plus he's lāuiloa i Giu Sila!' You exaggerate.

'We're having Dad's fifty-fifth birthday next Friday, don't forget. Why don't you invite Moses and his wife to come?' You can't escape her scrutiny. 'That's if you think we're good enough for them!'

You're trapped. You have to nod and say, 'I'll ask them.'

You're intensely worried about how you're going to ask Graeme, and how your asking is going to put Graeme in an awkward position, and if he and Melissa come, how they are going to react to your family and vice versa. And you're not going to feel good if you lie to your mother that you asked Graeme but he already had another commitment to go to. You've lied before about other things, but this is too important to lie about. So you keep putting it off and suffer the dreaded signs – unrelenting stress and lacerating stomach pains – of your recurring duodenal ulcer.

Four days before your father's birthday, while you're in your usual computer booth on the fourth floor of the new all-glass Student Study Centre, trying to finish your last assignment of the semester, your cell phone rings. You hurry out to the corridor to answer it.

'Still being a diligent student, Jonas?' Graeme greets you. You say hello, and try not to sound guarded. 'I'm also trying to finish my last essay, but have given it up and am now having a cuppa coffee, would you like to join me?'

Shit, accepting his invitation means you *can't* postpone inviting them!

A few minutes later, there's a flat white waiting for you as you join Graeme at one of the tables by the windows. And some Melissa-baked shortbread, Graeme's favourite. 'She told me to bring those for you.' He looks more fragile and vulnerable; a sickly paleness is pushing up through his skin, the wrinkles on his face are more numerous and deeper, and his coffee hand is shaking visibly whenever he lifts his cup to his mouth.

'Melissa was a VSA in a village in Samoa, eh?' You keep postponing the invitation.

He sits up, obviously excited about the topic. 'Yeah, in the village of Pou-tassy. Have I said that right?' You nod. 'On the north-eastern coast of Upolu. She was only seventeen, just finished high school. She lived with a family there while she taught at the school. Learned a lot of Samoan, loved it; loved the whole place and people. After she returned and graduated as a teacher she kept going back to visit her Samoan 'āiga during her holidays. She helped many of her 'āiga migrate here. When she left teaching and became an architect and ran her own practice, her visits to Samoa dropped off. But she still participates in her 'āiga's affairs here in Auckland.' You recall her telling you some of that the first time you were at their home.

You have to do it now, while he's least expecting it; while he's wowed about Samoa and Samoans. 'Graeme, mydad'shavinghisfifty-fifthbirthday ...'

'Hey, Jonas, slow down, man!' He laughs and, gazing at you, waits for you to calm down, then he says, 'Now, let's hear it.'

You swallow once, twice, look unflinchingly across at him, and say, 'My 'āiga would like you and Melissa to come to my dad's fifty-fifth birthday on Friday night next week.' You've said it, and it's like ridding your throat of a sharp fishbone.

'Thank you, Jonas, Melissa and I accept your 'āiga's generous invitation and will come on Friday, at what time, sir?' His eyes twinkle – are those tears?

'About 7.30 pm, my silver-haired lord!' You parody him. You start to write down the address for him, but he reminds you he has an 'infallible memory' like all pre-literate Samoans.

As you enjoy your coffee and shortbread, you find yourself telling him about your 'āiga – did he steer you to that? – and enjoying it. You tell him your mother had only a village education, your father graduated from Samoa College; they met here while going to the same church, in Māngere, 'fell in love, so the story goes', married and had three heirs: Jonas (named after his father's father), Ben (after Charlton Heston as Ben Hur) and Diana (after Diana Ross, his mother's favourite singer). You laugh with Graeme at that last bit. Your father, while labouring on a building site, attended cooking classes at night, then got a job as a waiter in a flash restaurant; worked his way into assistant chef, then chef. Your mother cleaned, and when you were born and she had to stay home, she cleaned at night. Finally a cousin got her a job at Foodtown as a shop assistant. 'By the way, in that whole saga of migrant success, my parents deliberately kept away from what they called "the wasteful, expensive fa'a-Samoa", so they could afford to get a good home and get us educated. They've not gone back to Samoa since they got here, even.'

'What do you think of that?' Graeme asks.

'In the last few years, I've felt deprived of the fa'a-Samoa and my roots. So have Ben and Diana.'

'Have you told your parents that?'

You shake your head and drink the remainder of your coffee – it tastes bitter and cold. 'We don't want to hurt them. They've sacrificed so much for us.'

'Jonas, I wish my spoilt mokopuna were like you and your sister and brother and didn't want to *hurt* their elders!' he declares. 'They don't even recognise there are such creatures as elders.'

You look at him with shrewdness and irony, and ask, 'And whose fault is that?'

His eyes light up with mock surprise. 'Jonas, you've got me there; right there where the blame should be.'

'But you didn't raise them: their parents did.'

'Yeah, I suppose, but to protect myself and Melissa from their rapacious free-loading and keep them at bay, I keep giving them anything they want.'

You recognise Donna's scent before Donna and a friend, Cushla (Samoan name, Teuaute), are upon you, right at your table, casting their shadows over you. Graeme looks up and smiles. You push back your seat and, without looking up at them, say, 'Graeme, these are Matagi and Teuaute!'

Graeme extends his right hand to Donna. 'How are ya?' They shake hands.

'Pleased to meet you, sir!' she greets him. Graeme moves to shake Cushla's hand, but she hunches up and shies away. 'And how are you, Jonas?'

You make no move to invite them to sit down. 'Good, good,' you mumble. 'Graeme and I were just leaving to go to a class.' You're relieved Graeme hasn't asked them to join you.

'Shit, I almost forgot!' Graeme improves on your lie. 'You, beautiful young ladies, want this table?'

'Yes, thank you.' Cushla speaks for the first time.

Graeme gathers his satchel, straightens his clothes and shoves on his Hurricanes sports cap while you all watch him. When he tries to get up, he grabs at his bad knee in pain, so you reach forward and help him up. 'I bloody well need that knee replacement Melissa and you keep urging me to have.'

'And when are you having that done?' you ask, trying to avoid Donna's intense scrutiny.

'Straight after our finals, and this time Melissa is going to kick the shit out of me if I chicken out again!'

'Good luck with your operation, sir,' Donna says, and you know she means it and recognise, from your past relationship with her, that she does have many appealing and decent qualities. 'And good luck with your finals,' she says to you.

'Thanks, Donna,' you say and mean it. 'And good luck with yours.'

'Lovely meeting you,' Graeme says to Donna and Cushla.

'I'll ring you,' you hear yourself saying to Donna, and gaze fully at her for the first time. Yes, she is beautiful. And as you and Graeme walk away from the table, the exciting, wild imagery of your sexual life with her starts capturing you.

'What was that all about, Jonas?' Graeme asks, softly.

'Donna and I used to have a relationship ...'

'Used to, and it's now called a relationship, eh?' Graeme slaps your shoulder.

'Yeah, used to.'

'She's a very beautiful young woman!'

'Yeah, straight out of Prof Thalmer's lecture and presentation on "Dusky Maidens and Gauguin in the South Seas", eh?' You start laughing at your own comment.

'Too right,' laughs Graeme. 'Too bloody right!' He holds himself up by leaning onto your shoulder as you laugh and weave your way down the corridor through the stream of students and staff now coming in for lunch.

Like most families that you know, you, Ben and Diana and your parents have *evolved* – or is it developed? – ways that enable you to live together fairly harmoniously. Some of that harmony you achieve through avoidance of areas of possible friction. For instance, if you watch the television news or eat together, you and your parents never discuss politics or current affairs or the behaviour and lifestyles of young people. On your political scale, but you've never accused him of it, your father is even right of Ayn Rand. You gave him *Atlas Shrugged* and it became his second bible, which he quotes from to justify his unshakable belief and faith in capitalism and his being a totally self-made man who has arrived where he is through the honest sweat of his brow and the strength of his own hands; Samoans who remain poor are that way because they're lazy and want to live off the sweat of hard-working taxpayers like himself and your mother. Mention things like socialism, the Labour Party, the welfare state, the rights of unions to collective bargaining and welfare benefits for single parents (especially unwed ones) and he (and your mother) become Emperor Nero at the gladiator games, callously turning down their thumbs for the final kill. You recognised early that that was why for them it was thumbs down on the fa'a-Samoa out of which they had come. It was socialistic: 'āiga before the individual, communal sharing, compulsory contributing to family and community affairs and projects, and what your father condemns as 'a bloody system of sweat-eating, with too many sweat-eaters and too few sweaters'. So over the past few years you've preferred to get your news coverage off the internet through your computer in your room. But tonight, you can't avoid being in the sitting room with them, in front of your mum's new humongous flat-screen television. It is Ben's and Diana's turn to cook dinner, so they're in the kitchen and dining room doing that. You'll watch the news – Dad prides himself on being 'well informed' – and then over dinner discuss and finalise the arrangements for his fifty-fifth birthday party, which he insists is your mother's wish.

You get stubbies for Dad and yourself and a Bacardi and Coke for your mother, as the signature tune for the TV One six o'clock news starts. You sit down in the armchair on your mum's right, away from your father. You take a deep drink on your ice-cold beer as the news headlines begin: Prime Minister in Beijing for free trade talks; two teenagers die in car accident in Māngere, alcohol and speed suspected; Minister of Justice accused of conflict of interest ... You don't pay too much attention to the headlines as you continue drinking and waiting for the news details.

You get a second stubby out of the fridge and start returning to your seat when the face of someone you feel you should recognise comes on to the screen, and the announcer is saying, 'This morning at his home in Freeman's Bay ...' It is old black and white television footage of a youthful long-haired Graeme; he is being interviewed without sound while the announcer is talking. 'Graeme Hudson, one of New Zealand's most distinguished architects, collapsed and died of a massive heart attack ...' You sit down quietly. You feel nothing. Not shock nor sorrow nor pain. '... Mr Hudson designed some of our country's landmark – and what some have called controversial – buildings and complexes ...' On to the screen come some of those, and snippets of Graeme and his staff designing and directing their construction. 'Graeme Hudson achieved all this despite suffering from a severe form of dyslexia. He went on to become the most generous patron of the Dyslexia Society ...' You watch the bespectacled head of the Dyslexia Society being interviewed about that. Now you refuse to believe the news: you had lunch with Graeme only two days ago!

'Isn't that your friend, Jonas?' you hear Ben asking. He is standing just behind you.

'Is it?' your mother asks, turning down the sound. 'Is it?'

Everything immediately sounds loud and demanding and focused on you. You now have to face it. 'Yes,' you whisper. 'Yes, it is!'

'The one who is supposed to be coming to my birthday?' your father asks.

'Yes!'

It is a calm morning full of sun and squawking seagulls and mollyhawks and the gullet-deep growling of the sea as it surges in from under the Harbour Bridge. You walk between your father and Ben, wearing formal 'ie lavalava and 'ulafala. Your mother and Diana walk a few paces ahead of you, holding the 'ietōga between them, displaying its ancient and silky beauty as it shimmers in the light breeze. Your mother told you it was the mat they were saving for your graduation; it has been in her 'āiga for years. The night Graeme's death was on television, you'd insisted with your parents that even if they didn't believe in the fa'a-Samoa, you wanted them to do it for Graeme's funeral. 'But your friend and his family know nothing about the fa'a-Samoa!' your father had objected. 'His wife knows a lot about it; she lived in Samoa for a long time and has Samoan 'āiga,' you had countered, unafraid of him for the first time, you will recall later.

You start up the long, massive front steps that lead into the house. You can't see anyone about. The wide sliding doors in the front are open, and you can smell fresh greenery and flowers. At the threshold, you all take off your sandals and line them alongside the footwear that is already there.

You notice that the pillars immediately inside the door and holding up the high ceilings of the house now have long garlands of flowers and nīkau palm leaves woven round them. Everything, including the art, has been removed from the massive room and the whole floor is covered with Samoan mats and siapo. You realise that the house has been transformed into a fale-tele. In the centre of the space, on top of a thick layer of siapo and 'ietōga, lies the white coffin. Beside it, at its head, sits Melissa in a plain white puletasi. Behind her sitting in a group are some of their children and grandchildren and a few of Melissa's Samoan 'āiga. To her left facing you are two grey-haired matai, bare-chested, wearing only plain siapo, their tatau glistening. It is obvious that Melissa has consulted and assembled the 'āiga. You are in awe. You look at your father and see that he is awed too, but there is also fear there: he'd not expected such knowledge and correct observance of Samoan protocol and customary funereal practice.

You have Graeme's cell phone number and, after you'd seen the news on television, you'd debated all night if you should ring it. Early in the morning, you'd done so, hesitantly. You'd jumped in fearful surprise, expecting Graeme to answer, when the voice said, 'This is Melissa Hudson speaking.' Clear, unemotional. 'You must be one of the thirty people Graeme allowed to have his cell phone number.' Is she amused by that?

'This is Jonas,' you reply softly.

'Tālofa, Jonas, I've been expecting your call,' she said. 'Why? Because being Samoan, you know what to do when a loved one dies and an 'āiga needs comforting and consoling.' That's not true for you, but you decide not to contradict her.

You'd rehearsed what you were going to say but lose all of that and blurt out, 'Mrs Hudson, I'm very sorry about Graeme ...' and go blank and try to control the sadness surging up in your throat.

'Jonas, he died the way he wanted: quick, unexpected, and reading *The Crocodile*, which you gave him ...' She stops, catching the first signs of sobbing in her gullet and holding them there.

'Is there anything I can do to help with his maliu?'

'Thank you for thinking about that, Jonas, but Graeme's Pālagi 'āiga and my Samoan one are arranging everything.' Her voice is clear again. She itemises those arrangements. 'By the way, there will be no Christian service. As you know, apart from being a loudly loquacious atheist, your friend Graeme considered all religions as "the causes of the worst massacres and wars on our planet". I've had to work bloody hard persuading my Samoan 'āiga about not having a Christian funeral. And we're bringing Graeme home for the day and night before his cremation.' She pauses. 'You bloody Samoans are so difficult; I had to persuade my 'āiga that cremating Graeme isn't inconsiderate and insulting!' She pauses and, breathing in deeply, says, 'If you want to come and see your friend, come here when he's home.'

Melissa nods and smiles at you as your party enter and sit down cross-legged on the floor. The two matai start welcoming you in high oratory, which you don't understand because the language is ancient, allusive and metaphorical. You glance at your father, whose head is bowed, beads of sweat starting to drip down his face, and you hope he can cope with the level at which the ceremony is being conducted.

When your father starts to reply, almost inaudibly, his head rises slowly, and when his gaze is directly on Melissa, his speech grows more confident and louder. He replies in the ornate language used by the matai, who nod often and congratulate him on his oratory. Then your father, unexpectedly, cracks what is obviously a joke in Samoan, and the matai and Melissa laugh. That immediately dispels the solemnity and seriousness. 'Because most of the people here today do not understand our language, I would like to speak in English,' he says, and doesn't wait for a reaction. 'I acknowledge and greet all the sacred 'āiga of Graeme Hudson. I greet the chiefs and orators of those 'āiga and, in particular, Mrs Melissa Hudson, the grieving wife and mother ...' As he speaks, your scepticism turns to surprise that, though he has denied you the fa'a-Samoa and you were convinced he didn't know much about it, he is now showing he does. 'We are here because of the friendship between our son and Mr Hudson. This mat is to acknowledge that friendship and alofa.' Your mother and Diana rise and, again displaying the 'ietōga, take it towards the matai.

'Mālō, fa'asaō!' The women in Melissa's 'āiga praise the beauty of the mat. Two of them come forward. Taking the 'ietōga, they fold it and place it beside the matai.

'The mat is called "Matagi Mālū", "Cool Wind", which is an apt name in the cool vocabulary of the uncool young people today,' your father continues. 'We kept it over the years to present to our son on his MA graduation, but he wants it presented to Mr Hudson on his graduation to Le Lagituaiva.' Melissa clasps her hands together and laughs. The matai and some of the elders laugh with her. You don't understand the reference to the Lagituaiva. 'For the benefit of uninformed people, like our children, the Lagituaiva is the Ninth Heaven in the Samoan cosmology of ten heavens.' He laughs softly with Melissa. 'Even this "never-been-to-university Samoan" knows about cosmologies.' You survey Melissa's Pālagi 'āiga: they too are enjoying your father's performance. 'In our ancient religion, when you die and you've lived a virtuous and generous life, your agāga, soul, goes to Le Lagituaiva, the highest heaven for humans. The Tenth Heaven is reserved specially for Tagaloaalagi, our Supreme Atua. This humble person is sure that Mr Hudson is on his way to Le Lagituaiva. To help pay for his fare, here is an envelope with a humble sum in it.' All the elders are now laughing openly. To Diana, he hands the envelope with the money you'd put together the previous night, and with bowed head she takes it to the matai. Your father ends by speaking directly to the casket: 'Lau susuga, Mr Hudson; go with our alofa, go safely and go well. The Atua will protect you all the way. Soifua!' Many of Melissa's Pālagi 'āiga applaud.

As your parents approach the casket, Melissa rises to her feet and embraces your father, then your mother. 'Thank you, thank you, for your alofa!' she tells them. They kneel down beside the open casket, and your mother, without hesitation, caresses Graeme's hair and then kisses his forehead. Your father does the same, then they turn and embrace the matai. 'Come, Jonas,' Melissa beckons you. The restrictive, terrible self-consciousness that usually infects you on public occasions like this is gone, completely. You slip into her embrace, she gazes up into your eyes and you kiss her on the cheek, and hold her and hold her.

The start of finals is only a week away. You wait outside Professor Thalmer's office for your 10.30 am appointment. Only a few minutes to go. You'd expected to be gripped by apprehension, fear and trepidation, but you're not experiencing any of that. Since Graeme's cremation, which was restricted to only his immediate family, the two matai elders and you, you've prepared yourself for this meeting with meticulous care: the kind of care Graeme would have taken. You've selected all the possible scenarios, worked out all the arguments and their supporting data, and then memorised all of it. You've been in Professor Thalmer's office a few times before, mainly to discuss the seminars you were giving. Those times, he did most of the talking.

You knock with confidence. 'Come in!' you hear him calling.

You open the door and meet the pleasant smell of books and papers – and is that strawberry yogurt in the mix? You see the opened yogurt container, with a plastic spoon in it, on his desk. Professor Thalmer is one of the few lecturers who hasn't adopted the more egalitarian, less threatening arrangement of not having your desk between you and your visitor. Behind his desk, he is writing furiously in a pad, and looking neat in his purple-framed glasses, his long brown hair freshly washed and combed. Without looking up he waves you into the chair directly in front of his desk. You deliberately focus on his shiny forehead. That does it. He drops his pen and glances up. His eyes brighten in recognition. 'Ah, Jonas!' Then he remembers, and his beaming smile changes to an expression denoting sadness. 'I'm so sorry about Graeme Hudson. I know he was a good friend of yours. So sudden, so quick.'

'Yes, Graeme helped me a lot with my work – and other things.' You look appropriately sad. Graeme is there beside you.

'He was a – a marvellous student who contributed a lot to our class.' He pauses and looks away from you. 'I understand he was also a good architect who contributed much to the development of that field.'

'Yes, all the media praised him for that.' You stop deliberately; you don't mind the awkward silence that is going to happen. You wait and gaze intensely at him.

He looks at you and away, fidgets and eventually has to ask, 'Now, Jonas, what can I do for you?'

You take your time. You hear Graeme's ironical chuckling. 'Yes, I have decided that I would like to do a PhD in New Zealand and Pacific literature.' Thalmer looks as if he hasn't heard you. So you repeat, 'I've thought about it very carefully, and have decided that I would like to do a PhD in this department.' You know he is going to give you the stock reply to such a request.

'For that, you need to make a formal application to the head of department, who will then refer it to our graduate committee, who will make the final decision.' He gives that stock answer.

You again wait and watch him. 'To succeed, what do I need to have?' you ask slowly.

'You need to have a research topic and a staff member in the department who can and is willing to supervise your research and thesis,' is his automatic reply. And then, trying to deemphasise its importance, adds, 'You need good grades as well.'

'I have a topic, Professor. I want to do a thesis on the topic "Politics and the Pacific novel: with special reference to the novels of Sia Figiel and James George".' You and Graeme wait and watch.

'Good, good,' he says. He stretches back in his chair, gazes up at the ceiling and asks, 'And do you have someone in mind as your supervisor?' You and Graeme continue to wait and watch. Thalmer names two possible supervisors on the staff.

You then attack. 'Professor Thalmer, I know you are the international authority on those authors.' You pause and watch his eyes, his ego, bloating. 'In all the four years I've been in your marvellous classes I have never doubted that. I have read almost everything you've published on New Zealand and Pacific literature, Professor.'

'Thank you, Jonas, it's very flattering that you believe that, but there are many others in the field who are admired and respected more.'

You and Graeme allow him time to enjoy his self-importance and then ask, 'What sort of grade average do I need to have for the department to consider my application seriously, Professor?'

'Usually, you have to be in the top two percent of your MA class, Jonas, but – but the department has made exceptions in the past. What sort of grades have you had for your MA courses?'

You pretend you're trying to remember. And then say, 'Nothing above an A-minus, I'm afraid. You've given me four of those. Two of my other lecturers have also given me A-minuses.'

You and Graeme sense Thalmer is now worried about those grades but that he is quickly finding a way out of that dilemma. 'A-minus is a very good grade, Jonas. When I give an A-minus it is a *very* very good grade. I will not hesitate in telling the graduate committee that!' You know that he is chairman of that committee. 'I will also remind our department that it has always been university policy to encourage and support students from underrepresented groups, such as women, Māori and Pacific Islanders. I will also remind the department that over the last twenty years only two Polynesians have ever finished a PhD with us: Meilin Hansen and Selina Marsh.' He is breathing heavily, triumphantly, as he declares, 'You should be the third one, Jonas. I – and I'm sure all the other right-thinking members of staff – will support your application.'

'I'd hate to be anyone who tries to stop that!' Graeme laughs.

Three Princesses

PAULA MORRIS

The picture hanging near the sliding glass door looked familiar. Fraser wondered if he'd seen the real thing in a museum somewhere else in Europe.

'It's not Estonian,' the elfin hotel receptionist told him. 'But I don't know who did it. It is a painting of three sisters. I can find out the artist name for you.'

She frowned at her computer screen, as though such information might be listed on the hotel's website.

It wasn't a real painting; it was a print in a gilt frame. Fraser supposed it was like the other pictures in the public areas of the hotel, chosen to make guests feel cosy and Baltic and medieval, despite the No Smoking signs and the shiny, spitting coffee machine. Tallinn had been a rich city once, the picture said, with merchants in fur robes and heavy gold chains who might have had blonde, smiling daughters like these ones. This part of the building would have been his warehouse, piled with amber and pelts, with sacks of flour or barrels of weapons. The merchant and his daughters would have lived upstairs, their windows looking out into the mist and the chimney smoke, gulls cawing from rooftops, snow flecking the thick glass.

This was how Fraser imagined Europe looked, once upon a time.

The women in the picture had bread for hair: burnished yellow strands braided, twisted and woven into rolls and pretzels. Fraser stepped closer. Their hair must have been very long; they must have had maids to help them plait and pile. Their scalps must have been pin-cushions.

His own wife had short hair, which she described as low-maintenance, though it seemed to require an expensive cut and 're-touching', whatever that was, every six weeks. She went to a salon, a word that Fraser thought affected and old-fashioned, on Jervois Road. He'd met her there once, when her car was being fixed, and he'd arrived too early. The place reeked of chemicals; his wife looked like a tinfoil hedgehog. The waiting-area chairs were fake leather, sticky with sweat when he tried to stand up. He'd been offered a coffee, and it arrived with a Hershey's Kiss half-melted on the saucer. The stunted chocolate in its fussy packaging bothered him most of all, because it was American and too sweet, and not even the colour of chocolate. In a *salon*, surely they should serve bon-bons?

The hotel receptionist handed him his key, which was an actual key and not a plastic card, attached to a pale wooden doorstop.

'You should not take this out with you,' she told him. Her hair was blonde but pale and wispy, unsuitable for competitive plaiting and weaving. 'Leave it here at the desk whenever you go. Anyway, it is too heavy.'

Three Princesses

'Yes, it is,' he said, feeling pleased at the sight of a real key, and the weight of it in his hand. He was pleased, too, to have to walk into an exposed cobbled courtyard to reach his room, and to step down two stone stairs, slick with rain, to unlock the door. The door stuck, and had to be rattled open; this pleased him as well. There was no point to Europe unless it was old and strange, creaky and quaint. Here it was fine for shops to be called salons. Here, men could wear pink jeans. Cars could be tiny enough to park sideways. Coffee could be served in tiny doll-cups. At the Christmas market down the road from his hotel, on a slanted square in the middle of the Old Town, people buying mulled wine could help themselves to a sprinkling of raisins, and take a sliver of biscuit to dunk.

In New Zealand all the biscuits would be gone in the first ten minutes. People would grab greedy handfuls of them as soon as they realised the biscuits were free. Larrikins would throw the raisins at loitering pigeons, and drink so much mulled wine they'd puke it up in the gutter. The streets around the Christmas market would be spiky with the fragments of smashed souvenir mugs, not handed back to the vendor as agreed, even though a deposit for their return had been paid.

The Three Princesses of Saxony. That was the name of the picture in the hotel lobby; the receptionist had told him when he was handing in his key en route to the Christmas market. Fraser was sure he had seen those princesses somewhere before, in some painting, in some museum, in some European city. There were so many museums in Europe, columned and echoing, built to resemble Greek temples. Castles would be better, he thought, swigging his mulled wine. Somewhere the three princesses might have lived.

The stench of the nearby pen, housing bales of hay and actual live reindeer – pale and indolent, lolling against the hay – was too much for him. In this oldest of old towns, he was a visiting merchant, and it was time to go shopping.

Once upon a time there were three princesses, beautiful and fair-haired. They were beautiful for a number of reasons. First of all, the rampant inbreeding among ruling European families was still far into the future, and afflictions like the Habsburg jaw were unknown horrors. Second, the general standards of beauty were more expansive and forgiving. If you didn't have bad teeth or a lazy eye, you could be considered a beauty. At various points in European history different notions of what beauty was surged and ebbed – sloping shoulders, long necks, small breasts, high foreheads, rosy cheeks. And if a girl was born into a wealthy family, then the sycophants, underlings, social climbers and alliance-seekers within her family's sphere of influence would all describe her as beautiful anyway.

These particular princesses were beautiful because they were young and well-fed and spent most of their time indoors, and because sugar cane was still growing in secret across the ocean, unknown to Europeans. So their complexions were soft and unlined, their teeth and gums were healthy, and they had a lot of time for preening, grooming and hair-brushing. Their skin wasn't scorched by the sun or lashed by the wind; they didn't have to subsist on boiled potatoes. Their faces weren't gaunt with malnutrition. Their hands weren't calloused or cut from work outside. Their backs weren't twisted from hauling pails of water or digging in a field. In winter they never risked frostbite or chilblains on their feet.

Three Princesses

They were never kicked in the face by a cow. It was much easier to be beautiful if you were rich.

The three princesses were fair-haired because they were born in northern Europe, surrounded by other fair-haired people and descended from other fair-haired people. The Mongols had yet to ride west; the Moors still lurked far to the south. Sometimes a person with brown hair would wander into their baronial hall or through their castle gates, but it's quite possible our princesses would live their entire lives without seeing someone with dark skin or black hair. They might have encounters with dwarves or witches, trolls or giants, but not with someone with brown skin and hair the colour of coal.

In any fairy tale with multiple princesses, one princess is the most beautiful of all. Sometimes it's the oldest; sometimes it's the youngest. Declaring the fifth of twelve, say, the most beautiful is too confusing for the reader or listener. Sometimes, even though the youngest princess is the most beautiful, the knight or poor guy or old soldier or whoever the heroic challenger may be in that particular fairy tale chooses the oldest sister to marry. She is the top sister, whether she's the most beautiful or not. Or perhaps she would be offended if a more junior sister was chosen. Daughters should be married off in order, especially if they are all beautiful and fair-haired, and the oldest is not over forty.

Beautiful princesses are never over forty. By that stage in their lives, they should be queens, or dowagers, or dead. If their husbands happen to die first, the women must remarry and become stepmothers, seething with jealousy because they're forced to live with their new husband's beautiful daughters. To be over forty and no longer beautiful is a terrible thing; revenge must be taken. Nothing good comes from outlasting a husband, or outlasting your own beauty.

Our three princesses don't know this yet. They've never thought much beyond the happy-ever-after.

Fraser needed to find a present for his wife. He'd already bought her amber earrings and a scarf, but these weren't enough. She would suspect him of buying these items in the airport: he'd been rumbled before, betrayed by a duty-free receipt. Apparently this suggested neglect and panic-buying. It suggested a generic tourist-shop approach, a sense of obligation, the dwindling of passion and respect. His wife was, overall, an intelligent and reasonable woman, but buying presents for her was fraught with peril. There was too much implicit symbolism, a symbolism Fraser never grasped until the present was handed over and the damage done. The various gift-giving days each year – Valentine's Day, their wedding anniversary, Easter Sunday, Mother's Day, her birthday, Christmas, and the return from a big business trip like this one – were his Stations of the Cross.

He'd mentioned this to her once, and it seemed to make her happy rather than penitent.

'Feeling scourged, are you?' she asked him. Then she walked down the long passageway of their house, her head thrown back, cackling.

In the Christmas market he paced the narrow aisles of stalls, looking for something that would be symbolic in the right way. Too many of the stalls were selling things that would be useless in Auckland. Fraser couldn't go home with a furry hat or a giant pair of knitted mittens: these were not things his wife would wear down

Three Princesses

Jervois Road, not only because it was never cold enough. He couldn't buy her shot glasses featuring the Estonian flag – or, in fact, anything featuring the Estonian flag, though he thought she'd approve of the colours. She might refer to them as a colourway, which would annoy him, or a colour palette, which was almost as intolerable. When they were redecorating their bedroom, and Fraser was forced to show interest in swatches of fabric and paint shades with silly names like Mouse and Mushroom and Mist, his wife kept saying 'colourway' as though it were an actual thing, like the underpass at O'Hare Airport with the rainbow-light installation.

He couldn't buy her anything made of beeswax, like candles or soap, because these would be confiscated at Auckland Airport as a bio-security threat, and he would end up appearing on *Border Patrol*, entrapped by a sniffer dog and denounced, on national television, by uniform-wearing functionaries and a satirical voiceover. The same applied to anything resembling Christmas wreaths, or reliant on dried flowers, sea shells and feathers. His wife had no idea how stressful it was to buy her a present overseas, even before the dark cloud of symbolism descended, obscuring all his good intentions.

One stall sold Christmas decorations, and Fraser spent some time there, staring so long at all the little faces looking back at him that the stallholder began handing him things, encouraging him to inspect the goods. Most of the decorations were small carved figures – trolls with dangling knitted legs, Vikings with axes, fair-haired girls in bright skirts and fabric floral wreaths. There were three different skirt patterns, three different 'colourways'. He could buy one of each – one for his wife, one each for his two daughters, although the decorations were fair-haired and his wife and daughters were dark. Fraser would tell them the tiny girls dangling from a shiny loop of thread reminded him of the girls in the hotel-lobby picture, *The Three Princesses of Saxony*.

Once upon a time there were three princesses, so beautiful and clever that their parents could not bear to part with them. No man in their kingdom was intelligent, handsome, brave, rich and/or important enough for them. No man was their equal. This is the fairy-tale part of this story, because in reality royal parents were unsentimental about daughters: daughters were expensive to clothe and house and tend, and their vocation was a strategic marriage followed by strategic children and then, hopefully, an early-ish death before they withered into harridans, shrews, witches, stepmothers, domineering dowagers or poison-savvy widows. Daughters were the pedigree puppies of the old world; their value lay in their sales potential.

The princesses were unhappy, because their doting parents kept them locked in a room high in the castle, hidden from the impertinences of inferior suitors. There they moped and muttered, and over-brushed each other's hair. They spent long hours devising elaborate hairstyles, braiding and pinning, twisting and piling, admiring their efforts. These were the pre-printing press days, so there were no books. Pianos were yet to be invented. There was only so much hand-sewing you could do, especially in winter when night drew in sometime in the middle of the afternoon, and the only illumination was the flicker of a candle and a smoke-spewing fireplace. The princesses wanted husbands and households of their own. Even the lowliest milkmaid in the realm had the chance to be seen and admired and kissed.

Their maid, who was brassy and over-familiar, kept them informed about social events at the castle, which mainly involved rowdy banquets in the big hall, but the princesses were never allowed to attend these. Lesser men might try to catch their eye, to make advances or proposals. The sight of these beautiful princesses might incite men to attempt a kidnap or start a war. Because they'd been hidden away so long, the princesses were like mythical creatures; some people didn't believe they existed.

One winter morning the maid had breathless news to convey: a strange visitor had arrived at the castle late last night, not long after heavy snow had begun to fall. He was tall and broad, with brown skin as warm as a piece of amber. Deep grooves were chiselled into his face – swirls and stripes and curls, somewhere between wound and pattern. He wore his long dark hair in a high bundle, pierced with a bone comb. Into his belt he'd tucked a white-tipped black feather, plucked from a bird no one at the castle had ever seen. He was a soldier and a traveller, born in a place far beyond the forest and the mountains, across many seas. He was on his way north, to look for a ship, and needed to rest his horse until the snow settled.

The three princesses were in an uproar. They wanted to see this dark-skinned stranger with his grooved face and magic feather, but they knew their parents would never permit it. So one of the princesses wrenched back the tapestry covering the open window, and the other two grabbed the maid. They dragged her to the stone sill and pushed her out so far that she was drowning in falling snow, moments away from plummeting to the slick white cobbles many floors below.

This is how they talked the maid into helping them.

That night, when the great hall was hazy with fire smoke and heaving with people, fresh reeds crunching underfoot, torches lit, drummers pounding, deer carcasses hissing on a long spit of lashed spears, the three princesses crept down the winding stone stairs to the kitchens. The princesses wore clothes the maid had procured for them – plain linen shifts and bright overskirts, kerchiefs tied over their heads to hide their elaborate, twisted piles of hair. The youngest sister wore a skirt patterned with pinks and yellows, the colours of spring; the middle sister wore a skirt patterned with blues and greens, the colours of summer; and the eldest sister wore a skirt patterned with russets and golds, the colours of autumn. The maid's face was white, the colour of winter, because she was afraid her collusion would be discovered and she would be put to death.

Hustled into a stone recess just beyond the hall, the three princesses waited for their moment. When the crowd fell silent, they stepped forward, though only as far as the threshold. The dark stranger had clambered onto a stool to address the assembly, and although he was standing at the far end of the hall, they could see him. He was taller than the tallest man they'd ever seen, and darker than the darkest man they'd ever seen. The white-tipped feather was tucked into his bundle of hair.

He was speaking in a language they didn't recognise, gesturing from one side of the great hall to the other. His words sounded like an incantation. The youngest princess wriggled forward, so she could see him better, and the others followed. Nobody noticed them, because everyone was looking at the dark man. His arms swept the room; his eyes swept the room. But he didn't appear to notice them either. The oldest sister, who was the most status-conscious, decided it was because they appeared too low-born and therefore unworthy of his interest. In the guise of maids, they would never attract his eye. And now she was down here, in the great hall, in the hot, throbbing heart of her father's fiefdom, she realised that it wasn't enough to look: she wanted to be seen as well.

Without saying a word to her sisters, the oldest of the princesses untied the kerchief entrapping her hair, and let it fall to the floor. Her hair was a golden city, woven with cobbled lanes and narrow paths, arched with bridges. In the light of the flaming torch on the wall, it gleamed.

It took just a moment for the dark stranger to fall silent, and look straight at her.

The middle sister wasn't having any of this. She had the best hair of all, a castle of butter, churned and moulded into turrets and gateways, encircled by a smooth yellow moat. There was no way she could stand cowering and simpering while her older sister got all the attention. She loosened the kerchief and let it fall.

The dark stranger's mouth fell open.

Privately, the youngest sister thought she had the prettiest hair, because it was the colour of buttercups, and just as soft. She tugged off her own kerchief and flung it onto the rushes underfoot. Her hair was a meadow, a field of undulating yellow, all gentle slopes and furrows. A draught caught the tendrils around her face and they shivered like flowers in a breeze.

Everyone was looking at them now, gazing at the three princesses few had ever seen.

Their father ordered them back to their room, and the dark stranger rode away the next morning. He didn't ask to marry any of the princesses, because he already had a wife at home, and she was demanding enough. He could have stayed here, he supposed, in this northerly place and never returned home at all, but it was too cold, the food was terrible, and bears, wolves and wildcats prowled the forests.

Where he came from, there were only birds and fish, to be eaten rather than fought.

The maid was about to be put to death, so he asked for her instead, as a slave, though really he needed someone to guide him to a port. She rode with him on his horse, covered by the coarse wool of his cloak, whimpering with either fear or relief. Her hair was fair as a sand dune, fluffy like toetoe. After she led him to the coast, he gave her six pieces of jade and let her go.

Back in the hotel, Fraser lay on his bed, watching ice hockey on TV because he could understand the match, if not the commentary. He admired the speed of it, and the slamming. The players wore bright armour and helmets, like knights built from Lego.

He missed his wife. She would have devised arch things to say about the youthful hotel staff and their cult-member smiles. She would have fed raisins to the reindeer in the market.

He hoped she and the girls liked the Christmas decorations he'd bought for them, the three fair-haired maidens dangling from shiny thread. One wore a skirt patterned with pinks and yellows, the colours of spring; one wore a skirt patterned with blues and greens, the colours of summer; and one wore a skirt patterned with russets and golds, the colours of autumn. They reminded him of the three princesses – not the ones in the picture hanging in the lobby, but a different three princesses he remembered seeing, through a haze of fire smoke, lit by a blazing torch. He'd almost forgotten them, but coming here had brought pieces of it back – just pieces, because it was so long ago, and too hard to re-assemble. So long ago, it felt like another life.

Killing Ginger

ALICE TAWHAI

ENTRY 1

Dear diary, I felt that Denise was a grasping person, anyway. She grasped at me as she fell. I know I haven't written for a while, but it's time again, so let me explain. Denise was my neighbour. She wasn't important to me. And that's very important, so remember that.

Last week, I borrowed some sugar from her. I wanted to see the inside of her house. Rhombus came with me, but she didn't invite him in. He had to wait on the step. Denise had cold sores; little white-rimmed doilies on her lips, as if someone had sprinkled her mouth with battery acid. Maybe she was low in iron or something. Her eyes were light blue, and their inner light made it seem as if they'd been scorched by the sun. That should have warned me that things weren't quite right.

I caught her just as she was coming home. 'You can come inside,' she said. 'It's always unlocked.' It was hard to believe she never locked her door. I have Rhombus, and he's a Rottweiler, but I still lock mine. I keep all the windows latched too. The world is not a safe place. She showed me her white ceramic swans. Crown Lynn swans; all in rows on her shelves, whole walls of them; each swan exactly the same as the others. She told me that every time she found one on the internet, she just had to have it. It was hard for me to imagine someone getting their mail and taking pleasure in opening the same parcel over and over again, but she said it was all in the numbers. The more she got, the more impressed she was with her own collection. And I have to agree that the pale blue walls of the small living room of her flat were overwhelmed by the parade of serene white birds. I pictured them coming alive at night in the dark; stretching their wings and separating their feathers before relapsing back into their china positions. Old habits die hard.

Marilyn and I used to enjoy getting mail too. (Marilyn's my sister.) And that's because we wanted the stamps. We collected them, and we were quite competitive. Well, I was anyway. Not so much her, because she didn't have to try. She was always prettier than me, and our father preferred her. Her eyes are brown, like hāngī sacks, and her hair is dark red, like the golden syrup we used to help our aunty pour into the steam puddings. I have blue-black hair myself; black hair with a blue sheen, like a bird's wing. Maybe Marilyn reminded our dad of our mum. In photos, our mum is a white girl, and Marilyn has her red hair. Sometimes I call her Ginger.

She says I'm jealous of her. 'After all I've done to look after you and protect you,' she says. But how could I not be angry with her, when our dad made it so obvious that he loved her the most? She's a lesbian now, of course. Running a women's collective. They do rape crisis work. It's not even a proper job. Our dad said she was doing it to get at him. She said she didn't owe him anything. I don't know how she can say that when he gave her so much love and attention. He barely noticed me, and I'm the one who cared about him the most. She feels good surrounded by sisters, she says. She knows this will hurt me. 'I'm your sister,' I say when I Facebook her. She says I'm too much about myself.

Some of the sugar Denise gave me spilled onto her dark blue bench. Little white nothings. Just part of the debris and waste of the universe. And then off I went. She'd showed off her swans, and that was it; thank you. Anyway, I'm tired now, dear diary. It's been a big night. I'll catch you up tomorrow.

ENTRY 2

Dear diary, I had to stop writing last night because I was getting a little bit off track, and I was tired before I knew it. I shouldn't let that stuff about Marilyn get to me. That will just lead to carelessness. What I was really supposed to be writing about was Denise, so I'll get to that now.

I knew her lover must be married, because he only came late at night. (I'm very observant.) And as far as I know, she never mentioned him to neighbours in the other flats. I stop and talk to them occasionally because I live in the house down the end of the driveway. I rented it to myself. I do a little bit of real estate work, and sometimes a little bit of PA work; mainly temping. Everyone knows that living in a house means you're better than someone living in a flat.

I saw him come, and I saw him go. It was dark, and the sky outside my window was hung heavy and low with thick black cloud. Starlight was dead. I waited patiently for his car to drive away, and then I waited fifteen minutes more, to be sure he wasn't coming back. I left

Rhombus at the other end of the driveway, where it met the footpath. No one comes past him. Fear is what gives us impulse control. Too much sometimes; and it holds us back from what we need to do. I have very little fear when it comes to doing what I need to do. But I have enough.

There were night noises. The sound of someone yelling, briefly, over towards E Street. The hum of heavy machinery from the industrial area over the way. Someone laughing; perhaps at a party. Everyone who was up was too busy to give a thought to what anyone else might be doing, which is how I like it. I felt as if I was on a conveyor belt as I walked up the drive towards Denise's door; gliding through the night towards her house. She had a crop of big creamy white puffballs growing near her back doorstep, and they caught the light of my iPhone, which I was shielding with my hand. No sensor light or alarm, of course.

I walked right in the front door. She probably thought I was her lover coming back, because she stepped into the end of the short hallway without talking. She was a black hole that a person had fallen into; a representation. The darkness was inky blue in comparison. I walked forward until she was so close that I couldn't see her properly, and I was more aware of the drifting, lilac smoke from her incense than I was of her silhouette. I was acutely aware of everything sensory. The hum of a heat pump. The smell of the joint she'd just smoked in the bedroom. I pulled my arm back, and drove the big kitchen knife I'd brought with me into her stomach as hard as I could. Then I continued pushing her in front of me into the room behind her.

She stumbled backwards until she tripped, and her head struck one of the shelves full of swans. As she drifted towards the floor, it seemed as if their feathers fell in slow motion with her; floating slowly down onto the dark lake that surrounded her body. When I looked again, they were just white shards of china lying on the ground; getting mixed in with her blood and her dark red hair; part of the debris and waste of the universe. Even old habits can be broken, I guess. Other swans, on shelves untouched, looked as if they would like to fly down too, and glide enigmatically to and fro, wondering about death. It's ironic that we chose to represent angels as men and women with the wings of swans.

I was glad that the person in the next flat from Denise was pretty much deaf, and that the other flat was empty, because there had been quite a crash. It's doubtful that the walls would have been soundproof in a cheap flat. The handle of my knife was stiff and black. It was harder to pull out of her than you might imagine. It was stuck inside her stomach for what seemed like ages. And I needed to get out of there as quickly as possible. Every second was an extra, unnecessary risk. I could have left unintended evidence, or I could have gotten caught. Although I didn't bother with gloves and that sort of thing. I have the perfect excuse for a strand of my hair to be on her carpet, and for my footprints to be on her doorstep. I borrowed sugar yesterday. People saw me. I made sure they did. Attention to detail. That's what it's all about.

As usual, it was hard to find exactly the right moment to leave, even when the knife came loose. When I was finally outside, the black cloud was even lower, and the orange streetlight was sulky and heavy. Above the light, the cloud had a filmy blue layer to it, like deep water. Rhombus ran alongside me, panting with excitement because he could smell the blood on the knife. Drooling on my feet. I soaked the knife in a bucket of disinfectant, super strength.

Then I had one of those OCD moments where I was almost overcome by the really strong urge to go back and check that she was properly dead. I mean, I didn't even check her pulse or anything. What if she had crawled to the phone? What if she gave them my name? What if she was still alive when they found her? I lay awake in bed with my thoughts gliding round and round like swans; never catching up with each other; until it rained hot, heavy wet drops on the roof, and then my tension was suddenly released. Rhombus's breath was black on my face. He loves me no matter what. Even if I didn't feed him, he'd still adore me. No matter what.

Anyway, dear diary, tired again. It takes it out of me.

ENTRY 3

I went out and stood with the others as the police took her away, dear diary. It would have looked funny if I hadn't. It's human nature to be curious. They were all talking about it. 'She was raped, you know.' I knew she'd have sperm between her legs, and I'm banking on them finding it. Not to get her lover in trouble as such, but I mean, he shouldn't be doing that; sneaking round in the dark, rooting someone he shouldn't be. Maybe he paid her. And it just makes it easier for me.

'I heard they found her with those swans all broken around her.'

'How did she afford them all?'

'Police lady says it was a mess.'

They had a lot to say. It was very exciting for them, but they had to make their faces sad.

The red and blue lights of the patrol cars swept around the dusk in the driveway, blushing and saddening the twilight in turn. A neighbour found her. The door was unlocked. 'Is she all right?' asked a woman from across the street, as they wheeled Denise out in a body bag. No wonder no one suspects the neighbours. A policewoman squashed the puffballs by the steps with her boots, and the white pulp clung to the side of her sole. She left three half boot prints on the tarseal drive, as if a ghost had walked there. Perhaps other police will find them later and decide they're a clue.

Later, they did the rounds, and a policeman came down to interview me. Police are so much more chatty in the evening. Like it's a more intimate time or something. 'That's an impressive dog you've got there,' he said to me as Rhombus growled at him. If I hadn't been there, Rhombus would have ripped his throat out. I told him I was a woman living alone, and that I kept Rhombus for protection. I am keen to send a message that I am fearful, a potential victim myself.

'It's a pity that your neighbour didn't have a dog too,' he said. Hiding in plain sight is easy. I'm not very memorable. People overlook me. They wouldn't if they really knew me. Then they'd be interested in me for sure. And they would write about me, and discuss me on Twitter; hashtag #ourmistake.

He had a fingerprint kit with him, and he rolled my thumbs and fingers in the fat black ink.

'I'm sure my fingerprints will be all over everything,' I said. 'I went over yesterday to borrow some sugar, and Denise showed me her swans.'

'That'll make you an official suspect,' he said, and for a moment I thought he was onto me, and I felt a little stab of fear. Initially, it was an unpleasant sick feeling, but it melted into a pleasant chill as soon as I realised he was joking, because he laughed. 'It's just a process of elimination,' he said, 'so that we know which prints to concentrate on, and which ones not to pay attention to. Sorry I scared you. We're not in the habit of arresting innocent people.'

That is the sort of attitude towards me that I like. I have dried off the knife and used it to chop Rhombus's meat into bite-sized pieces. If anyone ever decides to test it, all they will find is animal blood. You can learn a lot by watching *CSI*. The key to it is to have absolutely no motive. I was friendly with Denise in a neighbour sort of way, but not too friendly. No one will suspect me, or spray me with luminol. And this is the real thrill. The moment of death is good, but getting away with it is better. And I'm not greedy; I don't do it very often. I've lived here for two years now; a blameless life. They never keep tabs on me afterwards; I'm not important enough. I always move away. And no one remembers me.

'I'm just on edge,' I said. 'I'm not used to having someone murdered down my driveway.' (This is not true.) 'I keep thinking that it might happen to me next,' I told him.

'Oh, he'll be long gone,' the policeman said. 'Still, hopefully, we'll get some DNA from the rape kit. Maybe you should go and stay with family for a while though.'

I thought of my dad. I always felt safe when he was around. He had big, steady hands, and I always knew nothing bad could happen to me when he was with me. He's dead now, of course, so I have to keep myself safe. 'I'm going to put my house up for sale. I don't feel safe here any more,' I tell all the neighbours and anyone I see in the street. Everyone's still talking about it. Other people are saying the same thing as me.

And that, dear diary, is enough for tonight.

ENTRY 4

Actually, dear diary, it should be enough; that should have been my last entry for this time round, but I am weirdly compelled to discuss my sister again. Because she is at the root of all of this. I Facebooked her again, just to see how I felt now. She is still her patronising self. But we had some good times together. Like doing the stamp collecting thing when we were younger. In fact, what I do now is really just a continuation of my stamp collecting. I select a person, just as I used to select a stamp. I try to pick someone who won't be missed too much. I'm not a monster. I mean, Denise had no kids that I know of, and no one really visited her except her midnight lover, and people like me, borrowing sugar. Then I prepare them, and just like steaming a stamp off the paper backing, you've got to be careful. Too fast, and then you'll rip it and you'll ruin it. I think a lot about how I'll display the stamp before I stick it into place in the album alongside the stamps I've already collected. For a while, I'll contemplate it a lot, and my eyes will be drawn to it (so to speak), because it's the most recent. But eventually, the enjoyment of acquisition wears off, and I start to think about getting a new stamp to renew the feeling.

There's been a few. The woman in Paeroa, the girl in Porirua. I don't want sex or revenge or money or drugs. I don't get caught. Why would I? Obviously it requires brains, and luckily I have them, because I don't have people's permission to kill them, and they could fight back. Everything, both before and after, needs to be planned. No, I don't feel bad. Why would I? My problem is that no one realises how clever I am, so they don't treat me with the respect that I deserve. Marilyn is a good example of this. There's a part of me that would like everyone to know, including her, but I know that this is not possible, because then she'd be better off in life than I would, and I wouldn't enjoy that. My cleverness rests on nobody knowing. My work is necessarily anonymous. And that's where you come in, dear diary. Someone to tell.

Anyway, when it comes down to it, Ginger is worse than me. She wasn't even sad when our father died. And he was our father, not some stranger. She used to suck up to him when we were kids. Always doing what she was told, trying to take all of his love. The golden girl; the one with the big fat scorching neon halo hanging over her red hair. She still says she was just protecting me. Which is bullshit. She's just trying to twist me around to that feminist point of view that she feeds off in that lesbian collective. That's why our dad hung himself. Because of Marilyn and the things she said. It's like she wanted him to hurt. And he was always giving her a special smile, or stroking the back of her neck. But that was how she repaid him.

I suppose I hope he's at peace. I waited and waited for him to tell me that he loved me as much as he loved Ginger, but he never did. And there's no point waiting now. As for her, I guess I'm still waiting for an apology from her, not that I ever expect to get one. And do you know, dear diary, that she had the cheek to tell me that she was waiting for the same thing from me? She's not even on the same planet.

I find it funny that the person who's closest to you for all those years; who you do all your early growing up with, who you share all the same history with, can just drift off and not care to have you in their life. Even when you were one of the eight or nine at the time when they only knew eight or nine people in their whole entire life. I am the one who has done the best; I've made money in the real estate business, and I've kept my figure, while she's stayed poor and put on fat. I've got it all, except that when I want to scream, I'm the only one that hears anything. People are okay with me. They don't mind me. But none of them truly love me. Not Ginger, not our aunty. And our dad gave all his love to Ginger. Possibly even you, dear dairy, do not truly love me. And that is why I have Rhombus.

Each murder is like a little tape that I can play back in my head. But somehow, the result is never quite perfect. Even this time, something is nagging at me. Something wrong. It just doesn't feel as satisfying as it should. I play it through in my mind. The dark lake, the red hair casting its syrupy tendrils across the surface. The innocence of swan feathers. The puff of steam from her just-boiled kettle in the adjourning kitchenette hanging in a soft purple haze at the entrance to the room. She had a lamp with a dark blue shade and a TV with a screen the size of a big window and a surface like black water. It all flows together in a strangely pleasurable way. Until I get to Denise's blue eyes, staring up at me like a blue Friday afternoon sky. Staring straight at me, like she hates me, and it's not like she even really knew me. I should have closed her lids at the time, but I felt strangely intimidated, as if I needed to hide, and that was the moment I chose to leave.

Denise reminded me of Marilyn in a way. She had the same red hair. Most of them have red hair. No, not most of them. All of them. But Ginger doesn't have blue eyes. Hers are brown like our father's. And no matter how many times I kill her, I know that Ginger is still there; surrounded by her lover and her lover's children, and everyone and everything she wants. I can't touch a hair of her head, of course; she's the one person that I would have a motive to kill. There have been times when my fingers have itched, and I have thought; I could kill you now. But I haven't.

Our dad took us to live at our aunty's when our mum died. I can hardly remember our mum, except from the photos, where she looks like Marilyn. For a while, I thought the photos of her as a girl were photos of Ginger, until I realised that their eyes were different colours. Marilyn and I slept outside in the caravan, so that we weren't disturbed when the grown-ups had parties inside, although we could still hear them laughing and singing while they drank. When I think back, I can remember the inside of the caravan; wrinkled with pumpkin-coloured candlelight, and us huffing down into our sleeping bags. Marilyn's red hair would be fanned out on the pillow.

Our dad would come in. 'How's my girls?' he would say. And he'd give me a quick kiss. 'Turn over and go to sleep, there's a good girl.' He'd snuff the candle out with his bare fingers, because he was just like that. Big and brave. And in the dark, he'd climb into Marilyn's sleeping bag and lie on top of her, and I could hear him moving around while she lay perfectly still. It was always Ginger. He never once chose me.

And that, dear diary, is how my sister ruined my life.

Moontide

JAMES GEORGE

On the second day a pūkeko stalked among the river stones, paused for a moment in the wind coming up over the sand bars from the sea. Its eyes took in the glistening silver of the river water, the rustle of flax leaves. It stole a couple more steps through the sweep of stones at the water's edge, leaving four pointed starfish impressions in the sand. A shift in the wind and it stopped again, looked up into greenery, but it either didn't see her or took no notice. It walked on.

On Monday night we sit watching some sport on TV. Adam flicks the remote from channel to channel, sips from his flask of water. I get up and go and sit next to Lily's cot and just watch her in her sleep. She is lying slightly on her right side like she often does, with one hand raised next to her face, her thumb and middle finger touching. As if she's about to go 'click'. I reach and caress the dainty tufts of hair above her ears.

She stirs, so I lift my hand away, not wanting to wake her. When I get back to the lounge Adam is holding his weight-training grippers, opening and closing his fist. His forearms tense, and the veins go all spidery.

'What time's your Aunt Nesta coming by in the morning?' he says.

'Breakfast time,' I say. 'I'll get Lily's stuff packed and ready for her tonight.'

He turns.

'You sure about this?' he says.

I sit, take a couch cushion against me.

'Rache,' he says. 'Are you?'

'Yes,' I say.

He looks back at the TV, then away down the hallway towards Lily's room. He glances at the baby monitor on the coffee table.

'Okay, then,' he says.

'What does that mean?'

'It means, okay then.'

I reach for his hand. His fingers go jerky against the grippers. He sets them down and touches my hand for an instant, then stands.

'Adam?' I say.

'We should get a good night's sleep,' he says. 'We've got a long ride in the morning.'

When I was a girl I had an imaginary friend. She wasn't like a person I could see, even in my mind. She didn't have a face that expressions could roll over like shallow surf. She was made of sound; tiny bells and whispers that would be just loud enough to turn my head. The sounds would stop me while I was playing with my toys on the floor of my room, or in the walking bus to school. Once even as I was playing hopscotch, and stood poised with my left foot on the fourth square, my other foot caught mid-air like a kōtuku. Sometimes it came when I was sleeping, infusing a dream with its soft signature. No, not it, her. She'd ask why I had chosen strawberry instead of vanilla, which had always been my favourite, or who my new friends were, since we'd moved. And sometimes she'd ask me if she could stay for a bit, walk with me. Though when we walked she had no footsteps, she left no trace in the grass.

And sometimes she'd just sing to me, not words, but tiny melodies hanging like dust in a shaft of summer light. There for a moment, then gone.

On that first day only the sun had seen her, finding the yellow kōwhai flowers woven into the pattern of her teal summer dress. The wind had found her too, its zephyrs sending the fabric swishing. Her pupils still lay large within her irises, in the last moments before they'd start to contract hour by hour until they would be barely points. The sun's circle twinned in her empty stare.

We're on the motorbike heading south all afternoon, and in the evening we see the lights of Wellington sprinkled around the harbour. Reflections from the waterside buildings dive like tree roots into the black water. Adam has hardly spoken all day. I just hold my arms around him as we ride, my chest against the warmth of his back. Watching the silent conversation of his wrists, his hands on the throttle and brake. Whenever we stop I get off and lift away my helmet and take a long deep breath, needing air that has never been mine before. He fidgets with the buttons of his jacket, then looks up at me. Each time he does I wonder if I'm asking too much, but I don't say it.

I call Nesta.

'How's Lily?' I say.

'She's fine,' says Nesta. 'No trouble. Jeez, you're not gonna call me every fifteen minutes are you?'

I laugh.

'Nah,' I say. 'Every half hour maybe.'

It's getting dark as Adam slows the bike and eases us into one of the lanes queuing for the Cook Strait ferry, and the sky is a deep deep indigo by the time we set sail. We head upstairs and sit outside on the ferry's deck for a long time, nursing hot cups of tea. Then I walk to the rail and lean against it, looking down into the moon's path on the water. I raise a hand to keep the wind-rifled hair from my eyes.

'Don't get too close to the edge, hon,' says Adam.

'I'm okay,' I say.

'Sure wish I was,' he says.

I turn to him, where he sits silhouetted against the glow of the ferry's café, try to find his eyes with mine but he's mostly shadow. I reach for him and he stands and comes to me, presses against my side.

'What are you actually going to say?' he says.

'I don't know.'

'After all this time?'

'No.'

I shake my head, look down into the boat's wake as the ferry glides so easily away from the embrace of the land and out into the dark. I lean into him and he tightens against me.

We book in at a B and B in Picton and Adam wheels the bike around the side of the house, puts it on its stand between the water tank and the old rusting incinerator, so it can't be seen from the street. I've gotten used to this.

In the night I look over at him as he lies facing away from me. All I can see is the line of his shoulder in the faint wash of light from the streetlamp. I think I can see his body drawing in and out with each breath but it's probably just in my head. I shift closer, up against him, then roll over so we're back to back and skin to skin. When we were on the bike I was trying to glean, from the subtle electricity of his body, what he was thinking. Where that thinking is going to take Lily and me. What places it will go and whether we'll be able to come back.

I remember my parents arguing, Mum standing in the lounge doorway with one hand on her hip, making circles in the air with her other hand. The smoke from her cigarette making ragged suns and moons. Her brown eyes got harder with each day with him, the half-circles beneath her eyes growing fuller with each tear, curling up like a child.

He just sat on the couch with a glass in his hand, his chin getting taller and taller.

I reach back for Adam and just lie there, and it takes me ages to notice the rhythm of our breathing has moved into synch.

We're on the road to Nelson before the sun's fully up and the hills rise with us from their own sleep, twist and stretch like cats around the roads and riverbeds. We cut into more hills where mountains loom all stony and strict in the distance. We stop at some place with a concrete toilet block sitting against a rock face.

'You can slow down a bit,' I say, as I step off the bike.

'Yeah,' he says, 'sorry. Old bastard isn't going anywhere.'

I glance at him.

'Well,' he says.

'Adam, are you regretting coming?' I say.

'Not yet.'

Late on the second day the sky began to change from deep blue into golds, then the ruffled pink cloudscapes of sunset. In the night the river water held the moon's light in its tide. Above – way up high – a bird swooped in on the current, down over the bridge's framework to the splay of grass and gorse flowers at the water's edge. It drifted, the feathers pulled back tight against the wind currents. Then it wafted away.

I never went to see him. No one would take me, even if I had wanted to. I just remember the men in suits coming to the door and standing on the wooden porch, and him shifting up and down on his heels like he always did, his chest and chin stuck out.

'I dunno when she'll be back,' he said.

'A cousin said she was sitting having a cigarette on the porch,' said one of the men in suits. 'Then a car that fits the description of yours pulled up.'

'I haven't left Christchurch since I took her to the bloody airport.'

That first time the men just spoke there, only for a few minutes, one of them jotting into a pocketbook. I stood in the hallway for a while, watching them, their shadows inching into the hall. Then I went back to my room.

The second time they came he was in his dressing gown, and they told him to get dressed and then had to wait while Mrs Colway came bustling down from up the road and led me by the hand back to her place.

The third time, he didn't come at all and the morning after that the house was full of people sitting, standing, walking back and forth. I remember being picked up this time and carried to Mrs Colway's house. Then bits and pieces of my room arrived there too; toys, my colouring books. My ukulele and my stuffed animal friends.

But no one ever answered my questions about Mum.

We sit at a wooden bench, eating hamburgers. Leaves drift down from the trees. I flick through photos of Lily on my phone. Adam raises a drink can to his lips and I watch his throat dance. He fusses with his wallet, counts his cash, then reaches into his khaki army bag and takes out the map and runs his fingers across the paper.

He takes a bite of his burger, then his face sours.

'Is yours as bad as mine?' he says.

'Yup.'

We laugh; we haven't laughed since we left home. Then he stops.

'I can't promise you,' he says, 'you know, that I won't kill the bastard.'

I take a deep breath of the spiced woodland air.

'He has a name,' I say.

'What?'

'He has a name.'

'I don't give a fuck if he has a name.'

'You should. Because part of that is my name. Or at least it was.'

'Yeah, was.'

We take a few more bites then he reaches and hands me my helmet.

The hills steepen and grow into huge shoulders of deep green, draped with shawls of grey cloud. Adam threads the bike through sheer-sided apertures, burrows us down into gorges where water sparkles over shale beds. We stop at Murchison for another bite, at Īnangahua for a drink. It feels like hours before we see the ocean again, and when we do it is fronted by rocks standing stiff as petrified soldiers, looking up into the hills. Swirls of surf rush in and whip up through holes in the rocks, booming, twists of seawater set spinning like ice skaters.

Adam stands nodding.

'This is nothing like home,' he says.

'You don't talk much about home,' I say.

'Neither do you.'

I look away out over the water.

'Sorry,' he says.

I nod.

The road skirts the seashore for an hour then shies away. Just when I miss the sea it returns, and we inhabit a thin strip between the surf and the serrated hills. The bike's engine pitch rises and falls and I tighten my grip and close my eyes to it and think of the first time that I can remember the voice coming to me. I was in Mrs Colway's backyard and she was hanging washing and she lifted a peg off the metal clothesline and I heard it then, soft, humming a song my mother used to, to try and send me to sleep. I stood and walked to Mrs Colway and stared up at the vibrating wires and she looked down with a clothes peg between her teeth and I raised my hands to be picked up and she did.

'What's wrong, dear?' she said.

I reached for the plaited wires, my fingers stretching, but she bent and kissed my cheek then turned and carried me back inside where I couldn't hear the voice any more.

By dawn on the third day it had started to rain. Droplets slid and settled onto her eyelids, onto the delicate hairs of her eyebrows as she lay looking up beyond the criss-crossed Vs and Ws of the metal bridge, into the puffs of dust sprinkling down with each passing set of wheels. Tiny eggs of water settled in the dark, into the tiny lakes and valleys in her dress, into the palm of her open hand, spreading, growing. Water drifted, then fell from her knees and calves, into the flattened grass beneath where she lay. In a couple of hours it had even filled the trail of footprints leading away from her.

I tap Adam on the shoulder, and he checks his mirror and pulls over and we stop in a gravel turnaround. He looks to where huge boulders make a stone jetty out into the grey water. The wind here is bitter and it crashes against me, half spins me around when I step off and try to call Nesta. Adam laughs when he sees me teetering, then takes off his jacket and forms batwings with it and I step into them and he wraps me where the wind can't get me and I dial.

'Tell you what,' says Nesta.

I look at Adam.

'What?' he says.

I show him the image she sends, of Lily fast asleep with one hand raised.

The day Nesta came down to pick me up from Mrs Colway, the two women sat sipping tea and talking in the lounge. Mrs Colway had a multi-layered tea and cake stand thing she brought out when someone she wanted to think well of her arrived. They touched hands, then Mrs Colway, always so contained, so prim and careful, began to cry. Nesta handed her a handkerchief and they didn't speak again. I think the tea went cold.

My last glance of my street was through the rear window of a car in the rain.

Nesta had her son, Rickie, take her TV out of the lounge and put it into her bedroom. A year later she moved us north, away from everything. I found out later that the investigation, then the trial was on the news almost every night. A couple of years ago – just after he got out – a journalist sent me an email with an old film clip attached, that the email said had footage of the riverbank and the bridge and the scenes outside the court. And did I have any comment to make now and would I do an interview. I deleted the file, changed my email address.

By the afternoon of the third day the river had risen enough with the rain to cast a circle around her, and leaves and twigs and flower petals brushed against her. Against her right arm where it stretched in the grass. Her left arm and hand lay across her face. In the dark the water rose high enough to float her, once even enough to turn her full about, like a dinghy drifting from its mooring. She lay there, revolving, but the river never rose quite enough to acquire her still and silent figure for the last part of its voyage to the sea. In the evening it set her back down, turned quarterwise to where she had lain.

We walk out onto the first few boulders until we know we can't go any further. Adam looks at me.

'You sure you don't want to phone ahead?' he says.

'Yeah.'

'Okay. I don't know what kind of welcome we'll get.'

He puts on his helmet and stands fixing the chin-strap.

'He doesn't even know I exist,' he says, 'does he?'

I shake my head.

'Or Lily?'

'No,' I say.

'Reckon that's a good thing. I wish it was the other way round, too.'

I take a deep breath, look past him out to the charcoal horizon.

'I can phone for a taxi,' I say, 'if you can't do it. You can just hang here.'

'We're in the middle of nowhere.'

'When we get to Greymouth.'

'Nope.'

'You really don't have –'

'Nah,' he says. 'We're not having that conversation.'

He starts the engine and I swing my leg over the seat.

By the fourth morning the river had ebbed and the grass dried out again and the yellow flowers on her dress fabric once again caught the sunlight. Seagulls perched on the rails of the bridge, peering down at the form in the grass, clearer now, with its rotation. A couple of them sprung from the bridge's metal spine and ventured down and stood looking at her.

When we get there the driveway is overgrown with roadside bush, so we actually miss it, then turn around at the next settlement and have to go back. We sit on the bike, both looking up across the wooden bridge over the creek, to where the old house sits among trunks and branches. I think for a moment that Adam is going to ask me one last time if I'm sure I want to do this, but he doesn't. We roll to a stop beside a wheelbarrow full of random wood offcuts and he switches the engine off. Birds call in the trees, there's a murmur from the creek. I watch a thin trail of smoke drift from the chimney. Adam steps off.

The knock on the door breaks the silence. As it had when those two suited men came to stand on our porch when Mum hadn't come back from her trip home. She had crouched and kissed me and said, 'I'll be a couple of days,' but those days never ended.

There's a hint of footsteps, a tiny blur of movement from a window curtain. Adam sees it, then glances at me. He reaches to knock again but I do so instead. After forever the door opens.

'So,' the voice says, through the crack between door and doorframe. 'What do you want?'

I sense Adam's body stiffen and step against him, half in front of him.

'Well?' it says.

'Do you know who I am?' I say.

'Just another fucking nosey parker,' he says. The voice is raspy and starts to degrade into a cough. The gnarled hand on the door jitters. 'Ghoulish bloody tourists. I'm not a circus attraction.'

'Watch your mouth,' says Adam.

I shush him and step closer to the dim doorway and begin to make out an unshaven face, eyes almost submerged in blotchy skin. I push against the door and he tries to close it but he has no strength, and Adam reaches and just shoves it open and he staggers back against the wall.

'What the hell?' he says, blinking, as we step inside. I can't believe how much he's aged, even though I haven't seen him since I was a child.

'Rachel asked you a question,' says Adam, and the old man's body braces itself against the wall and he stares then glares at me with his pale blue eyes. The whites are cracked and seeping with red blood vessels. His crinkled upper lip jitters and he turns away then back to me. I don't move a muscle.

'You have no business being here,' he says. 'I've got nothing to say.'

Adam and I walk past him, down the hall to the unkempt lounge, the smell of must and tobacco and old sweat permeating everything. A half-eaten piece of toast sits askew on a plate. A chipped enamel cup holds anaemic tea. There are whisky bottles – empty – lined up against one wall. I turn back to see him close the door and stand with his arm against the wall; the weight of it seems to be the only thing holding him up. When he comes into the lounge and its light, his grubby checked shirt is open to his pink chest, and wiry grey hairs lie scattered.

Adam walks around the room, looking behind chairs and curtains, running his hand on top of a shaky bookshelf. He goes into a couple of other rooms.

'I don't have any guns in the place,' says the old man. 'If that's what you're looking for.'

Adam comes back in, nodding. The old man beckons towards an old couch and I sit, but Adam stays standing. One leg of the couch is wonky, and sits unevenly on a tatty paperback book stuffed under its foot. Stringy stuffing bleeds from a punctured cushion. The old man sits in a chair with a frayed blanket over it, rests his hands on the armrests.

'Why did you move here?' I say. 'It wasn't your people who were from the coast, it was Mum's.'

'How did you find out?' he says.

'Why did you move here?'

'Probably some journo, I reckon,' he says. 'Bastards.'

'Why did you?'

He stares hard at the dusty floorboards.

'You wouldn't understand,' he says.

'You could try,' I say.

He reaches for a pouch of tobacco and takes some papers from his pocket and rolls a cigarette. He offers the workings to Adam but Adam just turns away.

'Have her people been in touch?' I say.

'Oh, yeah. I've had all that. Sent a deputation, then cars parked in my driveway at night with their motors running. Even a brick through my window.'

'Yet you're still here.'

'They can't smoke me out. I'm not some rat.'

Adam turns back to the old man, shakes his head. He looks at me, taps the pocket of his jeans where he keeps his phone, then glances towards the hallway.

'I'm gonna check on Lily,' he says.

'Who's Lily?' says the old man.

'Fuck you,' says Adam. 'You think you have a right to know anything?'

'This is my house,' says the old man. 'No one tells me what I can and can't do.'

'So you want to talk about rights and wrongs?' says Adam.

'Piss off,' says the old man. 'You think you know stuff? You don't.'

'I know I'm about to rip your face off,' says Adam.

'Lout,' says the old man. 'Bloody lout, that's all you are.'

The old man hasn't moved a single bone in his rickety body. His sunken eyes just stare out like headlights in a tunnel. As strong as Adam obviously is, the old man shows no hint of apprehension.

'So, did she turn out to be a tart, too?' says the old man, smirking at Adam.

Adam kicks the low table out of the way and leans and lifts the old man clean out of his chair, arms flailing. Adam's hands grip the tattered shirt, bunching it, bunching the skin of the gnarled pink neck too. The old man reaches, attempts to pry Adam's fingers away.

'Hey!' I shout. 'Enough.'

Adam turns to me, his eyes skittery.

'Enough,' I say.

Adam blinks, hard. He lets the old man down and he just collapses, coughing, then dry retching. I push both hands, palms out, against Adam, steer him towards the door. We go outside onto the porch.

'Who was that for?' I say.

'What?'

'I said who's it for? It's not for me, or my mother. We don't need it. We don't ask for it and we don't need it.'

'He's a mean old prick!'

'I'm not talking about him. He doesn't matter. I'm talking about us.'

A gust of air hisses through the trees. Adam looks up into the branches.

'I know,' he says.

'Do you?'

'Fuck it, Rache. I'm here aren't I?'

I stare at him and he raises his hands, open now. And I try very hard to remember how soft they can be.

'I don't know if I can go back in,' he says.

I nod. He lifts his phone from his jeans pocket.

'I'm going to call Nesta,' he says.

I nod my head, touch a hand against his shoulder.

'I'll be just out here,' he says, leaving the door open.

I go in and sit back down.

'Say it,' says the old man, 'say it now. Whatever it is you came here to say.'

'She's my daughter,' I say. 'Our daughter.'

'What?'

'Lily. Just like Mum had a daughter.'

I reach and flick the switch beneath an old lamp and the room sharpens. I stare at him, looking for some flicker, but his eyes are just baby-blue ashes, nothing more.

'Hmmpf,' he says. 'Is that what you came here to say?'

'No.'

'Well, then.'

'You haven't asked me a single thing about my life.'

He nods towards the door.

'Well, you're with that ape,' he says. 'Now I know that.'

'Adam isn't an ape,' I say. 'And Mum wasn't a tart.'

'You'd know, of course. She was always coming back here. Back to that bastard I took her from. She thought I didn't know. Leaving me.'

'If she was leaving she'd have taken me with her.'

'He's dead now, too. Good riddance.'

'I don't want to hear any of this.'

'Well.'

I hear Adam say goodbye to Nesta, then footsteps.

'And I know you've got …' says the old man, but his voice trails off and he turns away towards the window. I watch his throat moving, swallowing, the movement laboured. Adam comes half-in, leans against the door jamb.

'How far are we from the bridge here?' I say.

'What do you want to know that for?' says the old man.

His breath is all shivery and the vein at his temple clings stark in the harsh lamplight.

'How far?' I say.

'About twenty minutes.'

'Jesus,' I say. 'That close.'

'Sometimes I go down there,' he says. 'Sometimes I need to.'

'I don't want to hear that,' I say.

'All right. Just making conversation until you lot clear out.'

'You still haven't said my name. You haven't asked me about my life and you haven't once said my name.'

'I didn't expect to see you here.'

'Well, I'm here.'

'*We're* here,' says Adam.

'I didn't want any of this,' says the old man. 'Bloody bastard of a thing. People always at me. Do you think it was easy in that bloody place for eighteen years?'

'I don't care,' I say.

'Oh, so it's okay for you not to care?'

'I've had about enough of this,' says Adam.

'Well,' says the old man, his voice rising. 'There's the bloody door!'

Adam reaches a hand towards me. I stand, look at the old man.

'I'm twenty-six years old,' I say. 'And two months, and seventeen days. I've been counting the days.'

'What?' says the old man. 'What the hell are you on about?'

'That's the age Mum was,' I say, 'when you left her under the bridge.'

He sits back, then forward, then starts to stand, his legs shaky. Adam steps and shoves him back into the chair, then goes back to the doorway. The old man slouches, crumpled like an old sock.

'That's what I came to tell you,' I say. 'But tomorrow, I'll wake up. Another day older. I'll wake up and I'll be miles and miles away from you again. And I won't ever think of you. Ever.'

He looks like he's about to try and stand again, but it's just his body twitching, all the wires frayed at the ends. He closes his eyes. I nod to Adam and get up and he puts his arm around my shoulder and we walk out of the cruel light and down the dim hallway. I can hear his voice behind me, snuffling, mostly a bunch of mismatched words, then:

'Bloody bastard of a thing!' he shouts. 'I loved her!'

Adam holds my hand tighter and we walk over the creaking porch and down into the leaf-strewn dirt to the bike. We get on, but he doesn't start it.

'Sorry,' he says.

'For what?'

'For – fuck it – for everything.'

I reach and take a tear from the edge of his eye, trap it between my index finger and thumb. We put our helmets on and roll forward. At the end of the driveway Adam pauses, turns and looks south. I know what he's thinking.

The bridge is twenty minutes away.

Her last resting place.

No. Her last resting place is in Karoro Cemetery in Greymouth, in the lee of a slight rise with a stand of sturdy trees between her and the cold westerly wind.

'If you see a kōwhai tree,' I say, 'let's stop.'

On the afternoon of the fifth day a man carrying a fishing rod and a knapsack saw her, where her body had pivoted quarterwise in the water then lain back on the grass. Her teal dress with its kōwhai flowers, which had blended so well with the greenery and hidden her, was sodden, as was her hair. Hidden from the cars as they rattled over the bridge, hidden from the searchers who walked, straddling the bridge's old metal rail lines and timber boards.

The fisherman crouched in the wet grass, took off his oilskin hat and looked across her to the rippled water.

He drove to the local pub, where the barman said, 'Righto, Kath, pour Des a whisky, will you?' and lifted the receiver off the phone on the wall. Within an hour the stalking pūkeko had retreated up and downriver, away from the group of men standing in a ragged circle, one of them unfurling a large black plastic bag.

At Greymouth we go to the cemetery and Adam picks up a jar of rancid water from an old concrete plinth and tips it out. He runs it under a water tap on a post at the edge of the driveway and swirls it a few times then brings it back and I set the kōwhai flowers into it, with the fingers that had wiped away his tear.

'Karoro,' I say.

Adam turns to me.

'It means seagull,' I say.

On the evening of the 7757th day, twenty-one years after she was lifted onto a plastic sheet and taken in an ambulance to her hometown and put into a cold room and placed on a bench, an old man stands at the place she had lain on the riverbank. She and he had left the town years before in a car with wedding ribbons fluttering in the wind. He closes his eyes and says something but it is lost in the gusts from the grey Tasman. He steps into the river and stands for a long time, then walks further until the water is at his waist, then leans and tips face-first into the moontide.

Back home again I sit on the couch, holding Lily against me, my arms a half-circle beneath her. My phone rings. I can't reach it without disturbing her so Adam lifts it from the table and answers. He turns to me.

'It's Nesta,' he says. 'She's asking if we're watching the news.'

He puts the phone down and flicks on the TV.

The phone rings again. It's not Nesta this time. It rings again a few minutes later and a few minutes after that, so I set it on silent, then just turn it off and we stay there – the three of us – in the silence.

Time

JACQUIE MCRAE

'Did you know, Frankie, that sea otters hold hands so they can't drift away as they sleep?' My daughter shows no sign that she heard me, but she's always been more of an adventurer than a listener.

She started accumulating bruises and broken bones the moment she could walk. She jumped off everything, including from the water tank into the pool, before she could swim. The only reason she didn't drown was that I heard the splash through an open window.

On her fifth birthday, she marched through the school gates on her own. That morning, as she was sitting on a stool and I was fussing with her hair, she cupped her little hands on either side of my face, looked me straight in the eyes and said, 'You can drop me off, but you can't come in.' I remember muttering something about walking her to her classroom and her adamant reply, 'I know where it is, Mum. I'll be okay.'

We christened her Francine, but from about age six she wouldn't answer to anything other than Frankie. She had a standoff with a teacher in year two, refusing to eat her lunch for two weeks as she wouldn't respond to the name she'd been given. I had no idea what was going on until I was called in to the school at the start of week three. Frankie sat in one of the office chairs, her arms knotted across her chest and a look of determination on her face. I knew that look well. With Frankie, you had to learn to compromise or be prepared to put on your battle fatigues. I was so upset to learn she hadn't eaten lunch for two weeks that I demanded Ms Rex call my child Frankie. From then on, everyone called her Frankie.

I wish I'd seen that her need to explore came from curiosity and not from a desire to make me look like a bad mother. I just wanted her to be like the other girls. I wanted to go shopping with her and take her to ballet classes. Ballet lasted one week, before everyone involved decided that something more strenuous than toe pointing was required.

I convinced myself that Frankie's interest in boundary fences was just a tomboy phase and that she'd grow out of it by the time she hit puberty. But puberty for Frankie was like finding another gear.

A sharp scream from one of the machines keeping Frankie alive makes me jump. A nurse walks calmly into the room, and after checking a few tubes pushes a button on one of the monitors and the familiar beep starts up again.

'No change?' she asks.

I shake my head.

'Can I get you anything?'

'Can we get some light in here?

She turns and looks at the open windows and the curtains that I've drawn back as far as they will go.

'I'm sorry, Mrs Faber, but I think it's the best we can do. Maybe a cup of tea?'

I shake my head and start playing with Frankie's hair. It feels like I'm taking advantage of her as I curl a strand of hair around my finger. As a teenager she could sense a fuss coming from me a mile away and would deflect it before it came anywhere near her. She let me help her get ready for her school graduation, but I'm pretty sure her dad bribed her. The climbing shoes she'd been going on about for a month appeared on her feet a few days later.

A nurse comes into the room with a basin, a mountain of towels, washcloths and a fresh gown.

'Hi, Frankie. I'm just going to give you a bed bath.' She switches her gaze towards me as she lays items on a side table. 'How are you doing today, Mrs Faber?'

A small bob of my head is all I can muster. It really is the most ridiculous question to ask, but I forgive her as she's talking to Frankie like a real person. Some of them come and go from the room like there's no one in the bed. I know technically that Frankie's not here, but while she's breathing she's still here and there's still hope.

She washes Frankie's face gently. 'I'm just going to undo your gown and wash your arms and your chest.' She moves the gown down and keeps her covered with a bath blanket, exposing only the area that she's washing. She lays a towel under one arm and squeezes one of the washcloths in water before rubbing soap onto it. 'Do you want to help?'

Tears spring to my eyes and I have to swallow a lump in my throat.

I nod. She shows me how to wring out the wash cloth in the warm water and then fold it around my hand like a mitt.

'I'll go first with the soap and you can follow me with the rinsing cloth and then pat her dry.'

I'm frightened I may pull some tubes out, but the nurse reassures me I'm doing fine. My thumb lingers softly along Frankie's forearm as I dry her. I help the nurse roll her onto her side so we can wash her back. I see a mark on her lower torso that I haven't seen before. I rub at the funny black smudge, and realise it's small letters and they're not coming off.

'Can you read what that says?' I ask the nurse, holding back tears as I'm hit with the knowledge that Frankie had to conceal something else from me.

She peers at it for a minute. 'I think it says, *Maktub*.'

'I don't know what that means.'

'I'm sorry, I don't know either.'

We finish the bed bath and the nurse disappears with the basin and the used linen. I inhale deeply as I look at Frankie lying back on her pillow.

'You could have told me you got a tattoo, Frankie? I wouldn't have liked it, but I would have tried to understand.'

My phone beeps and I read a message from Carl: *On way*. After twenty-five years of marriage, his ability to keep things simple still annoys and astounds me. I think that's one of the reasons why Frankie always went to him. He's the *yes* and *no* man. I'm the *let's look at every possible scenario before making a decision* one. I always knew that Frankie loved her dad more, but I worked my way through that. A lot of the books I read about children said it was normal for a child to attach to one parent, especially if they were similar. Even though I understood, it still hurt. I kept hoping I might get a turn one day.

I don't reply to Carl's text but type *Maktub* into the search bar of my phone.

Arabic word that translates to 'It is written'.

'Why would you want that tattooed on your back, Frankie? What's written?'

I think I feel a finger twitch and quickly look down, but her hand lies motionless in mine. I stare at it and will her fingers to move. The doctor has said that the movements I've noticed are just reflexes and aren't a sign of improvement. I wonder if he'd say it so harshly if it was his daughter lying in the bed. I want this to be an awful dream but I know it's not. I haven't slept since they brought her in three days ago, so I know there's no waking up. They said she wouldn't last the first night but they have no idea who they're dealing with. Strong will is the baby brother to Frankie's will.

Carl arrives looking tired and carrying a plastic bag. He leans down and pecks me on the cheek, dropping the bag on the floor, then moves to the other side of the bed.

'How's my girl?' He kisses Frankie on the forehead and pulls a strand of hair back from her face. I see the tears pooled in his eyes and hear the crack in his voice. 'Any news?' he asks, keeping his eyes on his girl.

'No.'

He strokes her arm, and in that small movement I feel swept aside.

'She's not a cat, Carl.'

'What?' I can see the confusion and pain in his eyes.

'Did you know that she had a tattoo?'

He looks at me and his brow is furrowed. 'No?'

An exhale full of relief escapes me, but then I'm flooded with loathing for my petty self and start to cry. He makes the feeling worse as he wraps his arms around me, crushing me into his chest.

'It's okay, Kate. It's going to be okay,' he whispers over the top of my head.

I nod inside my brain but I'm so tired I'm not sure that my head moves. Squashed in his embrace, I feel safe. The second he lets me go, fear rushes in and throws its ugly claws around me.

'They say she's not going to be okay, Carl. The swelling in her brain is stopping the blood flow. They're running some more tests but said we might need to consider stopping the mechanical ventilation.'

'I know.'

'Yes, but they don't know our Frankie.'

He attempts a smile but I feel like he's humouring me.

'Well, they don't, Carl!'

'No, they don't, but Frankie fell one hundred metres onto rocks.'

'So ... we just give up?'

'I'm not saying that.'

'No, that's right, Carl. You just say nothing.' The silence that follows screams so loud in my ears that I have to stand up and move about. 'You could have told her not to go!'

He closes his eyes and shakes his head. 'Let's not do this.'

'But she would have listened to you,' I wail.

He inhales and appears to hold his breath. When he speaks I can hear the tension in his voice. 'Don't you think I wish I had?'

Knock. Knock.

We both turn and see Frankie's girlfriend, Ari, standing by the open door. God knows how long she's been standing there.

'Sorry ... I can come back.'

'No.' Carl moves towards her and places his hand on her shoulder. 'Come. Come in, Ari.'

'Hi, Mrs Faber,' Ari says, still standing by the door.

I sense that she's waiting for me to invite her in, but I can't quite form the words. I motion with my hand for her to come forward. She looks at Frankie and hesitates at the foot of her bed. Ari's blonde dreadlocks fall across her face but don't hide the tears that run down it. A wave of sorrow rushes over me and I can't help but feel sorry for the girl who loves my daughter.

'Carl and I are going to get a coffee, Ari. It's okay if you want to sit on the bed and talk to her. We'll be twenty minutes.'

Carl nods and puts his hand on the small of my back as we leave. On my way past the nurses' station I check that they have my cell phone number.

'Don't worry, Mrs Faber. We'll come and get you if anything changes.'

'Thank you.'

The cafeteria is crowded. I take a seat at one of the only empty tables while Carl orders coffee. He comes back with a scone and places it in front of me.

'You should try and eat something.'

'I can't. I'm not hungry.'

We lock eyes and neither of us looks away.

'We're going to have to let her go, Kate.'

I shake my head sideways. The noise wraps around me and I'm grateful for it. I can't think. I don't want to think.

'She would hate this. If she lives ... she won't even be able to move her eyes. Do you want that for her?'

'But she might get better. I've read stories where people have made miraculous recoveries and the doctors got it wrong.'

'No ... you can see. They haven't got it wrong.'

'Two flat whites.' We both ignore the waitress as she places them in front of us.

'I'm not doing it, Carl.'

'Okay.' He takes a slow sip from his coffee and turns away from me to look out the window. I follow his gaze and watch a gaggle of geese meander across the hospital lawn and then slip into the lake. I envy their nonchalance. Looking at my watch I see that twenty minutes has gone by. I stand and leave my coffee untouched on the table. Carl takes a last sip of his and indicates with his hand for me to go first.

Ari looks embarrassed to be found lying down next to Frankie. Her slender frame reminds me of a gazelle as she leaps to sitting.

'I'm sorry,' she says, a blush colouring her cheeks.

'It's all right, Ari,' Carl says as he slumps down into one of the hospital chairs.

'Any change?'

She shakes her head.

'What does Maktub mean, Ari?' I ask, looking straight at her. 'I mean, I know what it means but what's the relevance to Frankie?'

'She said it's about being authentic and following your own path. Like, each of us has one and we just need to be brave enough to follow it. Like, it's already written so we don't have to sweat stuff.'

'Right. Like leaping off mountains and not worrying that you might die.'

'It was a dreadful accident, Mrs Faber.'

'That's enough, Kate.'

'I'm sorry ... it's just so wrong. She's not even twenty. She hasn't lived yet.' I lay my head in my hands. After a few moments I hear a chair being dragged towards me.

'Mrs Faber?'

'What, Ari?'

'This may be inappropriate, but I have some photos on my phone from that day. I feel like I need to show them to you.'

'I don't want to see any photos.'

'Okay.' She goes to put the phone in her pocket but Carl stops her.

'I want to see them.'

Ari swipes her phone a few times and then passes it to Carl. 'Keep scrolling across. I took a few.'

I can't help but look over as Frankie's face pops up on the screen, her favourite green bandana just visible under her helmet. Carl sees me looking and moves the phone over a little so I can see her better. I want to turn away but I can't. She's halfway up a vertical cliff, holding onto a climbing rope with one arm, and waving to the camera with the other. Her grin spreads wide across her face. Her muscled legs and arms tanned from the summer sun. In the last photo, at the summit, her arms are stretched victoriously overhead and her smiling blue eyes look directly at me.

I hear her voice in my head. *I lived, Mum. Don't worry, I lived.*

A wild animal sound comes out of my mouth. Everything I've managed to hold in for days comes rushing to the surface like it's trying to escape. I'm ripped open and struggling to breathe. I inhale deeply to try and calm myself but I can't control my sobbing. Carl puts his arms around me and I cling to him like I'm going to drown if I let go. He rocks me until my sobs subside and my breathing returns to normal.

I turn and look at Frankie lying in the bed. She's unrecognisable as the girl at the peak of the mountain. My fearless girl crammed more adventures into her twenty years than I managed in fifty. Machines and tubes are now the only thing keeping her alive.

The doctor and the intensive care nurse come into the room, and I can tell by their body language that the results of the second tests they were required to do are the same as the first. Both the clinical and the imaging show brain death.

I look towards Carl, close my eyes and nod. I'm grateful that he doesn't say anything to me before telling them our decision to stop the machines.

'I'm so sorry,' Doctor Sanson says, and he genuinely seems sorry. He's kept us informed from the moment she was admitted. 'Frankie's injuries are too severe for her to recover. The timing is never good, but I have to ask if Frankie ever discussed being an organ donor, or if you would like some time as a family to discuss this?'

The day Frankie got her driver's license replays in my mind. She was excited and flush with the thought of independence as she drove us home from the test. 'Just think, Mum, your days of being my taxi driver are over.' She flashed me one of her beautiful smiles and I tried to imitate it even though I was flooded with sadness. Another thing she didn't need me for. She told me that she had ticked donor and we got into an argument. I was upset that she hadn't had a conversation with me about it before she decided. She was adamant that it was her body and so no conversation was needed except to tell me her wishes. She made me promise that I would respect them if anything happened.

Time

'Frankie wanted to be an organ donor,' I say out loud.

Both Ari and Carl look towards me and I can see the surprise on their faces.

'Are you sure, Kate?' Carl asks.

'Yes, those are her wishes.'

'Then that's what we'll do.'

'Thank you both. I'll let the donor coordinator know. You'll be able to discuss any concerns with them and we're all here if you have any questions.'

The next hour passes in a blur as all sorts of medical people explain our options and what happens next. I appreciate them taking the time to explain the procedures and possible outcomes, but all I want to do is curl up beside Frankie. Carl and Ari leave the room for a moment so I climb up onto the side of the bed and place Frankie's hand in mine. I lay my head down next to hers so I can breathe in her smell and whisper in her ear.

'Maybe you were right, Frankie, and things are already written. Perhaps on some level you knew that you weren't here for long and I knew that I wouldn't get to hold you forever. I know I held you way too tight and I'm sorry for that. I should have spent more time telling you how brave and amazing I thought you were, but we don't get to go backwards. I don't know if you knew that Francine means *free one*. I didn't tell you because I didn't think you needed any encouragement. I love you, Frankie, and this is my time to let you be free.

I look down at my sea otter hands and release my grip.

Francine Faber died at 11.59 pm on 31 December. Her organs were donated and her gift helped to change nine lives.

May Board

ERU J HART

A sea-wettened wind curls along the hidden coast. The airport, nearby, catches and flings planes which moan airward. Miramar Peninsula fades into the dark as glittery traffic makes its way home.

The man next door is smoking. I am not smoking, I have given up. I considered the project an act of decolonisation. I teach English at the local high school. On a bad day I feel like a cog in the colonial machine; on a good day, a lever.

I am not sure if the man I can see through the slit in my road-facing blind is the dad, the brother or some non-relative. It was just me in this block for two splendid, quietish weeks. I grew accustomed to blasting my stereo. I am undergoing a 90s revival. All these recently dead celebrities (Prince, Whitney, Bowie, Jackson) have revived the public's interest in the idea that music – good music – existed before file-sharing, iPods and the new millennium.

The school holidays arrived and with them, the neighbours.

Two kids, under ten, leapt from the BMW. The man sat behind the wheel, gently revving the engine although he had apparently reached their destination.

'Far! Flash!' yelled one of the kids, pressing his face up against the glass next door. In the passenger seat a small woman in her twenties looked at the man, then at the children and slowly wound up her window. He finally cut the engine.

I was mixing my protein shake at the bench; I am trying to get ripped. One day on Facebook I saw a quote from Socrates which, as time stretched on, began to taunt me: 'It is a shame for a man to grow old without seeing the beauty and strength of which his body is capable.' With this in mind I have committed to eating 100 grammes of protein a day and working out three times a week. I want to see my abs before I am forty. Just once would do.

I cross the kitchen and slide along the living room wall. I lower the large blind. This cuts off the public's view of me, but I can still see a slit of Outside. I can still hear.

'Is this it, Dad?' asks the older boy.

'Seems so,' the man answers.

I hear the key click and a clatter of young feet through the wall.

I say goodbye to being the sole resident in this new apartment block. The last gulp of protein shake tastes unusually bitter.

So far, no abs.

Darnelle told me about the new apartment complex along Evans Bay Parade. I saw her at church. As is my custom, once Christmas was over I recommitted to attending after a year of hardly going. I get hungry for religion after Christmas. There's something about seeing Mum in her Sunday best on Christmas Day, while the rest of us burn in singlets and shorts under the Hawke's Bay sun, that makes me regret my godlessness. Sixteen years of top-notch religious indoctrination has its effects on an obedient boy.

Sitting alone on one of the long wooden pews the following January, I began to rethink my decision. The bright sun poked weakly through the gauzy net curtains. I could feel the pew shake slightly and turned to my right. Darnelle.

'Hey, stranger!' she said warmly. She wore a purple floral dress that stretched flatteringly across her rubbery body. Her light moustache begged for a waxing. 'How you been?' she asked.

'Finished my training. *Finally*. Got a job this year at the high school.'

She opened her mouth widely and her eyes followed. 'Good for *you*! Teaching what?'

'English. It's important to me that more Māori read. I'm hoping to do something about that. Half of all Māori leave high school with nothing.'

'Oh yah. It's a problem,' she agrees. 'What are you reading at the moment?'

'*Atlantis: The Mother of Empires*. It's from the 1930s, when some people thought they had found evidence of a lost civilization, specifically Atlantis in South America,' I say.

'How curious. You know *Signs and Times*? We're heading that way. It says so in the Bible. This was never supposed to last forever,' she adds.

Up towards the altar the pianist starts to play something like a dirge. A chorister pins the hymn numbers up on the board.

'I'm looking for a place. Heard of anything going?' I ask.

She grips my thigh tightly. 'Yes!' She grabs her phone and shows me a listing on Trade Me. 'I'll send it to you.'

Darnelle works for Te Puni Kōkiri – the Ministry of Māori Development. It's the default employer for Māori graduates. She has contacts.

'I heard about this from a friend. It's being built by Ngāti Toa, on a block of land that used to be a wool shed. Round near the airport.'

The ad shows an architect's drawing of a long concrete block, three stories high set against a hill. It has wide glass doors that open directly onto the footpath.

'Evans Bay,' she adds.

'That's a flash area.'

She raises her eyebrows. 'Not everyone's happy about it,' she adds cautiously. 'Be good for *you* though?'

The churchmen enter from the foyer, heading towards the pulpit. Three men in cheap suits claiming God's mantle.

'How's Tim?' I ask in a whisper.

'We're divorced,' she says plainly. 'Turns out he's still gay.'

'He was really trying,' I say.

'We both were.'

'His heart's in the right place.'

I open the hymn book. She and I begin the opening song: 'When upon life's billows you are tempest tossed …'

Nan's favourite.

The application form required my whakapapa. I had to dig it out from one of Dad's old boxes of papers. I haven't committed it to memory because I don't attend that many tangi or family reunions. Beyond the names of my grandparents, they are just characters in some disconnected historical drama. Iritana Iritana, a woman with the same first and last name. A man called Captain Tucker; not sure if *Captain* was his first name, or his title.

Dad's methodical pedigree charts show that my grandmother was one of nine children. Only five survived infancy. When a child died, the next one born was given their name. Three were called Te Atatuhi; a name thought so precious it outlived the child.

One of the sections asks: 'In what way do you support the kaupapa of this Papakāinga?' In neat handwriting I explain: 'Although I do not whakapapa directly to this area, I am a teacher at the local high school where many students do affiliate to Ngāti Toa. Our school is built on Pukeahu, a hill sacred to the first inhabitants. My understanding is that it was once a terraced garden.'

When I receive the phone call that I have been offered one of the brand new apartments, I am thrilled. I have been sleeping in the spare room of a teacher-couple from school. Sally teaches maths and her girlfriend Tarns works in student services. To minimise my impact I stay at school until it is dark and then drive around the southern coast until it is bedtime. It's become wearisome and a waste of petrol. In the moonlight the rough southern coast with its shadows of the South Island makes for beautiful, if grim, company.

When I tell Sally and Tarns I'll be moving out next weekend, Tarns refers to the cat.

'Olaz will miss you.'

Each night, Olaz waits beside the mailbox for me. He once placed a dead mouse on my pillow.

Olaz shoots me a stare suggesting that if he were larger, he would greatly enjoy eating me.

Mae is the other first-year English teacher in our department. She is fifteen years younger than me, with an obstacle-free path from high school to university to training college and back to high school again. She is an expert on NCEA, having sat it herself only four years earlier. I am a relic from the bursary system, where a whole year wasted could be overcome by a weekend of cramming for one enormous exam. Nowadays students glare under a regime of constant assessment.

Mae and I are of different consistencies. Mae admires my colourful PowerPoints. I admire her pert blondeness.

I spent the week before classes setting up my room. It was important to me that I stamp my personality on the space. I wanted the room to speak for me first.

'*Children should be taught HOW to think, not WHAT to think*' is one of my posters. This is to place the burden of learning content back on them. In bold 72-point Courier New font I printed a poster saying: '*The Master has failed more times than the beginner has tried.*' This was to provide a talking-piece into letting them know I have a Masters. I am desperate to be what they call in teacher's college a 'culturally responsive teacher', so I spent a morning researching Māori proverbs. I decided upon: '*He Waka Eke Noa*'. I printed off an A2 poster-sized image of a sketch from Captain Cook's voyage of a team of paddlers aboard a waka. The drawing has them in impossibly well-composed order, one man weeping, another clawing at his chest. The central figure is cloaked and elderly, brandishing a spear skyward, tongue lolling and eyes rolled back grotesquely.

May Board

Underneath I have written: 'Our Class Ethos: *He Waka Eke Noa* (A canoe which everyone may board)'.

I think I am trying to say that everyone is welcome. But truth be told, I will not tolerate much fuckery.

Before the students arrived on Day 1, Mae came in to scope out my classroom.

She wandered around the edge of the room, hands held behind her back. 'Hmm.'

'I went to a play last night,' she said. 'With my mum.'

I experienced a mild curiosity. As an English teacher I am now expected to take an active interest in dying art forms.

'*Call of the Barbarians.* It was written, directed and performed by a cousin of ours. She wandered around the stage wearing a horned hat and swearing at Romans.'

I think Mae's point is that Māori are making altogether too much fuss at having been colonised and that colonisation is an historical force, a modis operandi of history and not to be taken too personally.

Earlier this year, Mae and I and all the other first-year teachers attended a professional development conference in Porirua, on 'Confident Classroom Leadership'. It was run by an androgynous woman who, having taught at Mana College for fifteen years, abandoned it in favour of Norway, which can afford its egalitarian attitudes. It's much easier to give the benefit of the doubt, and possibly the Benefit, to people who are visually similar.

'One of the keys to working with Māori students in low-decile schools is to recognise that many of them come from gang backgrounds,' says the presenter confidently. 'Make those disruptive students who call out inappropriately your lieutenants. Give them some power, some responsibility. They'll rise to the opportunity. Make them responsible for keeping the class noise at an acceptable level.'

This presenter thinks back for a moment and says, 'One of my best lieutenants from Mana would call out "Fuck up!" if the class got too out of hand.' The audience laughs. 'We had to work on his manner.'

I am sitting next to Mae. She is wearing the long, red, gossamer cape which a student told her makes her look 'like Superman'.

I am feeling very big-brotherly towards Mae on account of our size and age difference. Truth is, she is bolder and five times more self-assured than I am. She comes from a family of readers and teachers. Chances are her parents are better read than she is. Must be nice.

Mae and I are gorging on the free plunger coffee.

'See, that's how colonisation works,' says a whispery Mae. 'Here's *your* way,' she says, holding out her left hand flat, as if balancing a tray, 'and here's a *better* way,' holding out her flattened right hand. I snort. Such a subversive Barbarian.

Mae completes the circle around my newly decorated classroom. She eyeballs my Captain Cook waka sketch, repurposed as a motivational poster.

'I bet that's what the boys call you: *A Canoe Which Any Man Can Board.*'

'Every sailor craves a port.'

Outside, January comes to a conclusion. The death of summer; the new school year.

'So,' queries Luke, 'this place is only for Māoris?'

We are lying in my darkened room. The bedroom door is open and a weak red light from my living room lamp is lighting up this scene like a darkroom. Luke's topknot has come undone. His thick black hair presses against the walnut skin of his neck.

'Not just for Māori. Apartments were offered first to descendants of Ngāti Toa. And then to anyone who supports the project.'

'Yeah, Māoris.'

'... And their white allies.'

Luke smiles. Even in the darkness it augurs a dim-bright end to years of loneliness. His and/or mine.

'How was work?' I ask.

'I've done six days this week. I'm wasted. Over it.'

I met Luke on Tinder, which is becoming, day by day, less embarrassing and easier to admit. We met up at Satay Noodle Kingdom because I like the dumplings there and they are fairly priced. Fifteen dollars for a main is not too steep to spend on a stranger whose photo looks hot but who might not be in person. Turns out Luke would have been worth up to a thirty-dollar main. He is half Samoan and has a strong well-built aspect complemented by impeccable manscaping. Favourably, he has the perfect ratio of listening to talking, 70:30, which suits a defect I have towards self-obsession.

Things went well, though I did misjudge his outfit.

'Have you just come from basketball?' I had asked him. He wore a drapey singlet with tapering black trousers. No, no he hadn't.

'It's Zambesi.'

Silly me.

Luke works for one of NZ's best-known high-fashion brands.

'But it's all smoke and mirrors,' he admitted proudly.

That was eight months ago, so this undefined coupling is something of a record for me.

Luke's mum is white, and his sister is dating an All Black. I found out this second fact when I visited him while he was house-sitting. I saw the All Black's name on a white bottle of prescription painkillers above the refrigerator. I like how Luke hasn't bragged about this. Actually, I think I have told more people that I am somehow moving about in circles that now include All Blacks than Luke has.

Although the 70:30 listening/speaking ratio suits my self-obsessive tendencies, it does mean I have to extrapolate a little on Luke's internal life.

He has a friend who lives in this neighbourhood who was part of a group of concerned citizens who thought the building was (architecturally speaking) 'too ugly'. This is another way of saying they found the prospect of tribal housing in this affluent area unattractive.

On our first drive through the area, Luke had pointed to a large building on the corner of my block, saying, 'Each of those shoebox apartments in that building is worth a million dollars.'

I acted unphased. 'Māori have been living on this coast for hundreds of years, Luke. The fact that they can no longer afford to is a sad indictment on late capitalism.'

Luke seems to enjoy when I go off on my liberal, race-based discriminatory rants. Or at least he never interrupts or counters me, which I am assuming is Luke's way of showing support. Luke had smiled. That's what I like about Samoans: they are like Māori, but happy.

After some sex that is not yet quite love, I get up and cut Luke and myself some cake. I have taken to baking as winter approaches, and my lowering mood begins to crave sugary adjustments.

In the darkness of my room, in one corner of the property built upon the proceeds of Ngāti Toa grievance, Luke asks, 'So who actually *were* the Moriori?'

My sister Joe has four kids now, and an unfinished science degree at Lincoln. She'll go back and complete it 'when the kids are older', but Sam is only two and a dream doesn't always outlast a child's dependence.

Sam feels utterly entitled to either of her fat heavy breasts, any time – day or night. 'They're his,' she jokes, but actually this is exactly how he treats them.

She and I were sitting in the Hawke's Bay sun last summer at the back of her place, beside the trampoline. Her lawns were unmown because Steve was depressed again. His negativity and the greenery were growing out of hand.

She was smoking Port Royal roll-your-own tobacco, which smelled like a wisp of rum-barrels on fire, and I was vaping my e-cigarette, which smelled like a half-sucked lollipop left in an old gym shoe. We were enjoying the post-Christmas anti-climax.

'I am going to sell Nan's cabinet,' she said proudly. 'Uncle Midge needs the money.'

Now that I am thirty-six, I call Mum about once a month, which looks negligent on paper but feels quite generous in practice. As Mum crawls towards seventy, her phone conversations are feeling less like conversations with a person and more like an activity where someone has cut her diary up into sentence fragments, rearranged them in non-sequitur ways, and is reading them back in her voice.

A typical snatch of such a call goes: 'I'm not talking to Margaret. Hera called and he's coming this way. Who's that out there? The twins! They don't listen, by crikey. What's she doing next door this time of night? Out in the garden, Aunty's garden. And they had such nice food at that baptism.'

One narrative I have managed to piece together is that Mum's older brother has dementia. They visited him last year in Tokoroa and his house was full of empty hot chocolate cups and hundreds of mince and cheese pie wrappers from Caltex. He shouted at them and denied having a daughter called Nicki.

The last I heard, plans were afoot to bring him back to a nursing home in Hastings. But no one had the money.

I looked at Joe, and past Joe at the washing line absolutely packed with drying kids' clothes. I could hear the twins bouncing on the torn couch in the lounge, screaming merry hell. I could see the sad outline of Steve's back through the kitchen window as he read *NZ Hunting & Fishing*, October 2014 Issue, in an effort to distract himself from suicide.

'How much do you think you'll get for that cabinet?'

'Three hundred dollars?' she reckoned.

'Is that really the best use of three hundred dollars?'

'Absolutely!' she said, without hesitation.

A cat-like whine came from the back porch. It was Sam. His gorgeous uncut ginger curls unrolled around his shoulders like a handful of measuring tapes.

'Tit-tit!' he screamed, pointing at Joe.

'Come on then my darling,' she said, one hand inviting him out and the other unbuttoning her torn t-shirt.'

Sam trundled over and when he got to us he launched at his breakfast, fastening onto my sister while looking suspiciously at me. *Mine*, said his energy.

We sat in the ovenish morning under the burning button of the sun. To the southwest rose Kahurānaki, the ancestral mountain, doing sweet fuck all to relieve the people.

'So,' asked Joe, 'what else you been up to, down there in *Wellington?*' She said the word like it was some extra-dimensional location, extremely distant, practically impossible to travel to and just as difficult to imagine. Compared to wherever this was.

'I'm thinking of writing a short story. Set about two hundred years ago in Hawke's Bay. It's from the perspective of a Māori boy, who sees a group of European whalers hunt and kill a whale while he watches from the shore. His reaction will be a mix of disgust – *how could you do that to a sacred creature?* – and amazement – *How incredible you have the power to do that to a god!* The final line will be something like: "He decided he would like to try that one day for himself. After all, the strangers were here to stay." I'm thinking of calling it "The Whale Killers".'

Her face wrinkles around the eyes. She watches me intently.

Her expression seems to be saying: *Is that really the best use of a brain?*

'Junior! Get the fuck inside! These kids needa go to bed,' says the woman I presume is his wife.

'Ettt,' says the man whose name I now know. Junior. 'Keep it down.'

Through the lowered blind I can just see him. He continues to smoke his cigarette. After a while he takes a small pair of scissors out of his pocket and in the darkness approaches the fenceline. There is a series of plaques tied with plastic strips to his end of the shared fence; promotional plaques from the official opening of the building. The Mayor came that day.

Snip. 'A Joint Venture Between Housing NZ & Ngāti Toa.' *Snip.* 'A Walker Architect Project.' *Snip.* 'Te Puni Kōkiri: The Ministry of Māori Development.' *Snip.*

A woman in jogging gear runs past as he gathers the plaques together.

'Evening, lady,' says Junior.

One of the boys opens the door and comes out in his pyjamas.

'Come on, Dad, come inside. The heat pump's on!' The kid grabs Junior's hand and they exit the evening together.

I decide that one day, but probably not this week, I will introduce myself.

The strangers were here to stay.

The Apology

HELEN WAAKA

Mum didn't have long. I knew as soon as I arrived.

'Hi Mum,' I said and leaned over the bed to kiss her cheek. My father was standing by the window, hands in his pockets, shoulders hunched. 'Why don't you sit over here by Mum?'

'I'm perfectly all right here,' he said, staring out the window, a misty rain blocking any view of the car park below. 'I'll leave all that up to you girls.'

'You girls' meant me and my sister, Ruby, who was on her way up from Wellington.

'Have you phoned Aunty Mere?' I asked. 'And it might be a good idea to phone a minister.'

'No. I don't want her interfering and I'm not having any Bible-bangers either.'

'But she's Mum's sister. She has to know.'

He'd always hated anyone else taking charge, and he was out of his depth in the hospital setting – that much was obvious – but to a certain extent so was I. Even with all the placements I'd had training to be a social worker, I felt vulnerable. This was my mother, and no amount of knowing was going to make it any easier.

'I'll go for a drive,' he said. 'Get some fresh air.'

Shortly afterwards Ruby arrived, all bones and sharp angles when we hugged, and there was the smell of alcohol on her breath too, a spirit of some kind. Her blonde hair was wet from the rain and lay flat against her forehead, emphasising her high cheekbones.

'She's slipping in and out of consciousness,' I said. 'We should each spend time alone with her – say the things we've never said – while we still have a chance.'

'You go first,' Ruby said. 'I need the loo.' She poked around in the depths of her patchwork shoulder bag and pulled out a silver hip flask. 'Want a swig?'

'No thanks.' I went back into my mother's room and pulled one of the vinyl chairs closer to the bed. I held her hands and traced the tips of my thumbs around the rings on her fingers – the worn gold wedding band, the single diamond engagement ring. I lay my head down next to hers and watched her chest rising and falling with each breath, amazed at how few she was taking. She mumbled something and I leaned in closer, straining to hear what she'd said. 'What was that Mum?'

'Was I good enough?'

'Sorry?' I wasn't sure what she meant.

'Was I a good enough mother?'

'You were the best, Mum.' I had to press the back of my hand against my mouth to stifle a sob. 'Ruby's arrived,' I said. 'I'll get her to come in.'

Ruby was chatting to a cleaner in the corridor. My father was nowhere to be seen.

'Rube. I need some fresh air. Have you seen Dad?'

'Not yet, no.'

Ruby's eyes were bleary and she tripped on the cleaner's vacuum hose as she walked towards me. 'Whoopsie,' she said.

'She's quite weak,' I said. 'The doctor couldn't give a time frame when I asked. She said it might be twenty-four hours, but it could be longer.'

'How come you always *know* everything?' Ruby brushed past me but went quiet when she entered the room and stood at the end of the bed staring at the small mound of our mother. For a moment I thought she was going to turn and run, but instead she moved closer to the bed.

'Mum?' she said. 'It's me. Ruby.'

'Ruby?' My mother turned her head slightly. 'Ruby.'

I found my father in the ward office complaining to one of the nurses about the car-parking.

'Bloody nuisance in this rain,' he said. 'I'm saturated. I've had to walk miles to get here.'

'You could use the staff car park,' the nurse said. 'If you give me your number plate, I'll let the warden know.'

'Ruby's with Mum now,' I said to him when we left the ward office. 'You could go in when she's finished. Spend a bit of time alone with Mum.'

'I don't need anyone telling me what to do,' he said.

'There's not much of it left, Dad. Time, I mean. When Ruby's finished we're going to get coffee. I can bring one back for you but someone needs to stay with Mum.'

He shoved his hands into his pockets and for a moment I thought he was going to protest again, but when we reached the day room he picked up a dog-eared *Time* magazine and sat in one of the easy chairs, flicking through it while he waited.

One of the nurses offered to set up a La-Z-Boy chair in Mum's room. 'You could use it overnight,' she said, 'and there's family accommodation available too – over in the old nurses' hostel.'

The door to Mum's room opened and Ruby came out, clutching her shoulder bag.

'Why don't you go over to the hostel later on, Dad?' I said. 'That way you'd get a good night's sleep. Ruby and I could stay here.'

'I can look after myself, thanks. You two can do as you please.'

'Ruby?'

'Stop bossing,' Ruby said. 'I'm going for a walk. I'll be back later.'

Two nurses manoeuvred the La-Z-Boy along the corridor and into Mum's room.

'You might need these,' one of them said, leaving a pile of blankets and pillows on the stool at the end of the bed. 'Use the sofa in the dayroom too, if you like.'

My father fell asleep on the sofa with the TV on mute. I tried sleeping in the La-Z-Boy, but woke whenever the nurses shone their torches into Mum's room. They came back in the early hours of the morning to turn and reposition her. My father woke then too and stood at the end of the bed, hair sticking up in all directions. One of the nurses suggested he go down to the kitchen and help himself to a cup of tea.

'Do you want some time alone with Mum now?' I asked when the nurses had finished.

'I'll spend time with her when I'm good and ready,' he said and settled back down on the sofa with his cup of tea.

Ruby appeared the next morning, eyes bloodshot and the smell of alcohol oozing from her pores.

'Don't look at me like that,' she said. 'Keep your sermons to yourself.'

Later that day Aunty Mere arrived. My father stood by the window and stared intently at the car park, still glistening from another downpour of rain.

'Why didn't you let me know sooner?' she asked him. 'She's my sister for God's sake.' But her anger was short-lived. She sat down heavily in the chair my father had vacated, then stood again to move it closer to the head of the bed. She stroked my mother's face. 'Why didn't you let me know?' she asked again, taking a tissue out of her pocket and wiping her eyes.

I'd phoned the Directory Service not long after I arrived from a pay phone in the foyer and managed to track her down, but I had to leave a message with someone else at the other end. 'I'm Rowena Scott,' I said, 'Mere Kingi's niece. Can you let her know Mae, her sister, is in Palmerston North hospital. She doesn't have long to go.'

Ruby and I barely knew our mother's family. My father had made sure of that.

'Get out,' he'd yelled at Aunty Mere once. 'Go on. Get out. Go back to the pā where you and your lot belong.' He'd stood tense and angry by the front door, holding it wide open.

'I'm not going anywhere,' Aunty Mere said.

Ruby and I stood shivering in our pyjamas, watching everything from the lounge doorway.

'Don't go,' Ruby blurted out.

My father turned, a frown of disbelief twisting his face. 'Get to your room!' he yelled. 'Both of you.' I turned to go, knowing how unpredictable he could be, but Ruby stayed where she was.

'No,' she said, moving closer to Aunty Mere.

His frown deepened. 'Don't you dare answer me back,' he said, and let go of the door handle to undo his belt. He yanked the buckle end of it out of his trousers and advanced towards Ruby, but Aunty Mere moved quickly and stood between them.

She was the same height as my father and her gaze never left his face. 'Leave her alone,' she said.

'Get out of my way.'

'You'd know all about it if our brother, Raymond, was here,' she said.

'Yeah well, he's not. Like I said, get out of my way.'

'Not on your life.' Aunty Mere turned towards us. 'Go to your room, girls. Pack your gears. You're coming with me.' But before she had time to turn around and confront him again, he'd shoved her backwards onto the couch.

'Get your hands off me,' she said.

'Those girls won't be going anywhere with you,' he said, leaning over her, poking his forefinger into her chest. She grabbed his finger and they both grappled for a moment, but my father was too strong and pushed her back onto the couch.

'It'll be all right, Mere,' Mum said. Up until then she'd said nothing. 'It's not as bad as it seems. They've got school on Monday.'

'Let me phone Raymond. He'll soon come and sort things out.'

'Like hell he will. I don't want that no-hoper anywhere near my house,' my father said.

'Come home with me, Mae. You and the girls. You shouldn't have to put up with this.'

'We'll be okay,' Mum insisted.

'Well, don't ever say I didn't try to help you. And as for you ...' she said, looking at my father. 'Time will tell.'

We'd seen Aunty Mere a few times since over the years, but never for long. She'd turn up briefly, whenever my father was away on one of his fishing or hunting trips. Now, here she was again, older and just as powerful, but this time grief-stricken at the thought of losing her only sister.

'Your cousins, Maria and Lizzy, are on their way. Uncle Raymond, too, as soon as he flies in from Oz,' Aunty Mere said.

A neighbour and a few old friends of my mother's called in over the next day or so, but not many. My father had scared most of them away over the years. They brought flowers and grapes and stayed for a few awkward moments, offering phone numbers and the promise of baking, then left. Ruby picked at the grapes and I found vases for the flowers. I gave them to the nurses for their office but kept a small bouquet of violets for my mother's room.

Maria and Lizzy turned up with Lizzy's husband.

'We didn't know,' Maria said. 'Mum phoned us when she got here. We came as soon as we could.'

'Neither did we until a few days ago,' I said. 'Dad didn't tell anyone.'

I hadn't seen my cousins since we were children, and it seemed strange to be greeting them now in my mother's hospital room. They barely knew her.

'Thanks for coming,' I said.

Lizzy introduced her husband, Joe, as a lay preacher. He asked if we'd like karakia. 'Prayer,' he said.

'Yes, thanks,' I replied, grateful for the offer.

My father wasn't there when she died. He'd gone for a drive, clearly irritated by the influx of visitors and the 'karakia'. My cousins had gone to pick up Uncle Raymond from the airport. I'd known all along what would happen, but when Mum's raspy breathing finally stopped, I panicked. For a bizarre moment I thought I might be able to shake her awake again. I stood up, leaned over the bed and grasped her shoulders, but in that instant I could see any life had been sucked out of her. I felt an odd sense of lightness then, and for a brief second the room seemed to glow. Everything – the drab furniture, the faded curtains, even the nondescript painting on the wall – shone, as though lit from behind. I wondered if the others could see it too, but Aunty Mere was asleep in the La-Z-Boy and Ruby sat on the other side of the bed, silent and staring.

I woke Aunty Mere. 'She's gone,' I said.

My father came into the room shortly afterwards and stood immobilised, gripping the end of the bed, his face drained of colour. I thought for a minute he was going to yell at Mum, demand to know

The Apology

why she hadn't waited. But then his face crumpled and he sat down heavily in a chair at the end of the bed.

I rang the bell and moments later two nurses came into the room. One of them left again straight away to phone the on-call house surgeon. The other nurse went over to the bed to check on Mum. 'I'm sorry,' she said. 'Would you like me to call a minister?'

My father sat upright. 'No thanks,' he said before anyone else had a chance to reply.

'Take as long as you need,' the nurse said. 'Come down to the office when you're ready and we'll talk about what happens from here.'

I'd supported bereaved families during my hospital placements and had a fair idea of what happened next. Mum would be sponged by the nurses and dressed in a paper shroud. They'd wrap her in a sheet, using safety pins to secure it in place. Afterwards she'd be taken to the morgue – a cold depressing place – and left there overnight until the undertaker arrived.

'I'll phone home, ' Aunty Mere said. 'See about taking her back to the marae.'

'Like hell you will,' my father said. He stood up and pointed his forefinger at Aunty Mere. 'She won't be going to any bloody marae.'

'Let's talk about this,' she said, 'and not here, not in front of Mae.'

'There's nothing to talk about,' he said. 'You have no rights here, Mere. She'll be taken back to Waitapu, where she belongs. I'm phoning the undertaker now,' he said and left the room.

The house surgeon came to confirm what we already knew, and a while later a nurse parked a trolley outside Mum's room. A sheet covered the wooden box on top and a stainless steel bowl sat on the bottom shelf.

'We'll come back later,' she said. 'There's no rush.'

'No need,' Aunty Mere said. 'I'll be looking after my sister. My nieces can help me.'

'I'll need to check with the ward sister first,' the nurse said.

Aunty Mere didn't wait for the ward sister's approval. She helped herself to the stainless steel bowl and filled it with warm water from the basin. She found clean linen hanging behind the locker next to Mum's bed. She wet a cloth, then gently washed and dried my mother's face. Afterwards she folded the top blankets down and undid the buttons of her nightgown. She rolled Mum towards her side of the bed and asked me to slip the nightgown up and over her shoulders. Aunty Mere handed me the bowl and cloth then, but I hesitated, not sure if I'd be able to wash my dead mother. I had to concentrate hard on rinsing the cloth, lathering it with soap and wringing it out. I used soft, tentative strokes across my mother's back and shoulders, fighting all the time to hold back tears.

I patted her dry with a towel and ran my fingers over the familiar heart-shaped mole on her left shoulder. Strands of her thick, shoulder-length hair brushed against the back of my hand and felt so alive I half expected her to roll over and speak. 'A bit lower down, love. There's still a wet patch.'

We rolled Mum onto her back again and I stared at her bare, soft breasts. I couldn't help myself then and choked out a sob.

'It's all right,' Aunty Mere said. 'Let me.'

She washed and dried Mum's chest and breasts and used a separate cloth to wash her lower body. She whispered something in Māori as she worked.

We removed the bed covers, keeping the top half of my mother's body covered in a sheet. Up until then Ruby had been watching from the end of the bed, but she moved closer to help us wash and dry Mum's legs. We both rubbed massage cream into her feet, something Mum had always loved. We dressed her in a clean nightgown and Aunty Mere brushed her hair out smooth on the pillow.

'We'll find something nicer for the undertaker to dress her in,' she said, 'but for now she looks beautiful, just as she is.'

She spoke in Māori again and Ruby broke down. She lay across the end of the bed, face down, sobbing like a baby.

A nurse came in to make sure we were all right and Aunty Mere asked if we could leave Mum like she was until Uncle Raymond arrived.

'I'm sure that'll be okay,' she said. 'I'll let the ward sister know what's happening.'

After she left, my father came back and sat slumped in the chair beside Mum. He stroked her hair, something I had never seen him do before, and he whispered something. 'I'm sorry,' I thought he'd said, but then he spoke, louder, and I clearly heard. 'I'm sorry.'

While we waited for Maria and Lizzy to bring Uncle Raymond back from the airport I felt it again – that sense of lightness. The glow came back briefly too, and this time I knew it was my mother, letting me know she hadn't quite gone.

Hey Dude

PATRICIA GRACE

I was looking for you to tell you that both 'places of accommodation' were full. I didn't know what else to call them but 'places of accommodation', as they didn't fit the description of any motel, hotel, B and B or any place I'd seen anywhere in the world. They were unlike any buildings I, or you, had ever come across, being large, single-storey, dome-shaped structures made of what appeared to be mirrors cut in triangular shapes. They looked like an imagined version of landed spacecraft, except that they were attached to the ground – dry ground, brown, dusty, as though there had been no rain for months. I was trying to remember rain.

There was nothing else in sight. I knew you would be interested in the buildings, which were about fifty metres apart, similar to each other but not identical. There were no roads, no vehicles. I didn't see anyone and didn't go inside as both places had their 'No Vacancy' signs out. Hand-painted boards. No neon.

I went looking for you to tell you about all of this so we could make new plans, but didn't know where to find you. So I wandered until I came to a worn track, so narrow that I guessed it must have been made by animals, though there were none to be seen anywhere. No sheep. No cows. Nothing for them to feed on anyway.

The track led me up a hillside. Halfway up I stopped and looked down. That's when I saw you, the back of you, walking away, following a crowd of people who were wearing an array of clothing, from formal, through costume and streetwear, to light casual.

This crowd was making its way to a gateway, and on reaching it began going through in a leisurely way, chatting to each other. There were no pearly gates. There were no actual gates, only two old, wooden gateposts, uncarved, the distance between them being that of an ordinary farm gate. You were about to follow through when you stopped and turned to look at me, as though you knew I'd be watching.

So, there you were, straight and bony, fit, well, old and happy, dressed as though going for a round of golf; sharp creases in your trousers, Michael Campbell designer shirt, shoes at high polish. I knew there would be a folded handkerchief in your right side pocket, your wallet in the back one. No golf clubs. Your hands were free. You waved, smiled, so I waved and smiled back. It was all I could do. You turned away and followed those others who were your people now. The sky was pale, stretched, pulled down like balloon rubber, to a white horizon. All right for some, I thought, going off happy with all those hunga mate.

Hey Dude

I was looking at a yellow ceiling, the soft yellow of under-ripe corn. It was the colour we chose for walls and ceilings when we decided to do up the bach. Your paint roller slicked across and back, across and back, stickety click, while I took charge of small brushwork.

And OMG, yesterday's earworm hasn't left me. It has survived the night. Could be with me all day, again, chewing.

Forever?

About taking a sad song and making it be-e-e-da.

I've been told you can get rid of earworms by singing the happy birthday song three times in succession. I'm reluctant to try it in case I end up with the birthday song on the brain.

There's a tent city outside. Four tents. You would like to know that we have kept coming here. One out front under the ngaio tree, one down by the water tank and two in among the nectarines. As for me, got a whole bedroom to myself, the whole bach to myself, for now. The kids are up already, chattering and running, there's a baby crying. Kids, parents'll all be in soon. Toast, cereal, coffee, whatever. Coffee? There's a thought. If I knew all the words to the song maybe it wouldn't be so annoying.

We came up in three loads – Tipi's van, the four-wheel drive and my car driven by Jay. Trailer with all the gear including the kids' bikes. If I could remember I might understand what there could be to make life bad for her or him, but I only know three or four random lines.

Jude, short for Judith? Or, the addressee could be male. For example, there's your niece's son Judah, called Jude, and that Jude fella at the golf club. As a name it's a bit androgynous. If I knew the whole thing I might know what could make Jude afraid. Of being alone perhaps? Abandoned? Of stepping out, standing out, standing back, speaking up, giving up, go-getting? Of darkness, the past, the now, the future? Most likely of losing a dodgy lover, as is the case with many songs.

It's good advice though, don't you think? To take a down song and give it ups, give it heaps, make it bedda? It's not about getting rid of sadness but keeping it, treasuring it as a fine ingredient. That's my take on it. It's about having a balanced recipe.

We used to watch *MasterChef* on TV, where amateur cooks competed for a major prize. Lots of hugs, tears and dramatics. Night after night there were cook-offs, with the least-favoured dishes sending their creators home. You didn't like the show at first.

Important to all good cooking was to have fine cuts of meat, fresh ingredients and not to drown what was to be the hero of the dish with too much fancy stuff. At the same time the judges looked to detect a complexity of flavours – sweet, sour, bitter, salt, heat and spice. Textures – smooth and crunch. They liked colour and inventiveness. All, combined with artistic plating, could produce a winner.

So, you don't attempt to ditch the sad, instead you keep it, give it its due, its own place. Let it be salt. Embrace it. That's what you do these days. You embrace. Not just lovers, kids or your relatives, but ideas, comments, histories, new-fangled stuff, other people's music. Instead of stressing out about people having loud, one-sided phone conversations in trains or buses when you're trying to read, or in cafés or other public places, you listen in, embrace, make the best you can of the situation. You could be rewarded. You never know what you might hear that will intrigue you.

Androgynous.

I watched *Project Runway All Stars* the other night. You wouldn't like it and I shouldn't either – female body image issues and all that.

A group of dress designers compete with each other to create outfits which are modelled on the runway by masked insects wearing stilettos, and judged. The designers are given a theme and two days in which to design and make. Every so often a mentor comes in to the workroom offering encouragement and advice. He's like the Wonderland Rabbit, pale and dapper, in and out. The theme this time was androgyny. Instead of having just one model to dress, the designers had to come up with two similar outfits – one for a female and one for a male.

I enjoyed seeing what they created: dresses for soldiers, harlequin swap, lace tuxedos, matching street strides featuring handkerchiefs lolling out of pockets. I liked the street stride outfits best, but according to the judges they lacked androgynousness, so the designer had to pack his scissors and things and go home.

You and I belong to the era of handkerchiefs. Hankies were compulsory items when we were at school and were inspected daily. Ironed and folded four times was how I carried mine in my gym dress pocket, not that the ironing and folding was compulsory, nor did it have to be a *real* handkerchief. A piece of ripped rag was permissible.

I felt sorry for the rag hanky kids and the ones who had handkerchiefs pinned inside their pockets so they wouldn't get lost. I thought they had mean mothers – mean, as in unkind. The word 'mean' can have a different definition these days. Said with a certain emphasis, it has an almost opposite interpretation to what we're used to: very good, excellent, something special. 'That's a *mean* haircut.' Or, 'How was the movie?'

'It was *mean*.'

'Yeah?'

'Yeah, *mean*.'

Handkerchiefs were commonly given as gifts. Women's hankies were often handmade, hemstitched round the edges and embroidered with flowers in one corner. Stem stitch, back stitch, lazy daisy, satin stitch, blanket stitch, hem stitch. Why am I telling you all this?

Why?

Because remembering can make sad songs bedda.

Handkerchiefs, men's or women's, could be bought singly, or in sets of four in flat boxes. I liked the boxes.

You had your own pile of hankies and I had mine – same old same old, for years and years, presents from way back. But one day it occurred to me, after a search through pockets and bags, that I was down to just a fragile three. I realised I had never bought handkerchiefs for myself. They'd always been given, probably forty years ago. Forty-year-old handkerchiefs about to give up the ghost. Can't stand tissues.

The next time I was in town I went to buy a half dozen, looked about in what I thought were likely shops – Farmers, Kmart, the Warehouse – but didn't find any. I didn't want to spend too long shopping as you were waiting in the car for me. We were to have lunch at Esquires before I took you to your appointment. In one store when I asked about handkerchiefs the shop assistant looked surprised. 'We don't have anything like that,' she said. 'Try the pharmacy.'

So I went across to the pharmacy and saw handkerchiefs, unpleasant, scratchy looking, dots and stripes, packaged in with rose or lavender soaps and lotions. They looked palliative, or at least geriatric. As said, I've never bought handkerchiefs for myself before.

Why start now? I thought. Why should I buy handkerchiefs? As though I was going to need them. As though inviting crying.

That night I said to you, 'I'm nearly out of hankies. Two or three about to fall to bits. Blow my nose on one of those and it'd all shoot out the other side.'

'Use mine,' you said. 'There's a whole heap.' So that's what I did, that's what I do. They're bigger. They're bedda.

They've all come in. They'll be making real coffee in the machine brought all the way from Paekākāriki. They'll pour Goodygrain into bowls for the kids. It's full of sugar, like all kids' cereals these days. Should be banned. Manufacturers should be thrown in jail for poisoning children.

Murderers. It makes you wonder who the real criminals are in this world. My phone gargles and I reach for it.

'cofi?' it asks.

'yip,' I reply.

I get up and go for a shower, take my time, put on a pair of shorts and one of your shirts, a pair of scuffy slippers from a hotel we stayed in where they give away slippers. You never wore yours. I return to the bedroom and make the bed. There's mooing, barking and meowing going on out there in the big room. Yoga. Downward-facing dog, cow pose and all that. Aunty Instructor is giving her instructions in te reo.

I open the door. Three-legged dogs all over the floor, the fourth legs, pretending to be missing, are waving in the air – fat ones, skinny ones, hairy ones, little ones, brown ones, white ones. There's barking, woof woof woof, which is not on the kaupapa, not in the spirit of yoga. Ought to be composed, serene, calm, peaceful, meditative, breath-controlled. But the sights and sounds go a long way towards bedda.

A father is at the table with a baby braced to him by a big arm. He's frowning, eating an apple and doing a crossword. Without looking up he stands, leaving the apple and the crossword, but keeping the baby and the frown. He makes my coffee into an All Blacks coffee cup and brings it to the table. I take the baby who looks straight into my eyes, bedda and bedda.

'What's "Rags to riches", ten letters?' the father asks. The yogaists are sitting cross-legged, quiet, eyes closed, or one eye.

Game over. They converge, give me morning greetings, begin making toast, dishing out porridge. I'm informed that the beach horse races are on at eleven o'clock and they're going to make sandwiches. They're going to get a feed of mussels off the wharf piles when the tide goes down. Swims. Fish off the bridge.

Porridge? Not a pop or crackle in sight. Much bedda. You always threw nuts and sultanas in yours. The kids take their bowls out on to the deck.

'What about Cinderella?' I ask, counting out ten letters on my fingers.

'That'll do,' the father says and writes it in the grid. I intend fixing small hooks to my hand line and fishing off the bridge when the tide comes in – after the horse races.

I could change Jude to Dude. Yes. That's bedda. That's you. Dude – classy, skinny, snappy, healthy, striding, laughing, old or not. Sharp shooting, with a bit of sting. Lah lah lah lah lah lah. Hey Dude, be not afraid. Except you were never afraid of anything. Ah, mmm, except failure. And owls. Just one owl, the white one in the pine trees a hundred years old.

The Tree House

TONI PIVAC

He arrived on the wind. It was a warm wind that vanished the moment he stopped walking, yet still he shook with a tremor he could neither cease nor control. The man had walked for hours but travel weariness was the least of his worries. He stood in front of the tree house and they looked at each other. The first thing he thought was that he'd have to duck. It would have to do though; he had no energy or will to go any further. It was the witching hour and only the faint moon lit his surroundings. When he looked up, the sky was kneeling. Trees were bowing at impossible angles in the now windless night. He shook his head, closing his eyes tightly like angry fists, and when he opened them again the trees had straightened up, standing tall once more. He reached out and the tree house door opened at his touch, whining like a dog's yawn and he stumbled like a drunk man towards his only hope of refuge and fell through. The night turned a darker shade of black and then switched off completely.

Hours later, once the night had given way to day, a little girl in ladybug gumboots ran down the track to the back of the farm. The way darkened as she passed through the trees, but little girls who live on farms do not scare easily, especially by silly things like tree shadows. She hopped over writhing roots without looking and high fived the low-hanging frond of a ponga as she sailed by. She barely slowed as she reached the tree house, dropping her shoulder to push through the low doorway. Then there he was. He lay there wrapped in the old woollen blanket she'd brought down from the house last winter.

She probably should have been more surprised when she discovered the lost man. She probably should have even felt scared. She didn't think about any of that until later, though. From afar the man looked like he was homeless, or at least what she thought a homeless man should look like.

Even though it was already open, she knocked on the door. Softly at first, a whisper of fingertips, and then a little harder when he didn't respond. She thought it would perhaps be clever to have a weapon, just in case. Finding only a piece of branch no longer than her forearm, she went back inside. She stood for a while, watching with her head cocked, when finally, inching closer with the stick clutched tight in her cold little hands, she gave him a gentle prod. Then again, a little less gently. He didn't move. Curiosity got the better of her so she moved closer and took a proper look at his face.

The first thing she noticed was the hair. He had a scruffy beard hiding his chin and an equally scruffy mop on top of his head. It was a safe face, though. Almost familiar even. The second thing was the dirt. He was very grubby. Sticking out the bottom of the blanket the girl could see once-white shoes, worn through to sockless feet. She wondered how long it had taken him to walk here. The closest town was seventeen-and-a-half minutes away. By car. She had timed it with her papa's stopwatch.

The girl cleared her throat loudly. The man didn't move. She stomped her ladybug boots on the boarded floor. Apart from an endless tremor and the rise of his chest, he didn't budge. Finally, the girl sat in the corner to think.

A while later a little girl could be seen running home, only to return with a bucket of food: bread smeared with peanut butter, two bananas that were more brown than yellow, and half a packet of rice crackers. She left it beside the lost man and backed out the door, a smile sneaking onto her lips as she left. There was a man in her tree house.

The lost man couldn't tell how long he had been unconscious for. He didn't want to call it sleep, it was far stronger than that and a whole lot deeper. On the bright side, he hadn't vomited since leaving the main road; that was a small victory. Hell, that was a huge victory. The shaking was getting worse, though. He rolled over, struggling to find comfort on the hard floorboards and saw the blue bucket. Had that been there before?

When she returned the next day after school, the man was still there and still asleep, but the food wasn't in the bucket any more. Most of it was on the floor, some in crumb form. She didn't want to think too much about what was in the bucket, but it had a sick smell to it. She was pretty sure she knew where the other food had gone. The lost man didn't wake and she snuck back out, taking the yucky bucket with her and leaving grapes and a bottle of water in its place.

Each time she found her way back to the tree house over the following days, she knew he'd be there. It was only a small part of her that wondered if he'd be gone. There were many things the girl didn't understand, but the main thing that didn't make sense to her was why the lost man hadn't woken up yet. She was sure he wasn't faking being asleep and she was also sure he wasn't dead. He barely moved when she jabbed him with the stick, but his chest rose and fell in a constant wave. No, he certainly wasn't dead.

The fourth day was noticeably different. Somehow, the lost man seemed closer to the surface. So she in turn edged closer to him. She watched as his eyelids flickered and then rose slowly. He saw ladybug gumboots and skinny brown knees. Instinctively, the girl backed away. She was too slow. The stranger reached up, his sleep-warmed palm clutching her wrist. The lost man felt her jolt and it moved up his arm and echoed like a gong deep in his chest.

'Sorry,' he said in a voice that sounded like stale cigarettes and regret. This must be where the food was coming from. This ladybug-gumbooted kid was keeping him alive.

The girl let her arm fall limp. He wasn't going to hurt her. He probably couldn't anyway. No, she didn't feel threatened by this man at all, not while he slept and, surprisingly, not even now that he had woken.

'That's okay,' she said softly. She stood there for a long while as the lost man held her arm. One of them was shaking. His brow had furrowed and his mouth was moving, searching for words that didn't seem to be coming. She opened her own mouth to ask the obvious question, then changed her mind.

'Don't worry,' she whispered instead. 'I won't tell.'

Later that evening, the girl who wouldn't tell lay sleepless in bed. She was brimming with excitement and fear. She wasn't quite sure which was winning. The man in her tree house was awake.

It wasn't until a full day later that he saw the girl above the gumboots in full view, from spotted boots to the curly thatch up top. Standing in the doorway it appeared that she had returned with a picnic. She brought it like any girl wearing ladybug boots should: in a bucket. She didn't apologise for its presentation.

He had spent the past twenty-four hours rocking in his makeshift bed, dragging himself from the gnawing sleep that seemed to pull him down. He needed to leave but he couldn't even sit up. Kids have big mouths. He knew what they were like. Secrets don't exist to kids, other than to tease others for not knowing. Any moment now he would be discovered and sent back. They'd take him and there would be nothing he could do about it.

When he'd heard the thump of her boots drawing nearer he'd strained his ears, listening for the cavalry behind her. But behind her was only silence. As the girl entered, the lost man's eyes were locked on the doorway. The only way in and the only way out. She sidled through the door, her eyes finding his. Clasping the handle of her bucket, she slowly sat on the floor in the middle of the tree house, carefully, as if she thought he might dash off like a wild rabbit. They watched each other for a long while. The man eventually closed his eyes again, vaguely comforted by his newfound companion.

What the girl quickly noticed was that the man shook a lot. Sometimes it looked like his whole body was nodding. When it seemed that the man had fallen asleep again, she rose to leave, swapping out her bucket of treats for the empty one beside him. Her eyes narrowed and her nostrils flared. The light in the treehouse was small and the smell large.

The next day there was soap, scissors, a hand towel and three flannels in the bucket. Once again she moved cautiously towards him, getting closer this time, and tipped the bucket to show him what it contained. 'Papa only has an electric razor,' she told the lost man with an apologetic shrug. After a long moment she straightened as if coming to a decision and added, 'I can help you if you want.' Then by the riverside where she had learned to swim, she learned to help a man wash.

She soon discovered that the trembling was worse when he was upright, and it had taken them a long time to get him to that point. He let her help him up and support him when he faltered. The girl took his hands in hers and gently cleaned the grime from his fingers. She bathed his feet with small movements as he sat at the riverside. The flannels were dirty and the light had started to fade before they were done. Once they made it back to the tree house, the man smelled better but he seemed to be even more lost. His eyes fluttered and his fingers wouldn't keep still. He stood with a sway, as if even the very clothes on his back were too heavy to be borne. The girl helped lower him to the ground. The darkness reached out and caressed him. He accepted the illusion of safety as the world once again faded to black.

The girl watched as he shook like a squiggle pen. She hadn't seen anything like it before. Mama had old woollen blankets in the horse truck. She wouldn't miss them. The girl would bring more.

The Tree House

Back at the house, the girl's parents noticed her wet clothes. She got a lecture about staying away from the river. If she couldn't be trusted to do that, she'd be forbidden from playing on the farm alone. She must be more careful. The girl hurried off to bed after dinner, apologies and promises spilling from her lips. She would never go to the river by herself.

As she lay in bed with her parents' hushed voices below her, her mind flicked back over the evening, the sideways glance she had caught her mama throw her papa. What was even more unusual was that the TV hadn't been on either. The girl fell asleep before she could make anything of it, and the curiosity had vanished by the time she awoke the next morning.

What she didn't know was that while she dreamed in blissful ignorance, down below, turmoil was erupting in her parents' lives. The parents had received a phone call. They had been listening to the news, they had been reading the newspapers and what they had learned was deeply disturbing.

The man in her tree house was a funny fella. He seemed to spend a lot of time sleeping. She watched him in his peaceful slumber and in his restlessness. She recognised when he was having a nightmare. At times he'd shake so much he couldn't talk, and when he leaned against the wall the whole tree house would shake. She was a bit worried it would come crashing down like the little pig's house of sticks, but she didn't say anything. She pretended not to notice the shaking at all.

He would sometimes spend long minutes talking quickly and quietly in the corner. There was no point talking to him when he was like that because he wouldn't hear anything anyway. She didn't mind that either, though. He became a regular fixture of the tree house and they developed an easy friendship based on buckets and words. It was nice because the tree house had been getting boring until he arrived. She only called it a tree house because her mama did. It wasn't until she had taken her friend, Morgan, to see her tree house that she discovered it wasn't actually a tree house at all, because, well, it wasn't in a tree. She liked it anyway. Her pop had built the treehouse. It was a rickety old shack that looked like an afterthought of off-cuts, and probably was.

Her real house didn't look much better than the tree house. She had always thought that the family homestead was more of a big sister to the tree house, because they looked pretty related, right down to the chipped paint job. The house and the family farm it sat on both seemed kind of tired. It was old but she didn't mind. It felt like a home because it had always been one. Her mama had grown up in the house. Even her pop had grown up there. Mama had lived here all her life, with her mum and her dad, a sister who had moved to Australia and a not-right brother who had ended up somewhere else. The farm was handed over to Mama to run, with her papa's help, when her nanny had gotten too old and her pop too fat. They were both dead now. The girl knew that her nanny and her pop had lived in the homestead for a very long time. Mama had told her so. They'd lived there until they didn't love each other any more. Mama said they stayed after that because they didn't know what else to do.

Day after day the girl in the ladybug boots returned, each time with a new experimental feast. Once he was sure she had smeared a bit of cat food on bread, hoping he'd mistake it for corned beef. Cat food aside, he found himself looking forward to her daily visits. She was like a clock. A clock that brought him some sort of respite from his thoughts and his demons. He could hear the voices coming back, but at the moment they were just a whisper. The other things she brought him were of less value, but far more amusing. In her bucket, she would bring something different every time: books, crayons, tubs of paint, string, a teapot.

Today, she came back with a blanket, a stuffed alligator, a doll, and a marmite and cheese sandwich, minus the crusts. 'Are you hungry?' she asked, pulling the sandwich out of the zip lock bag she'd brought with her. Looking closer, the man saw that there was an eight-legged squiggle on the front of the bag.

'What's that?' he croaked. He still sounded terrible, even to himself, but the girl didn't seem to mind. In fact, she didn't look up at all but instead smoothed the bag out flat in front of her. He cleared his throat and tried again.

'It's an octopus,' she replied, putting the sandwich on top of her bag plate.

'Why?'

'I dunno,' she said. 'I just think they're really cool. They're super smart and clever.'

'You know, there's a whakataukī my dad used to tell us about the old octopus. "Kaua e mate wheke, mate ururoa kē",' the lost man said, reaching out to trace the many legs of the picture. 'Do you know what that means?'

The girl tipped her head to the side, her eyes searching the walls of the tree house. 'Hmmm, don't die like an octopus?' she said at last.

'Very good,' he smiled. 'It talks about not dying like an octopus but to die fighting like the hammerhead shark.'

'That's a funny thing to talk about,' she said, a frown resting upon her brow.

'Well,' he began, 'octopuses were pretty well known for not putting up a fight when they were captured. Sharks, on the other hand, would fight to the end. Even once a shark's been caught and being filleted, its flesh will quiver under the knife, fighting one last time.'

After pondering for a moment the girl said, 'You could be a hammerhead shark.' Then her attention was dragged back to the doll whose hair she was braiding. 'But I still think octopuses are really neat. I'll bring you a book, ok? You'll see, you'll like them too.' And at that she jumped up, bent to gather her things and ran out the door. 'See you tomorrow,' she called as she flitted out. The lost man just stared after her.

Left on his own for seemingly endless stretches of time, the man spent lucid hours wondering. He was surrounded by evergreens, native trees. There were so many things he had been unaware of while he was inside. Time was only one of them. He had lost count of the days. Hell, he could barely tell what month it was. It wasn't searingly hot, or blistering cold. It was an in-between time. Everything about him was in-between, so it made a strange kind of sense. The tree house was definitely an improvement to the other place though. If he'd been a religious man he would have prayed, but as it was, he hoped only for dreamless nights and days of oblivion. 'Stop it, I know you're there. Go away,' he would end up growling, alone in the treehouse. He'd pick up the box of crayons and throw them, one by one, at the door, at the window, at nothing.

During a particularly bad episode, the girl, for the first time, wondered how sick the man really was. 'Should I get you some medicine?' she said. The lost man grunted.

'It's not more medicine I need,' he said, confusingly.

'Okay,' she said. Then, 'Are you gonna die?'

'I hope not.' These days he often found himself just as surprised as she was at what came out when he opened his mouth.

The heavens were dark and busy. Clouds danced in the sky, casting shadows across the paddocks. Ladybug gumboots could be seen skipping through the grass chasing the cloud shadows, climbing and jumping the fence between the trees. It was a familiar sight these days. This time, the lost man sat in the shade of the roof, below a swinging sign hanging drunkenly by only one chain.

'Your broken sign is very noisy,' he told her.

'Is it?' she replied, thrusting her bucket in his hands. He peered in to discover a handful of pebbles and a sellotaped pair of sunglasses. He smiled despite himself, and watched as she busied herself with a colouring book.

The smile suddenly vanished. He was going to be sick, he knew it. His body was tricking him and he knew that too. He felt like he needed to scratch his skin off. He hadn't thought it'd be quite this bad. Boy, had he been wrong. The girl was there though.

'Aren't your folks worried about where you go every day?' he asked her, moving inside and pulling a woollen blanket tighter around his shoulders. If he pulled tight enough maybe he could squash the crawling feeling. Yesterday a farm dog had gotten far too close. The farmer had called it back to the quad bike, but he'd been lucky. He couldn't be discovered. He needed more time.

'Nah, they've got other things that they worry about. As long as I don't go by the river by myself, they don't mind where I go. That's the only dangerous place here. I only come here though.' She didn't stop colouring her picture as she spoke, adding, 'Can you pass me the purple, please? I think the sky should be purple.'

He rolled the purple towards her. It still hurt to sit up. His head didn't like to be upright for long, so for now his world would have to be strictly horizontal.

'Ah, it's your safe place,' he said, nodding as if he had already gotten the answer right. The nodding had made him feel ill, but he kept talking. Distraction from his deceitful mind was important. 'When I was little I had a safe place. Mine was my tree house too. We have more in common than you would think.'

'What did you do in your tree house?' the girl asked.

'I'd go there to draw.'

'What would you draw?'

A shrug. 'Just my favourite things.' He watched her a while longer. 'Hey,' he said after a moment. 'You haven't asked me what my name is.'

'I just figured you'd tell me if you wanted me to know,' she replied without looking at him. 'Do you want me to know yet?'

The lost man didn't reply straight away but sat there, leaning on the scratchy woollen blankets that smelled of horse and leather, and blinked at her.

'You're a very strange child, you know that?'

She giggled. 'That's what my papa always says,' she said. 'But at least I don't yawn like a walrus.' The girl threw a look at his stretching mouth. He chuckled.

They spent the rest of the afternoon drawing together, and before she left, the girl turned towards the lost man. 'You never asked me what my name was either,' she said. 'But in case you wanted to know, it's Rika.'

The storm that had been threatening arrived like a shiver, starting small and then growing as it spread outwards. Beneath the heavy sounds of water, the broken sign creaked and banged outside the tree house door. The sound invaded his dreams and reminded him of corridors and locked rooms. The wind moaned outside the battered hut and the lost man moaned inside his tattered blanket.

The weather hadn't escaped Rika's parents' notice either. Mama was on the phone with her serious voice when Rika burst into the kitchen. 'Yes, I realise that, but I don't like the thought of him ...' Mama's eyes flicked towards Rika and she trailed off. A smile appeared on her face. It was the same smile she used when she was pretending to be in a good mood. She finished the call and turned to her daughter.

'You've been spending a lot of time at the tree house lately,' she said, instead of what Rika wanted her to say.

'I always do,' the girl replied, shaking her head, loose curls spraying water.

Her mama thought about that for a while and nodded. 'I suppose you do,' she said with a smile that was almost real. 'When we were kids, we'd spend all our time down there too.' The real smile started to droop.

Papa normally got grumpy when she mentioned her brother and sister. Rika wasn't sure why and she couldn't actually remember either of them anyway. This time, though, Papa just reached out to Mama instead of growling.

'It was the right decision, the best place,' he said quietly as he squeezed her mama's shoulder and her eyes began to refocus. Louder, to Rika he said, 'And you'd better go and wash up. Have a nice warm shower, dinner's almost ready.'

Confused, Rika nodded and skipped out of the kitchen, but not before seeing her mama rest her forehead on her husband's shoulder. She turned the corner as his arm reached around her mama.

Later that night there was noise in the living room. It stretched out towards the girl in her bed and shook her from her sleep. She lay still thinking of ghosts and cat burglars. Stay put, she thought to herself. Stay put. Yet no matter how big she made the thought, it wasn't big enough. The noise had disappeared and a hum of voices rose briefly before falling, then only silence remained. The quiet left too much space for imagination. Her feet whispered across the carpet, skipping over the spilled toys and books that littered the way.

It didn't take her eyes long to adjust to the dark and she was both disappointed and relieved to discover her parents, heads turned away from one another, at the kitchen table, a newspaper clipping clutched in her mama's hand. She watched for a moment, but the scene was like a portrait and she soon lost interest. She slid back to bed and fell into an anxious sleep to the vision of her parents and their silent conversation.

The days were beginning to seem gentler for the man. He wondered if it was something to do with the girl.

'What are you doing?' he asked his little friend, Rika. Maybe he'd turned a corner. The voices were there, but he found he could mostly ignore them. Their colours weren't so dark any more.

'Writing,' she replied.

'Writing what?'

'A letter to Mama.' She still hadn't looked up, and a tongue-tip darted out as a scowl appeared below her curly forelock. The scowl quickly turned into a tremble of the lips.

'What's the matter, bub?' he said. These days he sounded more like the man he used to know. Rika turned to him and words tumbled out, slowly at first and then faster as they cleared the way for the rest.

'Mama and Papa are worried about something and I don't know what it is. I want to fix it but I don't know how,' she ended, dangerously close to spilling the tears that had sprung up to settle in her lashes. The man drew in a quick breath.

'Some things in life cannot be fixed,' he said, 'they can only be carried.' Again, the surprise returned. He went to reach out but changed his mind. 'What I am sure of, though, is that whatever your parents are upset about, it's not you. Of that I am certain.'

At that, the tears welled over. Rika crawled over and wrapped her arms around him. He couldn't remember the last time he'd been hugged. At first he just sat there. But the longer she held on, the harder it was for his arms to stay at his side. His hands rose and pressed themselves into her shoulder blades; they felt like the budding of angel wings.

She stayed longer than she should have that day, and when it came time to go, she left the man talking in the corner. There was no one there to talk to but she didn't say anything. It was okay this time.

He seemed a bit lighter these days, like he'd taken off some invisible, heavy coats.

Rika spent the next afternoon at home with her mama. She wasn't sure why, but her mama needed her. Rika was at the kitchen table when Mama sat beside her and began looking through the pile of drawings she had brought back from the tree house. At first she flicked through the pages, but then a wave of recognition washed over her face and she stopped, growing unnaturally still, and plucked out a single page from the bunch.

'Marika,' her mother's voice warned. She knew she was in trouble. Eyes searched her face. Lips tightened, pursed. The next words would either be shouted or wouldn't come at all. A moment passed and so too did the shadow across Mama's face.

'Rika,' she said, softer now. 'Is there something you need to tell me?'

The wind followed them, chasing them down the track to the hut. It whipped their curled tails of hair into their faces, matching dark-haired figures, one a miniature of the other. They passed over bumpy tree roots and swinging ponga branches. They climbed fences. Ladybug gumboots thudded like a frantic little heartbeat. The pair arrived at the tree house where the once-crooked sign hung neatly where it belonged. On it, a freshly painted hammerhead shark, similar to the one on the page her mama was still holding, stood out brightly against the weathered boards of the treeless hut. Beside it was an octopus, two of its legs embracing the shark in what could have been a hug. Rika's mama pushed the door open. The tree house appeared to sigh. Rika pushed her way past her mama, taking a moment for her eyes to adjust, bracing herself. But all that was to be seen was a neatly folded pile of horse blankets and an empty bucket.

That Last Summer

K-T HARRISON

The last week of that fourth form year limped towards its end. My restless legs wanted to race out of that stuffy classroom and leap into the rest of summer. My wound-up desk-cramped body ached, just ached; surely, surely, and truly; ached to burst out of the too tight and too short school uniform that was keeping me in. *Wait*, I told myself, *be patient*. Ever since Monday it had seemed that the clock on the wall had been holding on to time, holding it back, holding it up, holding it still and holding it to ransom. So I waited as patiently as I could – I glared at the clock – I willed it to go the same speed as the thumping noise my racing heart made in my ears, but it only tick-tock, tick-tock, tick-tocked at its own sweet pace.

By eight minutes past nine each morning, the sweat that glued my white blouse to my back and stunk-up my armpits had dried and become wet again, dried and become wet again, and dried, leaving the salty residue to sit on my skin, prick at it and make it itch. But I wasn't the only one with itchy-prickly skin. My friends – Jo, Max, Frankie, Georgie and Belinda – itched too. Ever since the end of October we'd been moaning to one another about having to breathe in the fried onion pong that radiated out of our heating-up sweaty bodies. And although we washed thoroughly each day before school, dusted our skins white with talcum powder, sprayed ourselves silly with anti-perspirants, rolled on yards and yards of roll-on deodorant and dotted our face spots with anti-pimple cream, at fourteen years old it seemed we could do nothing to stop the hormonally predetermined sweat, stink, itch, and pimples that plagued us all. All except for the rich girls. They always looked so, so cool. So very cool.

At interval on Tuesday, I'd overheard Diana, Michelle, Paulina and Jacqui talk about the holidays they would have at their family baches at Whangamatā, Whitianga or the Mount.

'Again,' Diana said as Michelle nodded her head and Paulina and Jacqui rolled their eyes. In loud whispers, they shared their dreamed-up imaginings with one another – what they would look like in their new bikinis with their bronze tans, their sun-bleached golden hair – and the summer boys they would attract.

'Those boys,' Michelle said. 'They make those six weeks almost bearable.'

'Shhhh,' Paulina said. 'Big Ears is listening.'

'Oh, let her,' Jacqui said. 'Let her dream a little. God knows the dreary lives her and her lot must lead.'

'Oh yes indeed,' Diana said. 'Have you ever been down Rata Avenue? They live in such pokey little box houses. My driving instructor made me drive along that godawful street. They don't have cars, you see –

can't afford them, so what better place to practise? Of course, you have to mind out for the umpteen children playing on the street.'

'Really?' Michelle said.

'Oh yes,' Diana said.

'The actual road?'

'Yes.'

'It's a wonder they don't get run over.'

'Yes, isn't it?'

The houses on Rata Ave were mill houses, and we were mill children. Our fathers all worked at the paper mill in this timber town we all lived in. Number six Rata was our house, number eight was where the twins, Jo and Max, lived, and next door to them at number ten was Frankie's house. Georgie was across the road at number nine, and next door at number seven was where Belinda and her family lived. We'd all grown up together on Rata, and we called each other's parents aunty and uncle. In all our growing-up years, we'd never known such holidays at the east coast places of Whangamatā, Whitianga or the Mount, or any other beach we'd gathered seafood from, east or west.

For us, those times were day trips. We'd all pile into whichever vehicle had a space to sit in – we had a blue van, so we had heaps of room for lots of people. At low tide, we dug in the sand for pipi, and we collected pūpū – sea snails. Initially, as youngsters, we felt around in rock pools for pāua and kina and mussels, and with hammer and screwdriver we chiselled oysters from the rocks. As we grew we learned how to free dive, leaving the rock pools for the kids. And we went deeper. And all the times we gathered food, others sunbathed, and like pink pork sausages on a hot barbecue, they browned. Then they turned over to brown on the other side.

Sometimes a few of them gathered seafood too. And when the tide was in and our bags were full of what the sea gave us, we devoured the food our mothers had prepared and packed the night before, while those others swam, or splashed at each other and squealed as prettily as they could. But sometimes, instead of swimming, splashing and squealing, those others cooked and ate their seafood right there on the shore. We turned our backs on those people. They didn't know the lore we lived by. And, as in the classroom, it seemed we had nothing to contribute to their learning because all the learning we got came from them. So we ate the food brought from home and hoped nothing bad would befall us – because of them. We'd enjoy the sweet pipi and relish the pūpū that we'd dig out of their shells with safety pins, and feast on all the other shellfish gathered that day as we'd always done – when we got home. But only after they'd been shared out between all of us, including those on Rata who could not be at the beach that day.

As much as we all enjoyed those times at the beach, and as much as we relished the food that appeased our hunger afterwards and at each meal we had at home, there was a hunger in us that far surpassed the need to fill our empty stomachs. At fourteen years old, we had the rest of our lives before us, and the dreams we shared had nothing to do with the flimsy stuff of bikinis or the fleeting summer boys of the rich girls' desires. That we were all born with brown skins had everything to do with it – we had neither time nor necessity to oil ourselves and burn for the sake of affectation. We'd reckoned on how to pursue our dreams in the third form. With help from the guidance counsellor we'd worked out how we were going to make them come true. Had we not, our ambitions would have been as insubstantial and as transitory as a rich girls' summer. We had to work hard to pass our exams well. We knew that we'd have to work twice as hard to get half as far and be treated half as fairly as them. But in order for us to take ourselves out of where we were with what we knew, we needed money – we'd decided we were all going to the university in Hamilton.

At the end of that year, that fourth-form year, I'd come first in maths, English and science with a second in French. Jo and Max had come second equal in maths, English and science and first equal in French. Frankie was first in tech drawing, woodwork and metalwork, Belinda was first in cooking and sewing and Georgie was first in accounting, typing, and commercial practice. At prize-giving on Wednesday, after I'd received the prize for overall excellence in achievement, I looked for my parents amongst the sea of politely clapping mothers and fathers. They were not there to clap for me. Nor were Jo and Max's, Frankie's, Georgie's or Belinda's parents, to clap for them. So we clapped extra hard and extra loud for each other.

'We beat them,' Georgie said.

'We haven't finished yet,' I said.

With letters of recommendation from the principal, Mr Ryan, we all got holiday jobs. I was hired to help out at the town dump, Jo and Max were to work at the Stevens's Dairy in Kelso Street, Frankie got a job mowing lawns up Grandview Heights where the mill bosses lived, Georgie would deliver meat orders on Syd the butcher's bike, and Belinda got a job at the fish and chip shop down Roseberry Street.

So while the fried onion stink of our adolescence sweated out of our armpit pores, and the over-boiled cabbage stench of the paper mill wafted in and around the classroom, filling our nostrils with the putrid air it spewed out all day, every day, in our minds we were already out of there. When the bell screamed out our release on Friday, I froze, and then I was up and sprinting towards the rest of my life.

I spent all of my first pay. I bought Christmas presents for my brothers and sisters and my mother and father. Jo, Max, Frankie, Georgie and Belinda did the same. We also bought gifts for one another. 'Merry Christmas,' we all said, and that was the end of our first pays. My second pay went towards our power bill. So did Frankie's, Georgie's and Belinda's. Between them, Jo and Max had enough to pay their family's whole bill. So, despite knowing that after two weeks none of us had yet saved towards our futures, we all knew we'd contributed to bringing Christmas joy to the people we loved and who loved us, and that the lights would stay on in our homes for at least another month.

All through the rest of that last summer, we worked at our jobs and we saved as much of the money we were paid as we could. On our days off, we walked the roads of our growing up. And, along all the roads we went up and down, we roamed through our memories and we sorted through remembered stuff from earlier times. We rediscovered – for there was nothing new for us to discover in those places – the times we'd shared when we were younger.

'That's where ... remember?'

'You fell in.'

'You saved me from drowning.'

'We got chased by a boar.'

'Lucky for you a hunter from the club was there to shoot it.'

'You got stuck in the fence.'

'You waited for me.'

'Mr Scarlett thought we were sheep rustlers ...'

'We set fire to that hill.'
'We tried to.'
'Yeah.'
'You fell off your bike.'
'You laughed.'
'You kissed me.'
'You kissed me back harder.'
'I did too.'
'Kiss me now.'
'Nah.'

Once, on a Friday night, at Frankie's suggestion, we ventured up Grandview Heights. Diana, Michelle, Paulina and Jacqui all lived there.

'I'll show you my houses,' Frankie said. 'I mean, the ones I do.'

'Hey,' Jo said. 'All their streetlights go.'

'Holy Moses,' Georgie said. 'They do too.'

But no lights shone out from the houses themselves. At one of them, we gripped the bars of the wrought iron fence and peered in through the narrow gaps. A security light flashed on and displayed a white concrete driveway that curved through a manicured lawn and continued around towards the back of the house. Palatial splendour from out of a Mediterranean tourist guide magazine stood before us.

'Wow,' said Max and Belinda.

'That's one of mine,' said Frankie.

'All that space and they grow their flowers in pots.' I said. 'And their animals are concrete. How dumb is that?'

'It's beautiful,' said Jo.

We let go of the bars, backed away from the fence, and then the light went out. We stood at the white overstuffed mailbox and turned to look out over the town.

'I can see Rata, I can see my house,' Belinda said. 'See, down there.'

'There's ours,' Jo said. 'There's Mum's gumboots at the back door.'

'There's Dad, head beneath the bonnet of our old bomb, as usual,' Frankie said.

'There's mine,' Georgie said. 'I can see into my parents' bedroom.'

'What are they doing?' Max said.

'How should I know? The door's always locked.'

'Don't you ever wonder, though?'

'We'll know soon enough.'

'Stop being dumb,' I said.

Looking down from our elevated positions, we picked out the bits of our homes that we could see. I saw the potato and kūmara plants that grew in our front yard. I thought the corn waved. I thought I could see my only school blouse hanging out to dry; I thought I could see my mother at the kitchen table, counting out one- and two-cent pieces to buy a bottle of milk. I could see the family-sized talcum powder we all shared; I could see my mother's roll-on that I used, and I could see the cracked mirror that I squeezed my pimples at each morning. I saw how rickety and old our van really was and, leaning up against it, saw my baby brother Bobbie's rusted-up old bike with the wobbly back wheel that came off when he hit a bump or a rut in our crunched-up pipi-shell driveway. I could see us, all of us.

'Let's go home,' I said.

'Not yet,' said Max. 'I can see our garden. The tomatoes are red roses.'

'There's all our parents on the piss at yours,' said Georgie.

'Again,' Frankie said. And she rolled her eyes.

'There's our mum dancing with your dad. She's singing that old people's song,' Jo said.

'What song?' I said.

'You know, the one they always sing.'

Then, with Belinda in the lead, they began to sing.

Halfway through their singing they began to dance with each other. They sang, they danced and they pretend-felt each other up. They laughed, they sang, they danced.

'Stop making things up,' I said. 'Fools.'

Then a security guard came. 'Go back home you fellas – go on, you know you shouldn't be here. Get, before I call the cops.'

We walked towards town, down that well-lit street with the darkened windows – we walked back down to Rata in silence. And even though nothing more was said that summer about what we imagined they could see at ours from up at theirs, I thought it – every day, I thought about it.

One day some of the kids from down John Street, where the forestry workers' homes were, joined us at the lake. We smoked the Buddha joints they offered us. It wasn't that the weather was particularly hot, or that the water was exceptionally warm; it might have had something to do with the heat in our bodies and the uncontrollable urge to cool them down, it may have been at the insistence of the John Street kids, or it may have been because we were stoned out of our Rata Ave heads – we took our clothes off. Where through the cold days of winter we only dabbled our fingers in the chilly water, that summer we plunged in, smarting at the first hit of cold that smacked our sizzling bodies. And hissed the water warm.

'It only hurts at first; after that it's nice.' Belinda said.

We floated through what was left of the days – and nights. We laughed – screamed indecent and immodest loud laughter, our mouths wide open, too, too afraid to close them in case the uncouth joys of childlike boisterousness became swallowed up by grown-up manners and matters. We'd yearned for the knowledge of locked-door adult secrecy, so we ached our way through ignorant experiments to rid ourselves of innocence. So in the too-few nights and times that were left of that last summer, we frolicked beneath the waxing January moon, and then too soon the nights were over.

The driving-school car crawled its way along Rata. Bobby had been bumping his way up and down our driveway all morning. The car sped up. A bike wheel rolled onto the road, the car swerved to miss it, accelerated, hit Bobby, kept going, ran him over. The ambulance attendants rushed to the driver, who sobbed in the car as Bobbie lay dying on the road.

We took him home to our pā in our blue van. The grown-ups did what grown-ups do at tangi. We helped the cooks to feed the people who had come to farewell Bobbie. We gathered pipi and pūpū, mussels, kina, pāua and oysters. Others from the town helped out with food. Mr Stevens brought milk and bread every day, Mr Scarlett gave three sheep, Syd the butcher gave a whole cow, the hunters' club gave a deer and a wild pig, and the fish and chip shop up Roseberry Street gave two bins crammed full of fish heads.

As Bobbie's body went into the ground beside where our grandparents were buried, Jo and Max, Frankie, Georgie and Belinda sang. And time stood still.

The learner driver was discharged without conviction. Judge Geary said that this unfortunate mishap should not impact adversely on one so young. 'And may I add, one from such a prestigious and upstanding family who dedicate their lives to and are committed to building up this town. Let us not condemn one with such a promising future. Had young Bobbie not been playing out on the road, had he been appropriately supervised, we would not be here today.

'I strongly advise that the family of Robert (aka Bobbie) Jacob King reflect upon the joy that he brought to everyone who knew him in the four short years of his life. I exhort the family of Robert (aka Bobbie) Jacob King to extend kindness and understanding towards the young lady who will no doubt suffer the trauma of this horrific tragedy for the rest of her life. What occurred on the sixth day of February in this year, 1970, was indeed a tragedy of utmost proportions. We are all of us – all of us – victims here.

'Order – order in the court,' Judge Geary said.

My mother and the Rata Street aunties ceased their wailing. I wanted to bang his stupid gavel down on his pompous ass's head and tip him out of his high-up-there throne, stomp on him and all he stood for. I didn't, but I hadn't finished yet – later, though.

For some time afterwards, I grieved the losses of that summer.

'It only hurts at first,' Belinda had said. Afterwards I recalled the sting, but I couldn't remember where it hurt the most – or if it hurt at all. Had time already begun to heal the wounds of our loss of innocence? What then were we guilty of?

What?

Byron and the Bastard Blues

ANYA NGAWHARE

Dying is nothing like I imagined. In my head it was always more graceful, more romantic. I thought I'd be surrounded by people when I went out. Children and friends, the ones I loved most in this world. I thought at the very least it would be like it is on TV. My whole life flashing before me in snapshots, a rapid slideshow.

It's nothing like that.

The writers and directors and actors, they're all full of shit. They're a bunch of stupid, lying motherfuckers. They haven't got a goddamn clue. I don't see a tunnel leading to a bright white light; don't see my life flashing before me. No one is flooding to my side, begging me not to do what I'm doing. I don't see God or the devil.

I don't see a fucking thing.

It's just me, sat at the foot of a bloody bed. Poor dying me.

No, I never intended for my life to end this way, and I definitely didn't think I'd be the one ending it. But it's too late now, there's no going back. I've sent my goodbye texts. I can barely feel myself any more.

The silence is what's really bothering me, though.

This house is usually full of life, people talking and laughing and fighting. My family's absence has left it so eerily quiet that I want to think of something else. It makes me want to think about how I got to this point. This moment I never planned. The death I brought upon myself.

People can't usually pinpoint what pushed them over the edge, what made them decide that suicide was a viable option. A good alternative to living. But I know exactly what tipped me. I know who did it.

Byron. My only love.

I was thirteen the first time his green eyes met mine. They froze me, stunned me to the core. The beauty inside them was just, I don't know. Mysterious. He fascinated me.

My mother warned me about pretty boys and the secrets they kept. I wish I hadn't ignored her.

Truthfully, until I saw him, I never thought of them the way other girls did. Boys were nothing more than friends, silly idiots to destroy things and climb trees with. I even convinced myself that I was one of them: that maybe I was one of those kids who hit puberty and found out they were living as the wrong sex all along. I always wanted a penis so the stinky creatures would take me seriously; start tackling me just as hard as I did them.

But then I saw him, and I was glad when lumps grew on my chest instead of between my legs. I was thrilled when I caught him looking.

Byron and the Bastard Blues

While I was chasing after Byron, I ran into a long-haired goof named Andre. He was weird at first, pissed me off like nobody else could, but I kept him around. His hazel eyes had an odd affect on me. Byron's gaze made my heart double beat, sent butterflies racing around my gut like they were trapped in a jar. But Andre soothed them. He settled me.

It took a year to become Byron's friend. A painful year of me wondering whether he was worth it at all. He flitted between watching me and ignoring me, pretending I didn't exist. But I persevered, and with Andre's help he finally opened up to me.

The three of us were best friends before long. We were inseparable.

Maybe that's why Andre was confused when we started pulling away from him.

Byron and I began relying on each other like we didn't need Andre any more. We spent hours talking like no one else in the world understood us or what we were going through, like teenage hell was ours and ours alone. No one else could see just how fucking irrational parents were. It brought us closer, our shared hatred for the world and everyone in it.

The bond we developed took us to the next level, and we were hiding in the darkness of his bedroom whispering 'I love you' before too long.

Byron and I had all these plans, these dreams and theories about life. We knew how our lives were going to go before we'd even lived them. Babies and marriage; a beautiful home on a hill overlooking some clean, green valley. A lifetime of love.

I had these ideals about love and sex too: that they were intertwined. I thought that the only person you should give your body to is the one who puts a diamond ring on your finger, the one who says 'I do' and promises to keep you safe forever.

Byron didn't share my ideas. He believed that sex had nothing to do with love, but he didn't think boys should be dropping loads in everyone willing, either. He was all about liberation. Making each other feel good despite what the world thought of the means.

We were both virgins. What the fuck did either of us know?

He kept pushing, though. We were going to be together forever, but he didn't have the patience to honour my wishes. As far as he was concerned, I was wrong, and I was living a caged life because of that fact.

We were crammed up in his tiny bed one night, whispering about Andre and the girl he was chasing, when he decided things needed to change. One second his calloused fingers were brushing the rim of my bellybutton, and the next they were creeping through the curls inside my underwear.

I froze, body stilling like it had the first time our eyes met. He stared back at me with the same peculiar look. And we were both so silent, each of us processing the development in our own way.

Sparks were attacking my insides, little jolts of electricity shocking me all over. They heated the pit of my stomach in a way I'd never felt. I wanted him to do something, wanted his fingers to explore so badly that my brain short-circuited. My body ached for him even if I didn't really understand it at the time.

'I'm not forcing you,' he said, pale face as stoic as ever.

He pulled away before I could find my tongue, putting his bare back to me. All I could do was stare at the near-black resting on his pillow.

Byron woke something in me that night. His not-so-innocent touch sent my mind racing. It conjured things that had never happened; filled my head with images of his body on mine, his hands and lips and tongue. With one little brush of his fingers I lost my ability to function.

In that moment he captured me fully. He made sure I'd be his forever.

But something else changed too. His actions dislodged something between us, shifted the entire dynamic of our relationship. While I was fantasising about him, he was walking away from me. He built a wall around himself and shut me out completely.

I should have noticed it then, all the signs that things weren't right with him.

I'm a fucking idiot.

I was helping Andre ease the sting of rejection when I finally felt my own.

She was unconventionally beautiful. Like him. But he told me that wasn't why he chose her. Apparently they connected on a level we didn't, in a way I could never understand. She was different, new and unusual.

Except that she wasn't. Not really. There were stories about just how well she connected with other girls' boyfriends. Dozens of them, from at least three different schools.

My mum told me that a broken heart never really heals. All the tears and holes scab over and seal, but it never works as well as it did. It will always be damaged.

'But one day,' she said, arms around me while I snotted all over her shirt, 'One day you'll find a man just as damaged as you, and he'll treat you like the queen you are, and you won't notice the imperfections any more. You'll both feel whole. Brand new.'

My mother didn't know Byron, though. He took heartbreak to a whole other level.

The rumour mill started turning before long, and the school was flooded with stories about me and the many conquests I didn't know I had. And I wasn't picky, either. Apparently there was a threesome in the D-Block toilets during fifth period. A blow job in a garden shed at some party. I experimented with bisexuality too, same party. My personal favourite was a weekend away with a student teacher. I heard he took me to his parents' bach, tied me up and did all sorts of freaky stuff. I suspect the principal heard about the bach story too, because a few days later that teacher stopped coming to school.

Andre smirked when I told him what people were saying. He cocked his head and asked, 'So when am I being serviced, harlot?'

I wasn't amused, and his balls will never let him forget that fact.

Byron cornered me after school one day; green eyes narrowed, lips as straight as his shoulders. He scanned me from head to toe and I shuddered uncontrollably. I stared at the trampled grass beneath my feet.

'Is it true?' he demanded to know. 'Did you screw all those guys?'

I asked if it mattered, voice so low I barely heard myself. He heard me, though. Clear as day.

I pulled my shoulders in when he stepped closer. 'You tell me you love me, but you won't sleep with me.' His hot breath sent prickles down my spine when it washed over my neck. 'But you'll open your legs for a bunch of dumbass brutes who think of you as nothing more than a free hole.'

It was the first time he was openly cruel to me, and as much as my heart ached I wouldn't let it go. Couldn't.

'You told me you loved me, but you left me for a girl who had an abortion at thirteen.'

His breathing deepened and my insides shrivelled like a sun-baked worm. I forced my head up, meeting his gaze. The fire behind his beautiful eyes made my heart stop altogether. My trembling fingers curled into fists by my sides.

Byron turned on his heel swiftly, marching away from me.

I clamped a hand over my mouth, half expecting to spit my stomach out. My entire body thrummed like some ancient demon was trying to take control of it. It sickened me, the idea that our run-in could have ended very differently.

I never told Andre what happened that day; didn't tell him I was so terrified I could have pissed myself. I should have told him, though. It's one of the many things I should have done differently.

The last year of high school passed in a drunken haze.

There had never been a place for alcohol in my life, and I hadn't thought there ever would be. Losing Byron in every way made me see the appeal. It was a crutch, a good way to deal with all the voices in my head. The ones that pointed out every wrong step I made, every untaken path.

But without the bad, broken memories, I would never have found my guiding light. I would never have crashed into the unbending force that would quickly become my lifeline. An unwavering diva named Anna.

'Fuck him,' she told me one night, fingers wrapped around the near-empty vodka bottle we were sharing. 'He's a piece of shit, babe. And you're fuckin' gorgeous.' She shook her dark head. 'Fuck him, hon. You can do way better than that loser.'

She'd never met Byron, but that didn't matter to her.

I told her what Andre said to me every time he got the chance and she scoffed, full bottom lip twisted into a scowl. 'He's an idiot too. There's no such thing as soul mates, but if there were, I doubt you'd get stuck with an arrogant asshole like Byron.' She huffed. 'Andre needs to stop. He shouldn't be trying to get you back together.'

My mouth agreed with her, but the rest of me didn't.

With Anna's help I moved on. I didn't forget about Byron like she wanted me to, but I managed to convince her I did. I convinced myself for a little while, too.

There was a string of nobodies before I ended up with Taylor. He was nothing like what I would usually go for, and if we hadn't met through Anna, I probably wouldn't have given him a second glance. His ginger beard alone was enough to put me off. But he was sweet. He was good to me.

Too good, I think.

When Byron and I split, he got our friends. They all up and left like I was the problem, like I broke his heart. But Andre never turned his back on me. Not for a second.

Unfortunately, he didn't shaft Byron either.

I never told Taylor my best friend was turning nineteen, and I certainly didn't tell him that my ex, the guy I was still very much hung up on, would be at the party too. To this day I don't know why I did what I did. I didn't lie to him, but I didn't tell him the whole truth either. I was dishonest, regardless.

I shouldn't have gone to that party.

I made an effort that night. Anna gave me a dress and lined my eyes; she even gave me tips on how to ignore his 'stupid bitch ass'. I walked through Andre's front door fully prepared.

And then I saw him, laughing in a corner with some guy who made me think of a daddy long legs. I saw him, and every line Anna had taught me, every disinterested glance I had practised, vanished like they were never in my head at all.

Two years without seeing him hadn't changed a damn thing. My insides were a mess in milliseconds.

It was two hours and a bottle of chardonnay before he finally acknowledged me. He walked across the room easily, smiling like he hadn't noticed me standing there the entire time. He was polite, a perfect gentleman.

I looked at the boy he'd left on the couch, biting back the urge to comment on the things I pretended not to notice.

'Josh,' Byron said without prompting. 'My boyfriend.'

He laughed, amused by whatever he could see on my face. Disgust, I guess. A scowl caused by the bile bubbling in the pit of my stomach. It's the only thing that could explain the way his smile grew.

I wasn't surprised that he climbed the fence, but I never saw him being happier there.

'So you're a homo now?' I asked sharply, arms crossing over my chest.

His smile fell away before he replied with, 'I'm not anything. I care about his mind, not what's between his legs.'

I snorted at him; said, 'As long as you're between them, right?'

I walked away before he could speak. Partly because I didn't want to hear what he'd say in return, but mostly because not finishing the conversation would piss him off. And I was all about pissing him off right then.

He found me later on in the night, spread-eagled on Andre's bed with a belly full of booze. He wasn't surprised to find me, and I wasn't all that shocked to see him either. I knew he'd come sooner or later.

I noted how quiet the house had gotten and he nodded, told me that everyone had gone or passed out somewhere. He crawled over my body when I asked where his boyfriend was.

'Asleep on the couch,' he told me, fingers brushing over my shoulders. He cupped my left cheek and I leant into the touch, missing the way he'd do it when we were side by side in bed. I brought my own hand up to keep him there.

'Dre said you have a boyfriend now.' It was the last thing he said before I covered his mouth with mine.

I'd always imagined that I'd lose my virginity to Byron, but I didn't see it going the way it did. Fourteen-year-old me thought that it would be our wedding night, that it'd be sweet and slow and romantic, the way it is in the movies. Nineteen-year-old me thought we'd be dating at the very least.

Both versions of me were wrong.

He took a condom from Andre's drawers and fucked me right there on our best friend's bed. We didn't even undress. He just hitched my dress up and opened his jeans, moved in a rush like he didn't really want to do it at all.

He kissed the top of my head afterwards, and my heart sank when he left the room. When he left me for someone else. Again.

Taylor reacted about as well as I expected him to. His cheeks flickered from white to red and back again in a matter of seconds. He said that I was stupid to ruin a perfectly good relationship, that the last eight months of our lives were wasted. But if our relationship had been as good as he claimed, it wouldn't have happened at all.

That's what I told him, anyway.

He walked out of my life with tears in the corners of his eyes.

Anna was the one to confuse me. I expected her to yell or slap me, to tell me I was an idiot to let him suck me back in again. I thought she'd call me a cunt for hurting Taylor. But she didn't do any of that. She put an arm around me and rested her head against mine. She let me cry like I was the victim in the whole thing.

A smart person would have seen it then, would have realised that the relationship wasn't meant to work. It took another five years for me to figure it out. Five years and an on-and-off relationship with a boy I couldn't satisfy.

Byron and I were always careful when we got together. He asked me to go on the pill a few times, said he hated the restrictions that came with wearing condoms, the way they dulled the pleasure, but I always refused. I told him the doctor said it wasn't an option for me, but the truth is I didn't trust him.

If he was leaving his girlfriend's bed to crawl into mine, how did I know he wasn't climbing on top of someone else after me? How did I know he wasn't whispering sweet words and promises into her ear too? Or *his*, because history proved his lack of pickiness.

Two little lines popped the bubble I'd built around myself. They exposed the lies I was telling my two best friends and destroyed the silly dream I was clinging to.

I didn't cry when the test came back positive, didn't freak out like I always thought I would. I took a few deep breaths and reassured myself. I laughed about the pee stick being faulty.

I vomited four tests later, my body shaking so hard it made my head spin.

I told Anna over the phone, sobbing the entire time. She understood what I was saying even though I couldn't shape the words properly. She knew who the father was without asking.

Anna told Andre, and when he looked me in the eye he knew too.

'You told me nothing was going on,' he said, jaw stiff. 'You said I was paranoid, that you weren't stupid enough to go there again.'

'You're one to judge,' Anna bit back, left arm shielding me like she thought Andre was going to lunge at me and my unborn baby. 'You've spent years trying to get them back together.'

'Ages ago,' he spat, throwing both hands up. 'Before I realised he was a selfish prick who can't take responsibility for his actions.'

Anna scoffed. 'Why are you still friends, then?'

'Because his relationship fuck-ups don't affect how he treats me.' He sighed then, face softening. He rubbed the bridge of his nose. 'What are you going to do?'

The doctor didn't seem overly sympathetic to my situation. She didn't seem all that surprised, either. She just thrust a bunch of booklets in my direction and told me to pay at the front desk.

My stomach lurched when I saw the information on abortion, and I realised I'd already made my decision.

'You still haven't told him,' Andre said one afternoon, eyes flickering between my face and the small bump where my flat stomach once was. 'Why haven't you told him yet? You've known for weeks now.'

I rested both hands in front of my bump, eyes falling to my lap.

I don't know what he was expecting to hear, but I know he wanted more than my silence. He wanted answers I didn't have.

'He's going to notice at some point,' he continued, voice a fraction softer. 'And he may be selfish, but he deserves to know that he's got a kid on the way. That he's going to be a dad.'

'He doesn't have to be,' I mumbled, fingers threading together.

He exhaled sharply, and I peeked up to see him shaking his head. 'You're my best friend, and I'd support you through anything. You know I would. But I can't stand by and let you keep a secret like this.' He paused. 'If you don't tell him, then I will.'

When Byron and I first became friends, way back before life got complicated, his mum told me about his eighth birthday. She said that she organised a huge surprise party, that all of their family made an effort to be there. Byron got so flustered that he locked himself in the bathroom for the entire night.

At the time her story seemed pointless, but as I got older it made me realise a thing or two about the boy I loved. It made me see how much he hated the unknown. It's why I wasn't surprised that his green eyes widened when he saw me standing on his doorstep, why I didn't hold my breath when they narrowed just as quickly. I expected the reaction. Just like I expected him to hesitate when I told him we needed to talk, choosing not to let me inside right away.

He didn't say anything when we were stood in the middle of his lounge. Didn't even offer me a seat. His arms crossed over his chest and he stared me down, eyes even thinner than they were when I'd arrived unannounced.

I looked away, eyes ghosting over the pile of boxes stacked against the wall to his left. The evenly spaced letters printed on each one didn't come from his hand. They were too neat, too pretty to belong to any male.

'I'm pregnant.'

I ripped the scab off and waited for the blood to surface.

Byron's cheeks pinked swiftly. I expected that too, but it still made my stomach flip and turn and twist itself into knots. My body shook as hard as his white knuckles.

He said it wasn't his.

I told him it was.

'Get rid of it,' he demanded, top lip twitching uncontrollably.

I told him no, that I couldn't. I wouldn't.

'Fuckin' get rid of it,' he bellowed, face so red that tomatoes would be jealous. 'I don't want it. Abort it.'

'No.'

I backed up when he came at me, my hands shielding my stomach. My heart was pounding like hooves at a racetrack, and air was trapped in my lungs. Byron's green eyes were demonic, so ferocious they chilled my spine. In all our time together, after every fight and cruel word that had passed between us, never once had I been more terrified than I was now. Not once had I thought he might actually kill me.

Every piece of me stilled when I hit the wall behind me, and for a split second all I heard was white noise.

I had made plenty of predictions over the course of our turbulent relationship. Hundreds, even. And almost every single one was correct. I'd developed a knack for reading him. But in all the things I learned, all the quirks and ticks I loved too much to stop, I never once saw this. It had crossed my mind on an occasion or two, but I could never see him actually doing it.

The first fist to my stomach is the only one I remember, but I'll never forget the excruciating pain that shot through me like electricity. It knocked me to the ground and left me writhing. His strength shut my brain off completely.

I woke in my bedroom, body aching all over. I woke up and wished that I hadn't.

My sheets were a bloody mess.

I didn't call an ambulance. There was no point. Byron did what he had to do to get what he wanted. I wouldn't kill our baby, so he beat me until it died. He took away the one thing I ever wanted – a family with him.

Reality woke me for the first time in years, and I knew what I had to do.

I sent apologies to my parents and siblings, my best friends. I told them I loved them. I texted Byron too, told him I was sorry that I wasn't enough, that I couldn't make him happy.

I walked to the kitchen with blood caked on my legs, and I swallowed all but one of my father's diabetes pills.

Most people can't pinpoint what pushed them over the edge, but that's what did it for me. The boy I loved more than anyone in the world, the one I gave everything to, turned on me in a way I never could have imagined. He destroyed me. All I ever wanted was to make him happy, to have him love me forever like he said he would. To be his.

But forever is too long to measure, and Anna was right when she said that soul mates don't exist.

This Day Was Different

RENÉE

This day the horses came by was different, because this day one of them did a big shit on the footpath.

Nanny was furious. She'd liked the horses trotting past, liked the look of the shiny black hides, the straight backs of the two riders. Liked the way the riders lifted their arms and waved to acknowledge her as she stood watering her garden. At first it had been an exchange of smiles then a few comments.

'Nice day.'

'Such a nice garden.'

'Must be such a pleasure working in a garden.'

Nanny always smiled and nodded. *They have no idea. No bloody idea. Haven't a clue how much hard work was needed to make this garden. But that doesn't matter.*

It doesn't matter that they know nothing about that hard first dig which gave her sons' hands blisters. Serve them right. They should have worn gloves. She told them to wear gloves.

Then she made the dark earth hers. She crumbled every bloody sod in her gloved hands and not one worm. Not one. Then she did the second dig. Yes. And bugger. No worms. This land was sick. Sick things needed fresh air, sun, food and water, and the garden was no different. She gave it the best food she could afford. Sheep pellets, some compost, lime, and another turn over with the spade.

During those times of making the garden her back and the backs of her legs were so sore she could barely hobble inside and put the kettle on, but she thought *too bad*. You just have to keep going. She'd given herself a year. Nothing else but the garden. She was seventy-nine. She wanted to get this garden into gear because when she turned eighty she was going to China.

A woman to whom Nanny had given a table gave her a crabapple tree. A columnar.

'Nothing compared to the table,' said the woman. 'It's beautiful. How can you bear to part with it? For nothing? You could have got a good price on Trade Me.'

Nanny didn't say that when you're finished with something, when it had served you well, you shouldn't sell it, you should give it. The only vow she'd made when she started to get old was never to tell someone else how to live.

She was pleased about the tree. She'd not known there were trees that had been made to grow up narrow but still bear lots of fruit. 'Especially for small gardens, according to the man at the garden centre,' the woman said.

Turned out to be right. This last year she had picked three cups and made two jars of crabapple jelly. Good on toast and especially good with the slice or two of ham Nanny bought on pension day as a treat. She didn't think Michael Joseph would see this as a luxury. All that time ago he'd made the Old Age Pension for people like Nanny was now, and Widows' Pensions for women like her mother had been then. He was a proper prime minister because he cared. 'And when he was young,' her mother's smile was huge, 'Michael Joseph, he loved dancing.'

So had Nanny. She liked the foxtrot, the waltz, the Gay Gordons, the Maxina, and she liked the Excuse Me Waltz. She liked that one because you never knew who'd cut in, tap her partner on the shoulder and say 'Excuse me.' Even now, sometimes, when she heard a song on the radio, she thought to hell with it and danced in the kitchen.

Her granddaughters gave her a tree. An apple tree. Old, heritage, they said, supposed to repel cancer. Nanny crossed fingers. She hadn't liked dancing with that bugger, and no excuse me either, just hello Nanny, whether you like it or not, it's our dance.

She always thought of granny's bonnets as dancers. They danced in the wind but they also danced on a still calm day, just because they liked it. She knew their proper name was columbine but she liked the old-fashioned name because that's what they looked like. She had pale cream and yellowy cream, pinks of all shades and one or two mauve ones. Whenever she looked at them she thought of the Excuse Me Waltz.

When she was making the garden, Nanny planted far too many things because a lot of people gave her things and because she loved going to the garden centre. Garden centres don't sell plants, Nanny reckoned, they sell dreams. But that's all right. I don't mind, I'm a dreamer. Gotta get my garden dreams somewhere.

She bought roses, penstemon, a bay tree she put in a pot; she asked a woman in a garden she passed if she could have some borage plants. The woman laughed and said if you plant one borage you'll have a hundred next season. 'Are you sure?'

Nanny smiled. Exactly what I want, she thought. Bees love them, and there's nothing nicer than to stand quiet beside a big borage plant and listen to the buzz of bees happy in their work.

Someone gave her some swan plant seeds and she planted them all. Monarch butterflies liked swan plants and Nanny liked monarchs. She had a monarch butterfly as wallpaper on her phone. A woman who'd got into the habit of stopping for a chat, a blinking nuisance really, saw her phone once when it was sitting in the shade on the sill and said, 'Is that an iPhone 6 Plus?'

Nanny nodded.

'Pretty upmarket?' The woman's astonishment was clear.

Nanny wanted to say a number of things but decided to just think them.

'How did you get that butterfly there?'

'I went into system preferences and clicked,' said Nanny, and the woman looked at her like she hadn't heard right, like how could an old woman know that? Nanny was used to it. Attitudes to old women ranged from sympathetic to disparaging, but all of them had the same ideas about what lines on your face and a limp meant. In their eyes it meant you inhabited another place. It meant your brain had shut down. It meant you were stupid. You were the other. Strangers could call you dear or love if you were old.

This Day Was Different

When she got home, the woman tried out what Nanny said and now she's got a Hopper painting on her phone. That one where it's late at night and there's three people sitting at the bar and the bartender behind the bar, and it's like that lonely three o'clock in the morning feeling when someone is playing one of those sad blues numbers, just one instrument, maybe a trumpet? The woman liked that painting though. She thought the ones sitting at the bar knew what it was to be lonely. 'Makes me feel I'm not the only one,' she said. Nanny took a bit more trouble with the woman after that. Because you never know.

She'd remembered after the woman left that she'd put her crook, because the monarch background hadn't been one of the system preferences but a photo she'd found on the web, and somehow, God knows how because she didn't, managed to transfer it to her phone.

A friend from Dunedin gave her some iris corms. 'Don't know what colours, sorry, you'll find out when they come up.'

They were all colours. Yellow for one. Nanny liked to see yellow in the garden at the end of winter. When she looked out the kitchen window and saw the yellow flash in the corner she felt good, like it was true that winter was over and spring was here. It was hard to believe that sometimes, because the winter got so long and so sore.

Once Nanny had had larger gardens, because she made one wherever she lived. One she remembered as her favourite. That garden had been big enough to divide into places she'd loved. One was ponga, ferns, and another little fern she'd bought at a garage sale. That one was called Waikaremoana. No dry old dust from stupid cars on a sunny day though. One was Auckland, and it had some rocks and lavender, not hibiscus, and none of that bloody kikuyu grass. The Napier garden should have had couch, but, thank God, it didn't. The Wairoa one had a lemon tree and a tree tomato. Now they're called tamarillo. Should have had a willow and a wide river in the Wairoa one, but you can only do so much. The river and the willows were there in her head, anyway. And the whitebait.

Gradually this garden, like all gardens, formed its character. It was an old-fashioned garden, a cottage garden, bits and pieces, too full, but that's the way it goes. She put roses along the fence so passers-by would have something nice to look at. Pretty rumpty old fence, but a few roses galloping all over it would make it a beautiful old fence.

She had a vegie garden along the side. It got the morning sun first, then as the summer went on the sun times got longer and longer.

She hated cabbages, so she grew silver beet and spinach and didn't get any white butterflies, so there. She had wonderfully luxuriant basil and she loved the way people said, 'You grow *basil*? Outside?' And her parsley never went to seed early and the celery always grew green and tall the whole season, because they liked that she planted a few marigolds in with them. Well, that's what she thought anyway.

When she first started, passers-by smiled and nodded, then after a week or so made conversation. One man, fifties she thought, skinny, rode by on his bike and nodded and she nodded back. He did this for the first two years, then one afternoon he came along the footpath wheeling his bike. It was late afternoon in the second year of the garden, just after she got back from China, which turned out to be a great place – great people, busy but not too busy to help an old lady remember where she'd put her stick – but that's another story.

This Day Was Different

Now it was November, equinoctial gales were driving her mad. She hated them. They made her feel naggy and bad-tempered and the garden did too. It tossed its head and got very irritable. If ever Nanny got a bee sting it was during the equinoctial gales, and the garden got so flouncy that the worms, which had come later on in that first year, thought what the heck and popped back deep into deeper ground for a bit of peace.

This day, the man was very talkative. He got off his bike and said, 'Just had a few drinks with an old mate.' Then he said, 'I never pass your garden without thinking how beautiful it is.' Then he told her how his boy had died of cancer on this day three years ago, just before she came and made the garden, and how he had not been able to continue living here because everything reminded him of his son, and his wife couldn't leave because everything spoke to her of their son. 'Even your garden,' he said, 'because he and his mates played footie on the bare section before you came.' He looked down at the ground and said, 'Just couldn't stand it. Just couldn't.'

'Never mind,' said Nanny, 'never mind. You're back now.'

'Yes,' said the man, 'but she can't forgive me. I don't blame her. I rent a small bach up by the beach and sometimes I look out the window and see her walking on the beach.'

Nanny stood while the hose ran and she thought the water rates bill would be high this time, but someone had to listen to the man because in all the times he'd passed by he'd never said anything more than Hi, and this was his time for talking, and the tears ran silently down his face and he didn't wipe them away. So many men talk whether they need to or not, and most of them go on and on just because they like the sound of their own voice, but this man needed to talk and never had, and the few drinks had given him the courage to do it. So it didn't hurt her to listen.

Then he stopped talking and said, 'Sorry, I've gone on a bit.' He rubbed his face with the back of his hand. Got out a hanky and blew his nose. He nodded, hopped on his bike and pedalled off. The next day when he passed he just said Hi, like always, but he and Nanny smiled at each other this time.

Now those bloody horses had shit on her footpath. She got a bucket and a spade and boy, her legs were sore today, maybe she'd better start using that walking stick around the garden. But she knew what would happen. She'd forget where she put the damned thing. Or accidentally shove it in the compost like she had with all those scissors she kept for clipping deadheads. She kept that bloody supermarket going with all the scissors she bought.

She walked out the front and began sliding the spade under the piles of poo and realised she needed gloves on. So she walked back to her outside table and got the gloves from the little pot she kept them and her secateurs in, put them on, muttering to herself. Bloody horses. Bloody horses. She made her legs walk back outside to the footpath and the gloves were good. She scraped it all up into the bucket and carried the bucket, bloody heavy, around the back, dug a trench out from the two new roses she'd bought for ten dollars each, end-of-season specials, but no tulips in the sale which was what she'd really wanted. But that was gardening. Sometimes you had to settle for what you could afford and that was that. Anyway, probably for the best. You had to have quite a few tulips to have a show and she couldn't buy enough tulips to make a show so why not buy the roses? Roses made her smile. They made such a good job of conning everyone they were delicate fussy things that had to be cared for every inch of the way, but they were weeds really. You could dig them out in the middle of summer and plant them somewhere else and they'd always grow. That was the good thing about roses. If after a year or so you didn't like them in that possie, then you could move them somewhere else.

'I wouldn't move a rose at this time of the year,' said a skinny old guy called Climo who'd stopped to give her the benefit of his wisdom when she was moving Gertrude Jekyll a couple of years ago.

'No?' said Nanny. 'How much you bet this won't grow?'

'No need to take offence,' said Climo.

'Put up or shut up,' said Nanny and continued replanting the rose, which rewarded her with at least fifty blooms the following summer. So sucks to him. She'd known Climo since they were both in the primers at Porohiwi Primary and he'd been a pain then, and later always cutting in and saying Excuse Me when she didn't want anyone to cut in. He did it on purpose.

Now she dug the little bit of spare ground in front of Ingrid Bergman then made a wide trench and put the horse shit in the trench. Once the spade had sliced it all up small, she covered it over with earth, patted it with the spade and wondered what she could put in there. Then went back outside again. There were stains all over the footpath.

She smiled a bit to herself. *You're making heavy weather of this*, she told herself.

Well, I'm old, she said back at herself, *I'm bloody old. Picked up too much shit in my time. That's the problem.*

So? said the voice in her head. *You think you're special or something? Never too old to clean up shit.*

So she took the bucket to the tap and half-filled it with water, and she got the brush with the long handle and went out to the shitty footpath and scrubbed it. Then she walked back inside again, got another half-bucket, and rinsed it.

She was standing looking at her work feeling sorry for herself when the man on the bike came past. He got off his bike, wheeled it over to the footpath and said without any hello, 'My wife said I can come back. She said she'd had enough of looking at Hopper's painting and feeling sorry for herself. Time to make a new start. So I went back home on the weekend.'

His face was as clear and happy as the garden in summer after all those bloody winds had buggered off. He smiled at Nanny and Nanny smiled back. A proper smile.

'That's good,' she said, 'that's really good.' And it was.

He went to get on his bike, then remembered, turned back. 'I got some tulip bulbs I was going to put in pots at the bach,' he said, 'and there's no room in the garden at home. Would you like them?'

Neighbours

ALBERT WENDT

Apart from his lawyers, no one, including Anne, needed to know, Eric decided. It was overcast, with the heavy mattress of grey cloud hanging low, keeping the humid heat trapped in the city, and the nine o'clock sun hidden from view. He increased the pace of his walking, his thick-soled tramping sandals crunching mutedly over the footpath, sweat dripping down his body and soaking his t-shirt and shorts. He walked four times each week, for forty-five minutes, round the streets of Ponsonby, and had done so since he and Anne had shifted into Lincoln Street three years before. On the weekdays, if he had a full schedule of lectures and appointments, he walked early in the mornings. Otherwise, in summer, he preferred to walk just before evening when it was cool, and during winter at midday when it was less cold.

He turned into John Street and started uphill, on the last stretch of the walk before turning into his street. Hardly any traffic and only a young couple coming downhill, dragged along at a brisk pace by their magnificent husky. The couple glanced up at him as they hurried past, the young man raising his eyebrows in greeting. Eric acknowledged him with a nod. For a brisk moment, he inhaled the strong smell of dog.

His double-storeyed home was halfway up Lincoln Street, on the left-hand side. Just before it was the large white house, with the dark grey roof, that belonged to Jim and Mata Mein, a retired Samoan couple in their seventies – he'd been an executive in a supermarket chain, and she'd worked for Social Welfare. They'd been living there for over forty years. The Meins were the best gardeners Eric had ever known. Along the front of the house was a lush garden of ponga, nīkau and Tahitian pōhutukawa, with an undercover of ground ferns and grasses. Behind the house, taking up the second half of the back yard, was an even more enviable vegetable garden, which Jim was proud of showing them whenever they were over there. Bordered by feijoas, a couple of lemon trees and an avocado tree, the garden contained potatoes, tomatoes, green beans, carrots, different types of lettuce and other vegetables and herbs. Throughout much of the year, most of the street benefitted from that garden's abundant harvest.

Dressed in his usual gardening clothes – worn jeans, a faded Manu Samoa rugby jersey and Adidas cap, working boots and grey gardening gloves – Jim was in the front garden, weeding and pruning. He saw Eric and waved.

Eric stopped. 'How's the gardening?' Eric greeted Jim, going up to the white fence and into the fierce odour of freshly uprooted weeds and cut branches.

Smiling widely, Jim replied, 'Bloody difficult to maintain the gardens at our age and in this heat.' Ever since he and Mata had gone over, with a gift of vegetables, to welcome Eric and Anne the first week they'd shifted in, he'd grown to trust them, despite his wish, during the first year, to maintain a wary aloofness. Anne was the openly trusting one, and she and Mata soon became friends. Eric followed Anne into their affections. Now Jim and Mata considered them generous neighbours; the first Pālagi neighbours they'd allowed to be that.

'Looks great to me, Jim,' Eric said. 'And you're younger and fitter than anyone in our street!' He meant that: Jim looked as if he was only fifty-five at the most: Eric's age. On their second visit to the Meins' house, Eric had discovered that the Meins had a bench press and a full set of weights, on the back veranda, which they used five days a week in strenuous one-hour sessions. 'One weight-training session a day keeps osteoporosis away!' Mata had declared, jokingly. And they'd been doing it for over thirty years.

The strong enticing smell of coffee greeted him as he entered the house, bent down, pulled off his sandals and lined them along the wall. 'Hi!' he called as he headed upstairs to the bathroom.

'Coffee's ready!' Anne replied.

In the bathroom, he stripped off his drenched t-shirt and dried his face and upper body with a hand towel. On his way down and to the kitchen, he shoved on a clean t-shirt, combed down his long bristly hair with his fingers and suddenly realised he was hungry.

Dressed only in her blue bathrobe, Anne sat at the dining table, drinking her coffee out of her favourite mug and reading that morning's *Herald*. She'd just showered and washed her hair, so a white towel was wrapped round her head, and her face and arms were still red from the shower's heat. The coffee plunger, the small jug of hot milk, honey and his mug were in the middle of the table. He poured his coffee, put milk in it and, after honeying it, sat down opposite her.

She always looked neat, tidy and clean, an outward manifestation of her devotion to keeping the world around her in order, in logical symmetry and design and therefore easier to understand and manage. When he'd first met her, six years before, she'd just left her marriage and her lucrative partnership in the successful advertising company that she and her husband Bill had established, and was trying to establish a new company. The recession had stopped that, so for the past year, while working as a consultant, she'd been researching the financial feasibility of various business possibilities.

'Would you like some scrambled eggs, darling?' he asked.

'No thanks,' she replied without looking up from the paper. He waited but she didn't offer, so he went to the stove, pulled out the small iron frying pan, got out three eggs and, within a few minutes, was cooking scrambled eggs and some sliced tomatoes. 'Got any lectures today?' she asked.

'Just one at four,' he replied. He started laying out his breakfast on the table.

She got up and, unwinding the towel from her head, started drying her hair with it. 'Mata and I are picking up Jeannie later and going for lunch at the Fish Market,' she told him. Jeannie was Mata's only daughter, and Anne's age. Anne and Mata loved seafood, especially fresh oysters and ota, and lunched at the Fish Market on the waterfront once a week. He and Jim, who didn't like any raw seafood, sometimes went with them. She paused and asked, 'Would you like to join us?'

'I've got to prepare my lecture and mark some essays,' he lied, sensing that Anne really wanted only females there. She was gone swiftly.

From the windows of his study he could see into the Meins' backyard garden. His whole body tingled healthily from the pummelling heat of the fast shower and the hard towelling he'd given it. He sat down in front of his computer and switched it on. Jim was now hoeing round the potatoes, sweat dripping off his face and arms. Such dedication and care, he thought with envy. Before they'd bought the house, which they'd both liked on their first inspection, he'd hesitated when he'd found out that their neighbours were Samoan and retired, but when he'd raised his reservations with Anne, she'd confronted him with, 'What's wrong with Samoans and superannuitants?' Immediate affronted defensiveness on his part; he'd been lost for what to say. 'Eric, I don't give a damn about the racist stereotypes. I love the house and what we can do with it!' This was their first confrontation, his first glimpse of her frankness and intolerance of anything that appeared to be discriminatory on grounds of race, gender, age and so forth. 'And going on the huge price they're asking for this house, the Meins, being Samoans, haven't brought the property values down in this street!'

When Eric looked down again, Jim was leaning on his hoe and drying his forehead and arms with a dirt-stained hand towel. Jim glanced up and, seeing him, waved. He waved back. He was so glad that they'd bought the house, and the Mein family was one of the main reasons for him feeling that way. They'd even built a gate between their back yards the year before, and Eric had paid for all of it. You live and learn. People were what they were, not what prejudice dictated or predetermined.

He opened his email. The third email was a lengthy one from his lawyers, detailing their dealings with his father's lawyers and the contents of his father's will. He emailed them back, instructing them not to let anyone, including Anne and his surviving relatives on his father's side, know anything about the will or that his father had died.

For a long contemplative while, he sat watching Jim working, and remembering his parents with deepening sadness and regret. Even with his first wife, Pamela, in their ten-year marriage, he'd deliberately not told her the truth about his father (and his mother). For Pamela, he'd *created* parents with a brief history: at high school, his mother became pregnant – she never told anyone who the father was – and, after giving birth to him in a family and society that totally condemned birth out of wedlock and adopting him out, she'd died of incurable leukaemia. Later, when he'd realised that telling such lies – well, not really lies – only led to you telling more to make the first ones credible, and you had to remember those lies for the rest of your life in order not to contradict yourself and be exposed, he panicked every time someone asked about his parents.

He broke from his recollections and noticed that Jim wasn't in the garden any more and the newly hoed soil round the potatoes was a wet, glittering black.

That evening when he got home from work, Anne told him that the Meins wanted them to come over that Sunday for lunch. 'When I asked Mata about what we could bring, she said, "Bring only a large appetite!"' she added. This was the first time they'd been invited for lunch; until now it had only been for morning or afternoon tea, or a casual drink, and they'd reciprocated in that way.

Throughout most of his life, he hadn't been able to remember his dreams; not in detail anyway. However, since the day his lawyers had rung to inform him of his father's death, his dreams had become more detailed, and they felt starkly accusing, threatening, because at their centre was a ferocious presence – a creature? – that was creating itself slowly and, when it was complete, would spring into his awareness. He and Anne slept in separate bedrooms; her choice because sometimes he snored badly and she said she preferred to 'spread out'. As his dreams worsened he wished she was there to wake him when the creature was whole, and save him from it.

Tonight, the presence – first a featureless swirling darkness – suddenly assumed the face of a young man he'd never seen before but felt he knew. Penetrating black eyes under a high forehead, black hair shaved almost to the scalp, hollow cheeks, thin sharp nose, thin pale lips; a cocky, cynical, know-it-all face, with the assuming shape of a sneer rippling across it. Unexpectedly there was a close-up of his glistening eyes, of his silver-black retinas, in which were reflected the face of a young woman with long, wavy auburn hair framing a face that was shaped in a predetermined look of fear that was worsening, worsening, and in her eyes, in her retinas, was the enlarging reflection of the young man, clench-fisted right hand upraised, momentarily, and then lunging down at her, into the utterly exposed centre of her …

'… It's okay, darling, it's okay!' Anne was whispering into his ear, and he felt her reassuring arms around him. He buried his face between her breasts and sighed his fear into her warmth. 'I could hear you from my room, darling,' she said. He tightened his embrace. 'You were – were screaming, well, in a suppressed sort of way …'

'… Had a terrible dream …'

'About what?' she asked.

He hesitated and then lied, 'About a presence sliding into my room and into my bed, becoming the bed, which then enveloped me, wrapping itself around me, and pulling me down, down ...'

In a short while she fell asleep holding him.

The dreadful fear he'd experienced and his mind's refusal to release him from admitting to himself that the young protagonists were his parents kept him awake for a long time.

Mata had told Anne not to bring anything but Eric made a large mixed vegetable salad and French dressing and Anne roasted a shoulder of pork. They also had four bottles of champagne to take. Although, as they showered and dressed, they continued to feel apprehensive about what they anticipated was going to be a large gathering in which they wouldn't know how to behave correctly, that eased away when Jeannie came through the back gate and into the kitchen, exclaiming, 'Wow, guys, that pork smells absolutely delicious!' She hugged and kissed them on the cheeks. 'Dad wants you to come over now cos he wants someone to drink with – most of our 'āiga don't drink alcohol on Sunday,' she said. Early in Anne's life, she'd realised she had the knack of winning other people's trust and affection easily – not that she worked at it deliberately. Her father had said, 'My beautiful daughter loves people and animals and they reciprocate that automatically.' When she first met Jeannie, she sensed immediately that Jeannie possessed the same gift, and, though they were very different in other ways, Jeannie became the sister she'd always wanted. 'Champagne; wow!' Jeannie said as Eric pulled the bottles out of the fridge and packed them into an esky. 'Now I'm certainly going to have a drink!'

As they followed each other through the gate and up the path between the vegetable beds, carrying the food and esky, Anne saw that the wide back veranda was now the reception area, with all the sofas and armchairs from the sitting room arranged neatly across it. Each table had a large bouquet of flowers on it. And she knew this was more than a lunch.

Sitting alone on the central sofa was a thin old man with wispy white hair, dressed in a bright red floral shirt and black 'ie lavalava. Two elderly women, obviously sisters, sat in the sofa next to his. Jim and Mata occupied the armchairs opposite them. A young woman, with a yellow flower in her ear, was serving them snacks. On the corner on the ground was a hefty wooden table under a wide beach umbrella. On it were glasses and bottles – obviously the bar. Behind the bar was a young man who looked like Jeannie. A few men and women were coming in and out of the kitchen and house. Anne noticed that most of the people resembled one another, all sharing the prominent forehead of the old man on the sofa.

As soon and Jim and Mata saw them they waved them onto the veranda, but Anne and Jeanie veered off into the kitchen with the food, while Eric took the esky to the bar.

'What's this lunch for, Jeannie?' Anne asked, concerned.

'It's Dad's seventy-fifth birthday – and you're the only non-family guests,' Jeannie replied. 'Dad didn't want a party but we talked him into it.' She laughed. 'He didn't want anyone to know this lunch was his birthday party, so you don't need to worry about presents or anything.' She placed her hand on Anne's shoulder in reassurance, and Anne's anxiety eased away.

When Eric went onto the veranda, he walked round introducing himself, shaking hands first with the old man, then the women, and finally with Jim and Mata, who introduced the old man as Hans, Jim's older and only surviving brother, and the women as Renata and Effi, Jim's only surviving sisters. Such German names, yet so Samoan-looking, Eric observed.

When Anne and Jeannie and the young barman brought an opened champagne bottle and some champagne glasses, Anne kissed all the guests and offered them the champagne, which, shyly, they turned down. 'All the more for us,' Mata laughed as she took a glass.

'Eric and Anne, thank you for this!' Jim said, holding up his glass.

Jeannie quickly gathered everyone from inside the house. The five older men and women were Jim's sisters' children and Mata's cousins, the two teenagers and the barman were Jeanie's children, and the others were various nephews, nieces and cousins. None of them accepted Anne's offer of champagne or the young barman's offer of other alcohol. A young woman brought them mango juice. After they'd all been introduced to Anne and Eric, only the four oldest stayed with the elders; the rest returned to the kitchen and dining room to prepare the lunch.

'Like all true fundamentalist Christians and Samoans, most of our 'āiga do not drink the devil's water,' Jeannie remarked. Most of the elders laughed, the old man wheezing his laughter as if he was choking.

'You can laugh,' Jim accused Hans. 'You used to outdrink all of us until your heart started packing up!'

'And before I returned to God,' Hans continued. 'You know of course,' he turned to Eric and Anne, 'that Jim and Mata are the only atheists – or is it agnostics? – in our Christian 'āiga?'

In the conversation that ensued, Anne and Eric gathered that the Meins' surname had come from a German sea captain who'd settled in Samoa in the mid-nineteenth century, marrying into one of the prominent families in a village called Malie. Because of his European surname, the original Mein's oldest grandson was the first of the family to be allowed to settle in New Zealand, and he had worked and saved and sent for the next Meins. That pattern continued to Hans, who migrated to New Zealand after the Second World War; he had saved money and sent for Jim and another brother. Over the years, all of Jim's eleven brothers and sisters had settled in New Zealand, and mainly in Auckland.

'In case you're wondering why Jim's name is Jim and not a really hefty German one like all of ours,' Hans said, his body shaking visibly with mirth, 'it's because our father was apprenticed to a Kiwi plumber called Jim Katten, who he admired enormously.'

'Yes, Jim Katten Mein,' Renata echoed.

'What a handle!' laughed Effi. The two sisters were built slender and slim like Hans, and looked like twins.

'Better than Hans Bruno, Renata Eva, and Effi Johanna!' laughed Jim.

As this light-hearted banter about ancestry and naming continued, Eric grew aware that he was feeling more and more defensive. He was most alarmed when Renata asked Anne about her family, and Anne, without hesitation, explained that she'd been born in New Plymouth and, like Mata, was an only child. 'Well, I became an only child when my sister Ethel, who was born prematurely, died after only five months. My parents were both GPs. After Ethel's death, they never referred to her again; well, not in my presence. Beyond my parents, I know only vaguely of my grandparents and other ancestors before them. My parents seemed uninterested in any of that. They were more devoted to their patients and investing in property and getting me to do a business degree …' As she detailed her family history, Eric realised this was the first time he was learning a lot about Anne's family; a subject that, in their relationship, he'd avoided meticulously in case she asked after his family. And because he'd spent much of his life manufacturing a family history, he knew Anne, like the Meins, was presenting a censored, heavily edited version of her family. Despite that, he knew she was telling 'the truth'. He tried to remember what he'd told Anne about his parents, and grew more afraid when he started doubting his recollections. '… Like many GPs, my parents, while caring wholeheartedly for their patients, neglected their own health badly. My mother, a heavy smoker, died of pancreatic cancer when I was finishing my degree, and my father of a heart attack about three years later.' Anne stopped, traces of tears in her eyes. Mata came over and held her. 'This is the first time I've talked about them in such a long time,' she admitted. Jeannie refilled her glass. 'Thank you for making me do that.'

'Here's to Anne's parents and 'āiga!' Hans toasted, raising his glass of mango juice.

"Ia manuia!' Jim and Renata and Effi toasted.

And they all clinked glasses and drank. Eric reached across and held Anne's arm and, after clinking glasses with her, he again drank his champagne until his glass was empty. Now he needed to divert the conversation away from himself, so he got up and offered to fetch drinks for everyone, but Mata told him he was a guest. The young barman came and took their orders.

Over the three years he had known them, Jim had gathered much detail about Anne's life and work – she was always forthcoming about those – and much about Eric's career and work, but very little about his parents and his childhood. Now, as the alcohol eased throughout his body and head and he felt even closer to Anne and Eric, he *needed* to know. All autobiographies that individuals and families made public were heavily edited versions. No one wanted their so-called skeletons to come clacking out of the cupboard. If they did, they dressed them up to bolster their reputation or they laughed them away. 'So, my friend, Eric, what's your whakapapa?' Jim asked, and tried to sound casual about it.

Eric took a sip of his refilled glass, smiled, and stated, 'Nothing really as long and as interesting as the Meins'. No adventurous sea captain from a cold Europe and the start of a huge and illustrious 'āiga – did I say that correctly?' The elders nodded and grinned. 'I never knew my parents; well – only for the first five or so years of my life, and I can't remember much about that. The information I have about them, and my ancestors before them, I've gathered from my Aunt Sybil and Uncle Roger, who raised me, and from other people and the little research I've done. My Pākehā ancestors, poverty-stricken, migrated here from England. What they did and how they fared here in those tough settler days I don't know anything about.' He paused, now feeling *comfortable* and safe with that narration. 'My parents came along after the Second World War. Dad was born in Blenheim; Mum in Hawera. They met in their twenties while she was working in the railway café in Wellington and he was a railway mechanic. Fell in love, had me, and five years later she died in a car accident …' He had to stop; sorrow was filling his throat. He swallowed it back and then continued, 'Dad was driving and he blamed himself. He gave me to his sister Sybil to care for while he retreated into the interior, to Taihape, to work in the railway gangs constructing new lines. A few months later, he fell off a new bridge they were building across a river.' He paused again. Anne reached over and held his hand, tightly. 'My Aunt Sybil and Uncle Roger raised me. They were marvellous parents. They had no children, so when they died in the 1970s, I had no other relatives left. And here I am, fortunate to be married to this beautiful woman and being with neighbours we respect and' – he hesitated and then said it – 'love and admire!' He knew he had them believing utterly.

'Mālō, mālō!' Hans and Jim congratulated him.

'Here's a toast to Eric and his 'āiga!' Renata announced, raising her glass.

'To Eric and his 'āiga!' All the elders toasted.

Jim went over to Eric, embraced him and pulled him up to his feet. Mata pulled up Anne. 'To the best neighbours we've ever had,' Jim declared, and the whole veranda and neighbourhood resounded with another toast.

'Careful with the champagne!' Jeannie cautioned. 'We're going to run out of it before we can toast the birthday boy.'

Soon after, a woman came and whispered in Jeannie's ear, and Jeannie announced that lunch was ready.

They followed Hans and Jim into the spacious dining room. The heavy round rimu dining table was fatly laden with food, crockery and cutlery; at the centre of it was a small chocolate birthday cake with one candle in the middle. Anne had not seen such a magnificent feast before. She clutched Eric's hand. 'Wow,' Eric whispered.

'We know the birthday boy and Eric are not fond of raw seafood, Anne, but we made sure our favourite oysters and oka found their way onto this table!' Mata said. 'And there's more in the fridge because I know Hans, Renata and Effi are addicts too.' Some of the elders laughed.

'Good for the *muscles*!' Hans remarked.

'Speak for yourself!' Jim improved on the joke. Louder laughter.

Everyone came into the room, and those who were serving lined up behind the circle of elders. Anne realised that her appetite had been sharpened greatly by the champagne, the emotional happiness she was experiencing, the hypnotic aromas of the various dishes and not having had breakfast, but she knew she had to wait.

Hans stepped up and stood in front of the birthday cake. He looked round at everyone and then started speaking in Samoan in what was obviously oratory. Up until then, because all the elders had spoken only English, Anne had assumed their knowledge of Samoan was limited. But, as Hans spoke, and his whole being and voice assumed a charismatic strength that held her even though she didn't understand Samoan, she concluded that there was profound respect and love of the language – and other things Samoan – there. Hans was obviously welcoming everyone, acknowledging all the members of his 'āiga and Anne and Eric. He then wished Jim happy birthday: 'To our beloved brother Jim Katten, a happy seventy-fifth birthday!' he said, breaking into English. Hurriedly, Jeannie and the barman refilled their glasses and they drank a toast to Jim.

'Jim Katten, may you live for as long as you want!' Renata called.

'Yes, as long as the Atua Tagaloaalagi allows!' Effi added.

Mata lit the candle, Jim blew it out and they cheered and then sang 'Happy Birthday'. The singing was in four-part harmony, Anne identified. Obviously the result of family and communal singing over generations. The stereotype of Polynesians being superb singers was *accurate* in this case!

In Samoan, Jim thanked Hans and his sisters and Mata and everyone for the party, and then said in English, 'For the benefit of Jeannie and all the other younger ones who don't know, Tagaloaalagi is Samoa's supreme god and creator!'

'Of course I know, Dad!' Jeannie protested. 'You told me years ago.'

'Apart from Jim Katten and a few other pagan Samoans, no other Samoan believes in Tagaloa any more!' Hans tried to joke, but Anne detected a deep regretful tone in his voice.

'Time for overeating and adding on the calories!' Mata declared, handing Hans a plate.

Hans bowed his head and said grace in English.

About two hours after lunch, Hans, Renata and Effi and their children left, saying they had to go to a church function, taking with them a share of the leftover food. The barman and the other servers cleaned up and then left, with their share of the food. Jim, Mata, Jeannie, Anne and Eric continued drinking wine and beer that Mata kept producing from the freezer in the store room under the house. Though they were feeling woozy and bloated from eating and drinking too much, their absolute contentment at sharing the Mein 'āiga's love and hospitality kept them lucidly buoyant and aware and wanting that time to continue. Anne discerned her speech was slurred, and her limbs were not moving smartly to her instructions, but she was enjoying that too.

'The birthday boy's asleep!' Jeannie laughed, pointing at her father, who was half-slumped in his armchair, his chin resting on his chest, purring audibly.

'At seventy-five, he's earned it!' Eric exclaimed. 'He deserves it.'

'And the birthday boy's girlfriend is falling asleep too, from too much eating, drinking and old age!' Mata staggered up to her unsteady feet. Jeannie held her up. Anne rushed over and hugged them both.

Eric went over to Jim and, taking the empty beer glass out of his hand, bent down and kissed him on the forehead. 'Thank you for inviting us, Jim Katten.'

... This time, the sneering young man's upraised fist was coming down in slow motion into his eyes as he was gazing up at him. And he could hear himself screaming at the edge of his hearing, screaming, and he was belching up the vile burning taste of his acidy stomach, and desperately hoping for Anne to save him ... Thankfully he was awake, out of the recurring dream, but Anne wasn't there holding him, consoling him. He rolled onto his back and sat up, shaking and drenched with sweat, and wanting to rush into Anne's bedroom, but he forced himself not to.

Stripping off his pyjama pants, he staggered into the bathroom and into the shower, and switched it on. The cold water stung his body and head awake, and the dregs of the dream were gone, but the cold suddenly felt icy and he started shivering. He switched off the shower, rushed out and towelled himself with fierce ferocity until his body was warm again.

A short while later, dressed in the yukata Anne had bought him on a business trip to Japan, he sat in the computer chair in his study, gazing down into the shifting, murmuring darkness that now filled the Meins' backyard, at the bright reflection his study windows were casting across the vegetable beds. Such a happy, fulfilling family day; one that he'd never really experienced before and would not forget ever.

And as his parents had once again insisted on intruding, he welcomed them, without reservation, for the first time in years.

Because he'd created so many lies, a whole mythology of them, about his parents, it took him a long painful time to sift through those to find 'the truth' about them.

The night deepened and heightened the brightness of his window's reflection across the vegetables and made them look like black steel sculptures. Aunt Sybil and Uncle Roger were real, and they'd raised him after his father had killed his mother accidentally during a quarrel and was found guilty of manslaughter and sentenced to ten years in prison. He was nine when that had happened, and he couldn't remember much about any of it and had had to rely on his aunt and uncle to provide him with the information. As a teenager, he'd grown hugely ashamed of it, and had insisted that his guardians change his surname to theirs. (He would carry that shame and anger, he believed, forever.) When he went to university in Auckland he never returned to Blenheim. He kept in touch with his guardians until Aunt Sybil died unexpectedly of heart failure, and then, because Uncle Roger wasn't a very good correspondent, he'd let the connection lapse. Throughout his life, he'd kept well away from his father, but always ensured he knew where his father was and what he was doing, so he would never have to meet him.

Now, in death, his father was with him again, and with that returned his beautiful, beautiful mother. In the window's reflection below he saw – coming into focus – the wedding portrait of his parents that had occupied the central position on his aunt's and uncle's fireplace.

Pointing the Bone

ANN FRENCH

A ghost lives in my house. I glimpse him from time to time but I'm not as afraid of him as perhaps I should be. He tells me he used to live here but his family moved on and now he just waits. 'Wait for what?' I ask. But he doesn't reply and turns away.

Sometimes, my ghost carries a pipe, an old weathered thing with a black bowl and a stem that resembles a dog's much-loved bone, one that has been chewed and sucked on more than a thousand times.

He is a small man, who even as a ghost has a presence that demands respect. Around his neck hangs a greenstone adze, a toki. A feathered cloak, his only visible garment, falls from his shoulders. Like the pendant, it is a thing of beauty.

He tells me he is a tohunga. And this is his story.

Henare bites down on the pipe stem so hard it's a wonder it doesn't splinter and break. It is an old pipe, dark brown with a black bowl and one of his most prized possessions. He's not allowed to smoke in the house these days so if he wants to inhale 'poison', as his daughter-in-law puts it, he has to go into the garden or onto the veranda. Smoking his pipe is one of the small pleasures he still enjoys and it irks him that he is forced outside to do it, cast out like an old piece of unwanted furniture. Smoking, he thinks, while the comfort of the sun warms his old bones, should be something done inside, while reading a book or newspaper. And today the resentment is worse than usual.

Early this morning, his son William went to pick up his wife and new baby from the hospital. Henare sucks the stem of his pipe and makes a 'putt putt' sound he isn't even aware of. No aromatic fumes curl into his nostrils, just the taste of stale spit. *A girl! What a waste of the procreative process that is*, he thinks. *Why couldn't it have been a boy like my son, who would grow tall and strong with capable hands that could fix a broken car, catch a load of fish or carve furniture fit for a queen?* He snorts, imagining the years stretching ahead full of pink shoes, frilly dresses and dolls.

A car pulls into the driveway and William gets out, carefully retrieving a carrycot from the back seat. Helen, his wife, slowly unwinds herself and stands up with a grimace.

'Hi, Henare,' she calls. 'How are you?' And before he gets a chance to answer, she adds, 'Put the kettle on would you? I'm dying for a decent cup of tea before I feed the baby.'

Henare grunts and goes inside. Before the baby came along, the boot would have been on the other foot and Helen would have made a cup of tea and brought it to him. But that has changed. He sighs, a sound that comes from deep inside and makes his heart lurch as though caught off kilter.

He hears the sound of voices in the lounge, and without conscious thought, squares his shoulders, clamps the pipe firmly between his teeth, and walks through to where his son and daughter-in-law lean over the carrycot.

'Come and see your granddaughter,' says William and moves to one side so Henare can have a better view.

'I've seen babies before,' says Henare, 'and they all look the same. Like monkeys with squashed faces but without the bananas.' He thinks Helen and William will laugh or at least smile at the meagre joke, but instead both parents look at him as though he's said something distasteful, even vulgar.

Inwardly he takes a deep breath and then, stepping forward, peers into the cot. Inside is the most perfect human being he has ever seen. His hand goes to his chest again as he feels his heart lurch as it had in the kitchen, giving that funny jolt as though he's been shocked by an electrical charge.

The baby yawns, her mouth pouting while tiny fists pump the air and her feet kick. She opens her eyes and looks straight at Henare and bawls like a calf that's lost its mother. The old man steps hurriedly back and almost falls at the sound. *How could such a small creature make such a huge noise?* he wonders. It fills the room, a wailing cry that builds up and up, making Henare close his eyes. The sound goes through him, permeating his senses. Then suddenly it stops.

He opens his eyes and sees Helen has picked up the baby and is seated on the couch, feeding her. *Thank God*, he thinks.

Later that night, when everyone is sleeping, Henare gets up and goes into the room where the baby lies in her bed. One tiny hand has escaped its cocoon-like wrapping and is over her head while she sucks furiously and intermittently on the other. The old man reaches into the cot and smooths the tuft of hair that sprouts from the small head. It refuses to lie down and springs upright again with a life of its own. *As soft as a kitten*, he thinks, and stands for long seconds looking down while his heart slowly and surely falls in love.

They call the baby Miriamar, although she is rarely called by her full name. It is usually just Miri. Henare loves the name and even when she is still a baby, he tells her stories of princesses called Miriamar who are beautiful, have powerful magic and marry handsome princes or warriors.

'Why tell her such stories? It's not like she understands them,' says William.

'You never know,' says Henare, and sitting with the baby on his knee wrapped in a warm blanket, he launches into another tale of vicious taniwha, beautiful maidens and warriors who overcome tremendous odds to win the ultimate prize. Sometimes, the hero has to make a sacrifice to beat the odds, something of immense value that he prizes greatly, and at such times, the old man's voice takes on a deeper resonance. The stories are from his heart and soul, tales from the past and never frivolous or of minor significance.

As Miri grows older, she seems to recall her grandfather's stories and says, 'Koro, tell me the story about the lovely princess, the taniwha and the prince.' And although he has told it many times before, Henare always speaks as though it is the first outing of the tale, full of wonder and suspense, with deeds of great bravery and courage.

There are milestones along the way of Miri's growing up that, although they no doubt occurred with his own children, Henare does not remember as vividly or with such pleasure. *Perhaps that's what being a grandfather is all about,* he thinks, putting the finishing touches to the kite he's made, which resembles a taniwha. They will fly it later in the park.

When she is old enough, he buys her a small bicycle. It's pink, her favourite colour, with ribbons on the handlebars, and a wire basket. He watches from the front gate as she rides unsteadily, wobbling from side to side along the footpath, and breathes a sigh of relief as, gaining confidence, she swoops back into the driveway. He claps and smiles while his hand unconsciously touches the toki at his neck.

Six months before she turns five and begins school, William drives his father and daughter to the dog pound to choose a puppy. Miri is so excited she chatters non-stop the half hour it takes them to get there, and once out of the car she dances in circles on her tip-toes, sending little puffs of dust into the still air. It doesn't matter that Henare has a walking stick or is much slower, she grabs his hand and drags him with her to where, in a frenzy of canine exuberance, fifty or more dogs bark and wag their tails. 'Pick me, pick me,' they say and Henare sighs, knowing this could be an exhausting process and a long, long day.

Surprisingly, that is not the case, and within minutes Miri chooses a puppy. It is the ugliest and most unappealing of them all, with a shaggy coat, long droopy ears, a stump of a tail and enormous paws that would do credit to a lion.

Despite the best efforts of the adults, who put forward such names as Rover, Goldie, Duke and Jack, Miri chooses to call him 'Dog'.

In the new year when she turns five, Miri goes to school. Weeks before, she has her bag packed and even chooses the outfit she will wear on the first day. Henare feels sadness and knows with the advent of her going to school, a part of his life is over and will never return.

She is no longer his to care for and cherish on a daily basis. He will have to share her with strangers, and it is a painful thought.

He goes into town one day, catching a bus and getting off at the shopping mall. He wanders up and down the aisles, an old man leaning heavily on a walking cane, his breath coming in little gasps and gulps. Occasionally he finds a bench where he sits down for a while before standing and continuing on. Eventually he finds what he is looking for and, pulling out an old leather purse, hands over some money. The girl behind the counter asks, 'Can I wrap this up for you, sir? Is it a gift?' Too exhausted to answer, Henare just nods and his parcel is duly handed over, covered in pink floral paper. He has one more stop to make, and when that is done, he makes his way back to the bus stop and home.

He gives Miri both gifts the morning of her first day at school. She has hardly eaten any breakfast and is persistent in her query, 'Is it time yet? Can we go now?' Henare puts the presents on the table and waits for her to open them. Helen and William watch as the paper comes off and Miri gives a squeal of joy at the sight of the case filled with a selection of coloured pencils. In the second parcel are a variety of hair ribbons, every shade of pink that Henare could find on that long and tiring day at the mall.

The man and dog watch as she walks with her mother down the road, around the corner and out of sight. Henare feels a heaviness in his chest as though a lead weight has replaced his heart. Dog whines, wanting to follow, and when she is out of sight, gives a long howl and lies down by the gate, his head between his giant paws. He stays that way for the rest of the day.

Henare sits on the veranda smoking his pipe. Helen says nothing, doesn't growl or comment on how bad it is for him, and instead brings out a pot of tea with some scones on a tray. But both the tea and food sit untouched.

Miri returns home in the afternoon. She has drawn a picture with her new pencils of her family, Mum, Dad, Koro and Dog. They are stick figures with arms outstretched as though crucified and they have no feet, but despite these faults, all are recognisable for who they are. Henare pins it to the wall of his bedroom, where, over the next few months, it is joined by dozens of others.

School is an adventure and every day a new experience. The small dramas, dynamics and minor politics of school life are brought home and discussed, and Henare becomes adept at when to offer advice and when to shut up. He amazes himself. Miri learns to read, slowly at first, but she is a fast learner and is soon top of the class. Writing is more difficult, but she and Henare sit together and practise the letters of the alphabet every day after she comes home, until she masters that skill as well.

But one thing never changes. In all weathers, Dog and Henare stand at the front gate when she leaves for school, and both are always waiting when she returns home.

My ghost stops talking at this point and walks away. I wonder if that is the end of his story, although somehow I don't think it is. For some days I don't see him at all, and I'm concerned that perhaps I've done something to irritate or anger him, causing him to leave. I hope that's not the case. But a few days later he returns without explanation. It is a stormy day, rain falling in sheets, battering at the windows and causing the gutters to overflow so that they resemble waterfalls. Thunder and lightning boom and light up the sky, and draughts of cold air trapped inside cause the curtains to billow slightly and flutter as though phantom hands are shaking them.

Henare stands in the room where I spend my days writing and continues his story. His voice is soft but resonant and full of power, and I hear it easily across the noise of the storm.

One day Miriamar doesn't come home.

William is at work and Helen, who has a dental appointment, has arranged for a friend to pick her up and bring her back to the house. Initially Henare feels no concern, but as time goes by he knows something is wrong, and when Dog begins to whine, he is certain.

Helen arrives and immediately phones the friend, who says that Miri wasn't there to be picked up and apparently hasn't been at school since lunchtime. No alarm bells had gone off as the usual teacher was away sick and the reliever didn't know the class or the children in it.

William and Helen get in the car and scour the streets, using a cell phone to call friends who may have seen her or whose places she may have visited. She has vanished, and the police are called.

The hours go by and people come and go. Four police arrive, a woman and three men. They take notes, walk around the house, examine the garden and Henare's collection of drawings. They go into Miriamar's bedroom, the room where pink is the predominant colour; pink curtains, bedspread, small chair and table. Politely they ask permission and remove her toothbrush, some hair from a brush and a photo taken one Christmas when she was dressed as a fairy.

There are dozens of questions. Who are her friends? What are their addresses? Was she a happy child? Had she had a fight with her parents or with her grandfather? The last question is so preposterous that Henare snorts and goes to stand up and leave the room, but

William shakes his head at him so he sits down again and chews on the stem of his pipe. The questions continue on and on. Has anyone smacked or hit her? Has she ever run away before? Henare wants to stand up and shout at them, these stupid people, 'Why don't you get out there and find her instead of wasting time asking this nonsense?'

But the officers of the law won't be hurried, and they continue their questioning until there is nothing more to be gained by their inquisition. Somehow Henare is left with a feeling of guilt, a feeling he should have done something more to protect his grandchild.

Neighbours, friends, whānau arrive bringing food, then even more food and, to some degree, comfort. A doctor comes and gives Helen pills to help calm her, while William appears older every time Henare looks at him. He becomes a mirror of his father – a lined face, stooped posture, greying hair.

The first night comes and goes. On the second day, journalists and TV crews arrive, jostling for position to get a shot of the family or, better still, an interview. Helen and William decide to go in front of the cameras and make an appeal to whoever has Miriamar to let her go, to let her come home. Helen sobs uncontrollably and William is grim-faced but there is no response, no answers to the little girl's disappearance. She has fallen into the abyss.

Dog jumps onto Miri's bed, burrowing into the blankets, and no one has the heart to throw him off.

Henare doesn't sleep. He knows what is coming and wants to be awake when it arrives. He speaks to no one, and when people approach to begin a conversation, he closes his eyes and pretends to be asleep. He fools everyone but William, who, on the third day, sits with him and asks the question that he forces past his lips and that almost chokes him. But he has to know. 'Is she coming home, Dad?' he asks, and his large, calloused workman's hand closes over the frail, vein-lined one belonging to his father.

Henare looks at his son and knows he can't lie, though he would give anything to be able to say, 'Yes, she is.' But he can't, so he shakes his head, no.

William sits a little longer, tears streaking his cheeks. Then he gets up and goes inside. Henare remains, wrapped in an old blanket, waiting for the dawn.

In the afternoon, a police car pulls up, and this time only two policemen get out. One is the woman who came before and the other is a tall Māori with the build of an All Black. Both look nervous, as though wishing they could be anywhere but here. Henare stands, and as he does, Dog is suddenly at his side. He growls softly at the two officers as they go to mount the steps and they freeze mid-way, intimidated, but Henare says something softly and Dog backs away.

'We have found your daughter,' they say to Helen and William. 'But unfortunately ...' Henare doesn't wait to hear more. He already knows.

He goes out to the shed where the pink bike, waiting for its rider, leans against the wall. The ribbons are still attached to the handlebars, faded now and hanging forlornly. The basket contains an old teddy, ready to go for an outing, but it has seen better days. There is a missing eye and ear and some stitching has come adrift so that a small amount of stuffing pokes through. The old man covers all this with his blanket and moves back inside.

In his room, he removes the drawings, one by one, placing the drawing pins that held them in a wooden box. The art itself he puts in a large drawer at the bottom of his wardrobe, and when the last one is interred, he shuts it slowly and gently as though it were the lid of a coffin. Then he stands to face what he knew would be coming from the first day.

The tangi is a huge affair. Media from all over the country arrive in cars, vans and even buses. Henare feels dissociated from it although that is unsurprising, as few people seem to notice the old man who sits quietly in the corner smoking a pipe which, if they looked closely, they would see is unlit. Near him sits a dog with huge paws, droopy ears and a stump for a tail, whose eyes rarely move from the small coffin that lies on the porch.

At night, while others get their rest, he moves closer to the closed coffin and talks softly, occasionally crooning a long-forgotten song – long-forgotten by all except for a few like him. He tells stories to his dead granddaughter, of princesses who are beautiful and have powerful magic, of handsome princes who battle ferocious taniwha, all for love. When daylight returns, he moves back to his seat in the shade and waits until night falls again and he resumes his watch.

Words are spoken, hymns are sung, and tears, enough to drown the sun, are shed.

Henare speaks slowly, dredging words as though from a deep well. He tells me that the police arrest the man on suspicion of the abduction, rape and murder of Miriamar. Six months previously he'd been released from prison for sexually assaulting a seven-year-old girl, and although supposedly closely monitored, he has 'slipped through the cracks' and rented a house directly across from the school. His name is Poti Te Whanga.

In his house they find one of Miri's pink ribbons and her pencil case, but Te Whanga claims he found them on the side of the road. No one believes him, but it turns out that doesn't matter.

It takes eight months before Poti Te Whanga comes to trial. Prosecution and defence counsels work at collecting evidence and information, coroner's reports and witnesses, those who will speak for and against the character of the accused.

On the first day, William, Helen and Henare drive to the courthouse and park around the back, where a policeman directs them to a side entrance, out of sight of the waiting media. The jury has been chosen, six men and six women, and the judge, after he sits and thanks them for their service, warns that much of what they are about to hear will be distressing and afterwards, if they find they require counselling, that can be arranged. No one has offered counselling to Miriamar's family.

Poti Te Whanga is escorted into the dock and, like royalty, he waves to the public gallery where people have come to watch and listen. The judge cautions him to behave but he smirks all the more now he is the centre of attention.

The pathology expert who is called first gives medical evidence that causes Helen to sob out loud until finally William gets up and escorts her out. She does not return, and although Henare wishes his son would stay away as well, he knows he won't. The two men sit shoulder to shoulder, wondering at the monster who lived so close and yet was granted a cloak of invisibility.

The case drags on over two weeks, every day seeming worse than the one before. Helen hasn't come back. William is a walking shadow, neither sleeping nor eating and resembling one of the stick people his daughter drew so long ago. Henare feels himself slowly turn to stone though his heart beats strongly, fuelled by the anger and hatred that boils inside him and the single thought that justice will be done here, in this place.

But the monster has been clever. The DNA is inconclusive, evidence has been contaminated and defence witnesses claim Poti Te Whanga was with them at the time of the abduction and murder. Henare knows they are lying. He has looked at them, into their eyes, their hearts, and knows they fear to tell the truth.

The summing up by both the prosecution and defence doesn't take long, and the jury retires to reach a verdict. The judge warns, 'If you return a verdict of guilty, it must be because you are convinced without a shred of doubt that Poti Te Whanga committed this crime. If not, you must return a verdict of not guilty.'

When the jury returns, not one of them can look at Henare or William, and the verdict is not guilty.

Poti Te Whanga is released and walks from the court a free man.

Henare returns home with William, who goes and tells Helen the news. The three of them sit in the kitchen, not speaking. A spider's web of silence is woven, its strands entangling and choking them, each in their individual ways. Helen becomes withdrawn, only speaking when necessary. Not listening, not hearing. It's as though she is suffering a form of deafness. William spends hours in his workshop, hammering, sawing, lumps of discarded wood lying everywhere. Nothing constructed, nothing created or built. Henare walks, the distances becoming longer every day. Not that it isn't an effort as he grunts, groans and snorts putting one foot in front of the other, but when the day comes that he can walk around the block, he goes to William.

To begin with, William refuses and even becomes angry, his voice raised, his eyes wide, his fists clenched. But Henare tells him there is no one else who can complete the task, no other way to get justice, and the old man is unrelenting and persistent in his demand. Eventually William gives in.

My ghost stops the story here for a minute or two and I sense he is wondering whether to tell me what happens next. He looks at me closely, then gives a barely perceptible shrug and I gather I have passed the test.

The rain, thunder and lightning have given way to strong winds that batter at the doors and windows like vandals trying to break in, but this house is strong and I know it will withstand whatever the elements throw at it.

William makes everything ready, then calls to Henare, who is sitting on the veranda, smoking his pipe one last time. He gets up and walks to the workshop and stands at the bench, placing his hand palm down on the folded towel William has prepared. Father and son look at one another and things unsaid are passed between them in that glance that could never find a voice otherwise.

William holds a hammer in his right hand, and with his left, places an adze just below the middle joint of the index finger on Henare's right hand. For a second he steadies it then lifts the hammer and with a grunt brings it down.

My ghost, Henare, doesn't say much for a while, but when he does it's to ask me to look for a name in the newspaper. Every day I scan the Death Notices but there's nothing, and I think he will be disappointed but he appears not to be, so I continue looking and, like him, I wait.

It's not such a long way to Miri's school but it still takes Henare the best part of an hour to get there. He takes Dog with him and goes at night. Although it's cold, he wears only his feathered cloak, unworn for many years, which has been lying with the drawings of his dead granddaughter in the wardrobe. It is a beautiful thing, made of feathers, and as he walks they lift and flutter as though they have a life of their own. Only someone like Henare, a tohunga, has the right to wear such a cloak.

He reaches the house he is looking for and marvels at the audacity of the man who still lives there, secure in the knowledge he cannot be touched for the terrible crime he has committed. Henare knocks on the door, and after a few minutes hears footsteps and it's opened. Poti Te Whanga!

He sneers at the old man and says an obscenity, but his words are swallowed up and fall into the night as empty and useless as sand in the desert. Henare stands tall, the dog at his side. He points a silver-white bone, the length of a man's finger, and says the words first in Māori then in English, words full of magic and power that ring out and cause the man they're directed at to shake and put his hands over his ears. The air becomes heavy with the smell of blood and fire, breathing life into the terrible curse. The dog watches impassively, his eyes unwavering, watching the man who stands trembling in the doorway.

Then it is done and the old man and the dog turn and slowly make their way back home, where William and Helen are waiting.

Today there is a small paragraph in the newspaper. A man has been found dead in a house, a possible suicide. It's hard to tell as he's been there for some time and the body is badly decomposed. Neighbours say he'd become a recluse over recent months and was rarely seen.

There are no death notices. No one mourns him, no one cares.

It gives his name and when I tell my ghost, he smiles.

I notice he touches the toki at his neck and that the index finger of his right hand is missing. It's no surprise, and I remember the words, 'Sometimes the hero has to make a sacrifice, something of immense value that he prizes greatly ...'

For the first time I see a little girl standing at his side. She has ribbons in her hair and tugs at his hand, wanting him to come, impatient to be gone. By their side is a dog. It's an ugly beast, with a shaggy coat, long droopy ears, a stump of a tail and enormous paws that would do credit to a lion.

The storm is passing and the sun comes out. Everything sparkles and is clean and new. It illuminates for a moment my three ghosts, and gradually as I watch, they fade away. And I am poorer for it.

Frau Amsel's Cupboard

TINA MAKERETI

Frau Amsel sat with her knees together and her hands folded in her lap. To her left, the window was slightly open and a breeze lifted the frayed edge of her curtain so that the light shifted over her table and walls. She could hear the sounds of traffic outside – a few cars, bicycle bells, the light pummel of many feet, all pushing through on their way to schools and jobs that wouldn't abide lateness. She felt giddy, or nauseous. She couldn't tell.

The flat was clean, everything was in order. He would arrive soon. She wondered, if she held herself still enough, if she kept the clean lines of herself tucked and uncreased, if she kept her fingers from twitching and her feet from shifting, she wondered if she could slow his arrival. Perhaps she could stop there, just make everything stop. Herself. Could she ever just make herself – stop? She pushed the thought down with the bile that threatened to rise in her throat. Of course not.

The children. Her Soul. She almost laughed at this. Damned. Either way. And she would make do, as she always had. They would make do, her and the children. They had survived worse, she thought.

The last time she saw him, she had not known what to expect. On the previous Tuesday, the telegram had told her that Paul was gone, but it had taken her days to know it. *He will not come back,* she had whispered to herself again and again as she prepared cabbage and a little bread for the children on Thursday; *he did not think of us,* she had chanted under her breath as she made soup from the last potatoes on Sunday. All that time tears silently ran down her face. She did not sob, did not wipe them away, did not know how they continued to come all through the day and night without the normal tremors of crying. The children had watched her warily, and did not make the sounds children should make.

And then when Tuesday came again it brought the summons to his office, and she finally wiped her face with the bottom left corner of her apron, untied it, and put on her coat. She walked several long streets to a building she had not seen before, and up the five flights of stairs to the right level. When she arrived she was frightened, but she made a decision to draw an impassive face across her features, to remain calm and quiet and obedient. She sat with her knees together and her hands folded in her lap. This was what survival told her to do.

She was taken into a barely furnished office, and told to sit at a spare desk. An official came into the room with a small pile of items which he placed on the desk without looking at her. The official sat and opened a folder, and read her a statement about her husband's death. He had not carried out his orders. His cowardice put the other soldiers at risk. It was therefore necessary and prudent to place him with the group of partisans he had refused to execute. Thus he met the same fate as them.

'There is some poetic justice in this, Frau Amsel,' the official said. 'Your husband did not act to protect his country. But a price has been paid. Perhaps the shame will not stigmatise his family forever.'

Frau Amsel heard in his voice that the official meant this to sound like he was being kind. But she also heard the steel vein of mockery that ran beneath his words. Why had he brought her in if not to put her in her place? She fixed her eyes on the space between the wall and the sharp edge of the desk, and did not let her thoughts change her expression. Though perhaps her defiance did not matter, since he had not once looked at her since he entered, and all she could see of him was his chin and nose beneath the ring of hair that surrounded his balding pate.

Then, finally, his speech finished, he lifted his head and looked her full in the face, and told her that her husband's few possessions were now hers to collect. At this, she looked properly at the official, waiting for the signal that she might leave. His eyes widened slightly, his mouth slackened. She saw it then, something familiar, something from the past, a resemblance to someone she once knew. But she couldn't place him. Couldn't remember. She wondered if her lack of attentiveness would cost her. His mouth was open in a small ring of surprise, and then he gathered his features in, shuffled his papers back into their file, returned to his face the veneer of control that was so important to his rank.

'Frau Amsel, you were once a Klein, I believe, before your marriage?'

'Yes.' She did not know what else to say. How did he remember her so well?

'I knew your brother. Perhaps your husband did not do well by his country and his family, but your brother made the ultimate sacrifice. Indeed, on balance, you may hold your head high.'

She did not need to be told how to hold her head, or who she should be proud of.

'I remember.'

'Yes, Carl and I were friends in high school. Your mother would invite me for supper.'

'Yes.'

She did not allow her expression to change. If she could only hold still long enough, she was sure it would soon be over. The official watched her. There could be no gaps through which he might enter.

'How is your mother, Frau Amsel?'

'She died almost a year ago.'

'I am sorry to hear this. And your father?'

'He died long before the war.'

'You are very much alone then.'

She thought of her in-laws in Hamburg. They were far enough away that contact was difficult. Travel was almost impossible.

'Yes.'

'How will you feed your children, Frau Amsel?'

She could not hold it. Her eyes twitched and lowered and looked to the side. When she looked back he was watching her even more closely than before. She hoped her voice would not shake.

'There is my cleaning work. The Winter Relief.'

'Yes. Of course. Our destitute are provided for. But this will be only the minimum, barely enough for survival without some other income.'

Frau Amsel's Cupboard

They were both silent. The silence stretched between them for too long. It was all she could do to stay in the chair now.

'I would like to visit you, Frau Amsel, to make sure your brother's niece and nephew are well taken care of. But it is better that the children do not know.'

The silence sat between them again. She saw what his request would mean. She saw that a refusal would not be received well. Even so, a good woman would leave immediately. A strong woman would turn her nose high and find a different way. She saw her bewildered children and her bare cupboards and a war stretching out beyond the horizon and no knowing the end of things.

She let her chin lower, just a little, to signal her assent.

And so he came each Thursday at 11 am, with a basket of food. Sometimes he brought soap and items of clothing, once he brought an accordion for the children to play. The extra items were not new, but she did not ask where they came from. That first day, when Frau Amsel finally heard the boots on the stairs, she had to clench her thighs together so that she did not wet herself. He knocked, softer than she had expected, and when she let him in, he told his guard to wait outside. He showed her the basket, and she said thank you and took it to her kitchen. When she returned they stood in silence again, until he cleared his throat and asked why she had not offered him a seat. She apologised, gestured for him to sit, sat herself and then stood again.

'Pardon me, Herr, Herr –' She had not realised until that moment that she did not know what to call him.

'I am Fuchs,' he said.

'Yes, pardon me, Herr Fuchs.' She could no longer stand the game. Frau Amsel was a practical woman. She felt like prey waiting to be pounced upon. It would be easier, she was sure, to be direct. 'What would you like from me?'

The officer's eyes widened slightly, but he quickly drew himself back into the seat and narrowed them again. He stood.

'I must admit, Frau Amsel, that I am surprised by you. I thought you would remain coy for much longer. It is a shame that you speak so bluntly because I do like the coyness of women. But I will not leave just yet.'

He let his eyes roam down her neck to her left shoulder, where he held them for a long moment. She felt the restraint in his gaze, his thoughts roaming further down her body, his control of the impulse for his eyes to follow. He looked up again, the reason for his visit bold in his face.

'I do not have a family. My work demands much of me and thus I have no time to pursue such things. But, of course, I am a man. Certain arrangements can be beneficial for two people in need of something from each other. I can offer a little protection, some food. You can offer me ... other comforts.'

A noise escaped from her mouth before she could hold it in.

'Ah, Frau Amsel, do not be afraid. It is very simple. What I would like now is for you to go into the bedroom with me.'

There were worse things. She thought of the space in her cupboard that should be occupied by food. She thought of her dead husband and parents and brother, but they seemed far away. She allowed herself to move, keeping the clean lines of her shoulders straight and her spine upright, as she had been directed.

And so that was how it was between them each time he came – routine, mechanical, she attempting to conceal as much of herself as possible even as she stood or lay before him naked; he trying to rouse some response from her but, failing that, taking his pleasure as he could. It did not hurt her, she was relieved to find, it was not such a high price to pay. She did not feel anything for the activity that happened to her body for that half hour each Thursday morning, but she did find an anger grew in her for the husband she had loved and admired when he was living. He had left it all to her, the work of raising their family – he had made her responsible for the clothing and feeding of two growing children. She would never have been put in Herr Fuchs' path if it hadn't been for his selfish choice. Now she was forced to make this sacrifice because her husband had not cared enough to sacrifice his morals. Did it matter that he took a stand? Those people died anyway, and he along with them. Frau Amsel became a cynical woman.

One day, after Frau Amsel had tolerated Herr Fuchs' proximity for long enough to see a film of sweat form on his back and hear a small grunt of satisfaction, Herr Fuchs asked for a cup of tea. This was new, and she did not like it. While she worked he watched her, and cleared his throat a number of times, and looked, for the first time she had seen, rather like a shy school boy. Her kitchen was tidy, but there were badly patched windows that had shattered during air raids, and cupboards that hung from their hinges unless she carefully lifted them to swing them closed. All of her tea cups were chipped, except the special collection she had wrapped and packed in their own box, in the bottom cupboard. She would give him her least favourite of the good cups. She did not want his pity.

'What are those?' he asked, holding her arm, which in turn held the cupboard open as she tried to retrieve a single cup.

They both looked at the collection of porcelain jugs and cups that peeked out from their wrapping in the box. Each had a different pattern, or different glaze; some were large and some small. Several showed different kinds of animals, or characters from stories.

'They are nothing,' she said, 'some old family relics, that is all.' She quickly closed the cupboard door.

'But Frau Amsel, you move so quick to hide these nothings. Are you keeping something from me? Please open the door.'

She looked at the cupboard, now closed beneath her palm. Just one thing, she thought, just this one thing.

'Frau Amsel?'

She opened the cupboard. He reached in and pulled three pieces out, replacing them without re-wrapping them.

'Ah, what a collection you have there. You must bring them out. You must show people.'

'They were my mother's.' She let the statement hang in the air. It was not possible to tell him how she felt about his commands.

'I am sorry. I have been too inquisitive, and now you are unhappy with me. I will leave. But you must know, this collection of yours, it has a certain beauty.'

She did not want to share her treasures with the official, but she could not help the small smile that tugged the corner of her lips. 'Each piece comes from a different place. This is the secret of them. They must each tell a story of a different journey, or I do not keep them.'

Sometimes, at night, she took them out and lined them up on her table and rubbed a soft towel over them as she recounted the story of

Frau Amsel's Cupboard

how each came to the women in her family. The truth was the collection had begun with her grandmother. Before the war, she had added to it as well. The children were allowed to listen to the stories as long as they did not touch. When they went to bed, she would think of different ways to categorise the porcelain, putting those of the same region together, or placing the animal-shaped vessels in one group, or sorting by colour. When she had been a child, she had imagined a personality for each piece, and given each a voice that only she could hear.

'You like them very much.'

'Of course.'

He grinned momentarily before regaining his composure. Then he left without drinking the tea after all. She did not know whether to be pleased or fearful about his odd behaviour, though she did not trust it.

The following week Herr Fuchs did not come to her door, but his guard arrived at the appointed time. He told her to come, and so she found herself in a strange car, on her way out of the city. As she watched the familiar buildings become scarce, she felt a cold stone-like weight in her belly. She clenched her knees together and sat erect. After half an hour, they stopped at a place she did not recognise. The guard took her through a back door, then down to a basement entrance where Herr Fuchs stood. She did not know what they were doing there, but she hoped very much it was not what they usually did on Thursday mornings.

'Ah, Frau Amsel, I apologise for not coming to your flat to bring you here. There were arrangements to be made – I could not be in both places at the same time. But trust me – you will like this.' He opened the door, and gestured for her to enter. The room they entered was dim and smelled musty. So far, she did not like it. He switched on the lights and it took her several long seconds to understand what she was looking at.

There was a table in the room, with pieces of pottery lined up along it, many just broken pieces or orbs of some kind she could not distinguish. But lined up along the walls were several long shelves, and on these were many giant pots and bowls with faces and patterns moulded and inscribed on their rims. She looked from one to the next and the next, each with an impish face that stared from the edge of its vessel. There must have been hundreds.

'You may go closer,' Herr Fuchs said. She looked at him and saw that his face was open and eager. He wanted to please her. He meant this as a gift.

She went closer. The faces on the pots were so strange, but each gave a different impression – serene or joyful, severe, bewildered. One looked on wisely and had a trunk-like handle for a nose and patterns like a beaded necklace where a mouth should be. They each had individual decorations like this, thumbed in repetitive patterns or dotted with circles and holes. Further in there were bowl-like vessels, though they were big enough to hold a meal for thirty. These had smaller faces on the inside rim. She recognised their features as if the other pots were their kin.

She reached out a hand, and hesitated.

'Yes, yes, touch them if you wish. They are fire bowls from German New Guinea. The women made their cooking fires in them.'

She looked at him.

'It is a hobby of mine, to know something of their provenance. I have a colleague whose job it is to keep this collection safe until the bombing ceases. I have taken a personal interest in such things for some time.'

She ran her hand along the smooth contours of the bowls, felt the fullness there, the expectation of being filled with something – a hearth fire, sustenance for a family. The pots were black in some places, tan brown in others. She wondered if it was fire that blackened them, or if the clay was made that way.

'But, why are there so many? What do the faces mean?' What of the women they belonged to, she wanted to ask, but was unsure she really wanted the answer.

'They can teach us something of the history of man. The ethnographers have their reasons for collecting as they do. Do you not think they are wonderful?'

He was right, they were wonderful, but that was not enough. She ran her hands along the rims, traced the faces and patterns with her fingertips. Tried to gain the measure of them with her eyes and arms. And all the while she wondered at the mysteries behind their features. Eventually, she let her hands fall to her sides. She wanted to ask more, but she did not want to give the official the satisfaction of her curiosity. She remained impassive, silent. She felt him watching. Then he cleared his throat.

'You will not fit any of these pots into your cupboard of treasures, Frau Amsel.' He liked his little jokes. But she kept treasure in other places too, where he could not look.

When she looked at the official again, his expression had changed. He seemed smaller, as if he had been puffed up with air before and had now let it all go. 'I am sorry. That is not what I meant to say when you came. I cannot show weakness, Frau Amsel. It would not do for me to be soft. But you ... You do not let me in, and I would like it if we could be ... friends.' She did not allow her expression to change. He took a step closer, so that he could whisper. 'Please. I could take care of you. After the war –'

'There will be no "after the war" for us, Herr Fuchs. This is it.' She had interrupted him. Her voice was hard.

'Of course. How foolish of me.' He straightened, stepped back towards the pots. 'There is a story I know,' he said, clasping his hands behind his back and nodding towards the shelves, 'about an ancestress with magical powers. She could command the clay, the pots and the firewood. The clay would come to her and she only had to form the pots. She then ordered the firewood to pile up. She only had to light the fire. Then she ordered the pots to hop in. After they were baked she told them to go to the market. All the pots would run to the market to stand in line waiting to be traded for food.'

She imagined the pots bouncing along – they already had personalities – it was not hard.

'One day the ancestress got married. On her wedding night, after she had been with a man for the first time, she lost all her magic. Since that time women have had to work hard digging for clay, collecting firewood and carrying pots to the market place.'

She thought of them, the women with skin the colour of their pots – she could see where their fingers had worked circles and ridges, where they'd lovingly smoothed until the face on the pot relaxed. She could sense their tiredness and their steady determination. The fire, the collecting, the carrying. All the while children at their heels.

'These fire bowls represent the ancestress herself. She was called Kolimangge. They are from the Sepik River. The face on the large

Frau Amsel's Cupboard

storage pots is Meintumbangge, the eagle man, her father. He was a head-hunter.'

She did not know what a head-hunter was, but it was gratitude she felt when she looked up at Herr Fuchs again. More gratitude than she had felt for all his baskets of food.

That afternoon, he took her home and did not stay with her. She found she could not hate him quite as much. At least for the moment. Perhaps it would be easier if she could like him. Would it be so bad to let him in? She considered it, the next time he came. She tried to see the part of him that was not the Official, the part that was hungry for her approval. But when he touched her, she could not respond. She thought of her husband, her gentle husband, who had no stomach for the things war makes men do. He had been stronger than she could have been. She thought of dark women in a land she couldn't imagine, who worked their hardship into mud, and made things of beauty from it. Herr Fuchs could not reach the part of her that thought these thoughts, but when she smiled, he thought it was for him.

When her children came home, Frau Amsel went to her cupboard and took out her treasures. As she unwrapped each one, she recited her mother's stories. Then she placed the collection on her table in a circle, so that no particular order could be discerned. When her little girl asked, she said yes, they could touch the cups and plates, and even make stories with them. While she watched her children play, Frau Amsel sat with her knees together and a treasure cradled in the palms of her hands.

Late Antiquity

PIRIPI EVANS

Raining now. A few warning drops at first, and then it comes down in a dense curtain, threatening to drench you if you don't find cover. You can't say this city lacks for natural resources. Fresh water falls abundantly and there is plenty of natural ventilation. You shuffle under a bus shelter, wait for the shower to pass and listen to the hissing of car tyres on the wet road and the sound of the wind. How much later – half an hour? – the shower thins out and you cross the road, the headlights picking out the little swirling raindrops.

You scrape along the pavement with worn soles, the front of your shoes opening up like a mouth and the end of your sock poking through like a tongue. These shoes know more about this pavement than any other pair. They shuffle over manhole covers, blobs of chewing gum dark with age, pavement cracks that branch out into complex tributaries. Then the rough geography of the cracked pavement ends, replaced by a geometric, newly installed surface of brown tiles. And here's a whole cigarette – it's squashed into the gap between the hexagons, but you're going to pocket that one none the less. Lots of tobacco left in it.

Numb fingers push the ciggie into your pocket, and you take the chance to look up, feel the wind on your face and hear it in your beard. You're walking against the flow of the foot traffic, which is flocking towards the train station and the bus stops. People in dark suits, guys' ties flapping, coats ruffled. These people belong to the false world. They're soft, domesticated, they don't know hunger or cold, all their needs are trivial. They're keen to get inside, out of this late afternoon with its autumn sky, grey and heavy like a dome of concrete. Amazing how the shitty low cloud manages to hang around even with the constant wind. Broken umbrellas poking out of street-side rubbish bins are a common sight. Black cloth clings to the inverted steel frames like pieces of fluttering, shredded batman costume.

Nearly bumped into that guy there, a little student huddling into a black coat. '*Whoa*,' he says, brushing against you and holding his hands up in a non-aggression gesture. That's about the only way to get noticed by anyone in this false crowd. Mostly they treat you like just another street fixture – a bollard or a mailbox or a lamppost or something. Goddamn wino, nothing to be particularly regarded. Do you envy them, going home to their false comforts? In a way you do, but you've tried that conventional life and it's always gone wrong. Used to have a job, quite a respectable one as it happens. You often remind anyone who will listen – *used to be rezbegtible, you know*. But God didn't make you to hold down a job and pay the rent and mow the lawns. God had different ideas for you, Billy-boy. God – or was it the other bloke downstairs? – gave you sight that sees through the false world and its plastic layers. There's always a simmering frustration inside that you know will finally burst into a fireball, mushrooming like a real big bomb going off. You know the feeling coming on, it takes you back to the word in the old army code book, NCLRSTRKWRNG, and Sergeant Collins outlining procedure if this message is ever received in the field – *get low to the ground, tuck your head between your legs and kiss your arse goodbye*. How do you deal with such a violence of feeling inside, your head full of stupid thoughts?

You drink. First the job, then the house, then the wife and the children all slip away. Lots of empty beer and wine bottles pile up instead. The green, green glass of home. Soon enough you find yourself emaciated and living in a bare room with no furniture, until that goes too. So you try knocking off the booze, but that only gives you the shakes and provides your anger with clarity and focus. The only thing left, short of blowing your brains out, is to keep drinking. And that becomes your life. So when the do-gooder social workers down at St Luke's try to talk about Maslow's hierarchy of needs, *food, shelter and group belonging*, you see straight away that Maslow is just one of these false pricks. A man's greatest need is a drink. It's always there, nagging.

You shuffle on and cross the road again, away from the foot traffic. There's a ghostly light coming from the windows of the public library. It's closed for the day; the librarians are visible in the window, closing up the counters and picking up stray books from floors and tables. The leather-covered reading chairs are teasing you through the window, wonderfully comfortable to lounge and go to sleep in. No chance of getting in during closing hours, though, because they have big-time security on these places. Now you enter Civic Square, where the paving is dark with recently fallen rain and the wind is coming straight off the harbour. People are huddling into their coats as they head for the bus stop. Even the bloody seagulls are shivering, hunching down as the wind ruffles the feathers on their backs. You go through the bins on the way through, but there's nothing much doing. The birds have had the best of the scraps and there's not so much as a cigarette butt to be found. You walk on, passing the broad windows of Chinese restaurants. Your mouth is watering for some of the noodly stuff piled up on the plates. Could even eat those bung-eyed goldfish lazing around in that big tank there. The next-best thing is to put your extended middle finger, *ponk*, against the window as you pass, and watch the surprised diners looking up.

And what is the object of this hike? Not going back to the night shelter, no way, not now that nutter Jacko's back in town. And Sam Gordon will be there, snoring like a sawmill. He will keep Jacko and the other jokers awake and there will be a real nasty fight. A man wants nothing to do with it, and would rather take his chances out here.

Besides, you happen to have something those other no-hopers don't. You've discovered a little church with a window that won't quite close, having cased it out pretty thoroughly in the early hours of this morning. You only paid attention to the place at first because of the huge billboard they've put up outside. #GLY is all it says. If you hang around long enough during the day, you can overhear one of the church people explaining that it's hip language for *God Loves You*, that's how young people speak on their phones or something, and God wants to bring young people back through the doors on a Sunday.

Your pins-and-needles fingers check your possessions: soft ginger-nut biscuits in one pocket, cigarette pieces in another, along with your lucky coin. This is a big old fifty cent piece, no longer legal tender, but the remnant of a big win on the pokies and a piece of luck that you carry around with you. You tap the strap of your backpack, make sure it is still over your shoulder, and head down to the church. But your heart collapses inside your chest when you get there, because there's a bloody big roadworks going on right outside. An area of the street is coned off and swarming with guys in hi-viz jackets. There's a huge floodlight aimed into a hole in the pavement and some guy bringing over a jackhammer. #GLY is lit up in the background. This is going to take a careful approach, which has to be made by walking around the block and getting onto hallowed ground through a little path at the back, which is unlit. Soon enough there is a shout from the work site and you hear the clang of something heavy being dropped on the ground, the foreman abusing someone. With this distraction under way, a man can move a rubbish bin up to the open window and prise it a little wider. The window ledge is a bit hard on the old ribs these days, and the landing on the lino floor isn't elegant. However, you stand up, check that nothing's broken and you find yourself in the rector's office. You daren't turn on a light, even though it's pretty gloomy in here: just the dim shape of a desk, a computer and a noticeboard with white paper pinned up on it, probably service schedules or something. You creep through another door, which is a wrong turn and you find yourself in a Sunday school room, more generously lit by the floodlight outside. You can make out kids' pictures on the walls. The figure depicted in thick blue paint with a zig-zagging beard must be Jesus. You retrace your steps and find the kitchen, where the Zip's still hot and a man can help himself to an instant coffee with lots of sugar and a good cloud of steam coming off it. You look around for some biscuits, but there's nothing edible around, only a pile of pamphlets that are readable by floodlight: *Thorndon Bible Society Autumn Lecture Series #3: Late Antiquity – The End of Classical Civilisation and the Triumph of Christianity.* You pocket one of these, not sure why. Maybe you can attend the lecture and hope for tea and bickie-wickies afterwards.

So you carefully carry your coffee through to the main church, settle on a pew and then grab the blankets out of your bag. The pew's not a waterbed, but it beats the hell out of a park bench with all its wooden ridges digging into your back. It's hard to sleep, with all that racket going on outside, but it's pleasant enough to lie back and think. Always pays to plan for tomorrow. Might try the old line on a few people. '*Zcuse me sir, haven't any zpare change have you? Haven't eaten today.*'

In the old days you worked as a teacher. You couldn't stand it though, the education system. Your job was not to teach them, but to package them up for the false world – here they come off the production line, Pretender 72519, Pretender 72520, Pretender 72521 ... You hated it and so did they. They toyed with you, making fun of a man's name. Christ knows how many times in your life you've had to spell it out to people – *No, it's Ngutu. N-G as in sing. November, Golf, Uniform, Tango, Uniform.* The kids saw it written down and wanted to pronounce it Mr In-goo-two, which sounded too much like Nigger-oo-two. You'd hear *Hey nig!* shouted anonymously in the playground, or come back from your lunch break to find NIG written on the blackboard, a classroom full of sniggering kids. Pretty soon they find out where a man lives, and you get NIG notes at home, or answer the doorbell to find nobody there, but your mailbox ablaze. You start telling yourself there's no harm in a couple of drinks during the day to help deal with it, but you get in trouble when they smell it on you, and then some do-gooding little shit will mention it to a parent, who will mention it to someone on the school board who will tell the headmaster. Then you catch one of them in the act of the blackboard prank, and you end up manhandling him down to the principal's office, only to find that you are in deep trouble and the kid is screaming and nursing his shoulder. You're made reckless by the drink, and you can feel it coming – NCLRSTRKWRNG. The school office staff are gaping and a small boy who's come to deliver a message is now cowering in the corner as you give the principal the benefit of your thoughts, chiefly about where he can put his job. With infuriating calm he tells you that he accepts your resignation.

The jackhammer stops, bringing your attention back to church and pew. Sleep is instant, deep, safe and beautiful. But you find yourself waking up again in the depths of the night. The stained glass windows are still dark when you sit up feeling alert, your ears sharpened and listening out. At first you think you are imagining small noises somewhere inside the church, then you hear the creaking noise of someone opening a door – slow, stealthy, cautious. Then you hear the light switch and the whole place is flooded with light, making you blink. There's a tall guy standing there, red-faced, brick-coloured shirt, fascist little grey moustache.

'*Oi, you,*' he bursts at you. '*What the heck are you doing here?*'

And you mumble 'God loves you,' as if that's any kind of explanation.

'What?' he says. 'You need to get yourself down the night shelter mate, you can sleep there. Can't have you in here stinking the place out and who knows what.'

He's come to throw you out into the night, so you have to gather up your bag and blankets, and shuffle blinking to the door that he's opened for you. You get to the door, feel the cold, hear the wind.

You turn around to say *Whatever happened to Christian charity?* But the anger is streaming through your blood, and you know it's not going to come out quite how you intended.

You roar back through the door: 'Call yourself a fucking Christian?'

Obscenity echoes through the rafters of God's house and the false Christian reels as if he's been struck between the eyes with a hammer.

'Get out. Just get out and stay out.'

You escape into the night. You fish in your pockets for a bottle cap and carve a couple of deep scratches into the paintwork of his silvery new car outside in the church car park.

The wind is still moaning and swirling, a piece of litter skittering across the street. The church is no good now. They'll fix the window, and they might even get one of those bloody alarm systems installed.

What to do now? You once knew a young guy, Tyrone, who knew how to find his way into a nice warm police cell. He would wait for a passing cop car, chuck a rubbish bin through a shop window and flag down the car like a taxi. But the thought of confronting the cops – *oh no, not you again* – is not appealing tonight.

You end up settling for the night at the back door of a cycle shop, next to a couple of rubbish bins and some rusting bicycle frames. You pull out your blankets and try to cocoon every part of yourself, your bag doing as a pillow. Now that you're not walking, you realise how cold it is. It starts working on your skin, making the goosebumps rise. Soon it's into your flesh and you've got a good shiver going. You feel a pang of longing for that church pew. You ball yourself up tighter, knowing you can't let it penetrate right into your bones or that will be the end of it, you'll just be found wrapped up and snap-frozen. The sound of the wind is sorrowful in the trees and telephone wires, like the wailing of women over Christ's body. You go to sleep wondering whether you'll ever wake up.

But you always do wake up. You take some time to remember where you are and how you got there. Find yourself looking at bicycle rubbish, a couple of big blue wheelie bins, and, in the slab of sky between the roofs, a hint of dawn, orange and pink. You pick yourself up, stretch your shoulders, rub the pins and needles out of your bony arse, make several attempts at stuffing the blankets back into your bag, before sitting down again to fold them properly. You start walking, which brings out all the complaints in your body: knee, hip, back. You start to wonder what to do with the gift of another day.

Stop for a moment. Now here's a discovery: a half-finished bottle of piss standing on top of a concrete wall, waiting to be found by the right passer-by. It pays to take a sniff and an experimental sip rather than just knocking her back, because you got to be careful that it's not literally piss, some guy having emptied his bladder into the bottle before staggering into a taxi. A quick sip shows this one's just flat beer, quite drinkable as it turns out, but it's only half full and pretty soon you are left looking down the neck of the bottle like a telescope. *Bastard*, you say to this prick-teaser of a half drink, and down the bottle goes, crash on the pavement, breaking into green shards.

The wind has stopped and the cloud thinned out overnight, so that the sun comes out now and then. Pretty soon the false world starts to move. The traffic gets heavier, jokers and sheilas in suits walk by quickly and importantly. They'll be off to their false work – not too many of this lot have ever rolled up their sleeves. Suited guys, Mr Pretenders one and all, are seated at an outside café table, their sunglasses shimmering like flat-screen TVs. Your own breakfast is a couple of soft ginger-nut biscuits, which is the last of your food. After this, there is no choice but to milk the soft tit of charity, which never runs dry. Unlike government, that shrivelled bitch. *Taxpayer*, they caw, *taxpayer's money*, like some skinflint old crow. Give a man a break. Taxes go to much shittier causes than buying an old man a drink. But Charity, that's a beautiful shabbily dressed goddess and the mother of last resort. So away you go across town, towards the St Luke's Mission. Here comes the wild old goat who's eaten the last scrap of weed on his barren hillside. Come in, says Charity of a thousand teats, I even have succour for the likes of you.

Wonder if Sam will be out busking today? That's his solution to this thing of poverty before benefit day. He puts down his greasy beanie hat and stands there singing, or howling, more accurately. His hat usually has a handful of coins in it, which he has put there himself to make it look like people really appreciate his voice. He sounds like a dying stag.

St Luke's Mission is on the seedier side of town. It's an old converted hotel or something, well past its glory days. She's all worn carpets, lifting wallpaper and sloping floors. The front office has a dreamy feel to it, with the sun beaming in through the window and lighting up lots of drifting dust and warming the donated furniture and flaking filing cabinets. The whole show looks like it belongs to another era, maybe the 70s. The office is manned by a nameless bloke with mouldy blond stubble and a dumb thin face that looks familiar. He's a fellow no-hoper – not so far gone as yourself – and they've given him a job; that's their way of helping this bloke. He removes his feet from the desk and when you walk in, you ask: 'Is Robbie Vermouth in today?'

He scratches a cheek thoughtfully, making a hollow rasping noise, and goes to a thick ledger book. 'You mean Robbie Vermeulen? Yeah, you're in luck mate,' he says. 'Robbie's with someone at the moment, but he's got time for walk-ins and should be free in about half an hour. What name shall I give him?'

So you give him your name, and have to spell it out, of course – *Ngutu, that's N-G* ... and then you settle down to wait on the armchair with a big gash in it and all its stuffing spilling out.

Robbie's got his business face on when he comes into the waiting room. He looks tight-lipped, tense, prissy; like you're supposed to get the message that you're on thin ice here. Last time there was an argument and raised voices. Home truths and tough words were spoken, and poor Robbie got called a fucken twerp, or some such choice phrase. Let's hope he's not still sore about that. Hello – there is something different that could explain his mood. Today he has his arm all bound up in a sling. This fills you with sudden joy, and you have to fight the urge to laugh. But, keeping an admirable grip, you sympathetically ask what happened, and he explains that he came off his bike. *Condolences*, you say, and – formalities dispensed with – ask him straight out for some money. Of course, he's got to say no to that. So you ask for some food, and he comes back at you: 'Where have you been sleeping, Billy? They tell me that they haven't seen you at the night shelter for a couple of weeks.' And lying to this guy is as natural as breathing. You explain that you've been staying with a friend of a friend, but that he doesn't do the shopping and there's no food in the house. He says, 'Well I hear you've been sleeping rough.'

You're not gonna answer. This guy Robbie can really try a man's patience. He breaks the awkward silence by saying, 'I can give you a note for the food bank, that's no problem, but I want you to do something for me. You're still a strong guy, I reckon, but if you keep avoiding treatment and sleeping rough you're just in a big downward spiral. I want to see you in the night shelter tonight.'

So you say: you got it. Thanks cobber.

He looks right at you, full of doubt and pity. Then he sighs through his nose and opens his book to write a chit for the food bank, shaking his head just a little, so it's almost not noticeable. He's accustomed to dealing with the likes of Billyboy. That's his cross he has to bear.

The old backpack feels heavier as you step back out onto the street, now supplied with some tins of beans, tomato puree, rice, biscuits, heat-and-eat noodles, dried fruit. You feel almost like it would be good to go and sit by the waterfront to have a bit of this grub. But on second thoughts, no – you'd be an eyesore down there, surrounded by successful businessmen, successful women in dark stockings, successful boats at their moorings, successful fat seagulls. So you head up towards The Terrace, up towards the old cemetery there. Can almost hear the old man's voice: not right to eat in a cemetery on account of the tapu, etcetera. You tell his voice to piss off; fight him out of your mind – then he usually won't bother you. The point of coming here is to find a place to eat without being molested. Sure enough, there's a convenient patch of grass under some trees, which is a pleasant spot to hurt your teeth on the dried packet noodles, and then have a bit of a lie down in the morning sun.

Wake up with a start. *Shit* – must have dozed off. You stand up and brush off the grass, then you nervously check your belongings and make sure that nothing's been pinched while you were asleep. You start down the hill, as the sun is well past noon and it's time to look for somewhere to spend the night – which ain't gonna be here. It's not that you worry about ghosts and shit like that – it's just that a man can't feel comfortable out in the open. A city man needs concrete and steel and wood nearby; maybe the enclosure of an old doorway or the feel of a park bench under his back.

The sun is well past its high point now. It takes you a long while to get down the hill again. It's late in the afternoon when you get down to Vivian Street – near St Luke's again. This is a good place to scavenge at night time. It's just a matter of sitting around and waiting, without looking too obvious, in case Robbie shows up and drags you off to the night shelter. You sit at a bus stop and let the buses go by and the sun creep down until it slides behind the rooftop of the shop across the road. You watch it disappear blindingly, until you are in shadow, and a lemony afterglow is stuck on your retina. The traffic has increased. The cars sit in orderly herds, inching their way forward, the drivers in their sheepish trances, thinking ahead to the motorway and the leafy suburbs. A couple of birds, the last of the day people, waggle past in Lycra, talking importantly. As the sky becomes duller, some of the cars creep past with their headlights on. It's that moment just before the streetlights begin to take over from daylight. Now it is time for the night people to come out. There are two sets of high heels tapping on the pavement, one of them a slow, scraping gait that belongs to a hooker called Brandy who you know by repute only. Even if you had money in your pocket, she wouldn't consider providing any services – she can afford to be picky. Mr Pretender – wedding band and all – is her preferred client. Still, looking at her damn near gives you a heart attack. Your body can still surprise you with this hormonal shit. You feel yourself jolt, feel the old engine turn over and cough, like when the key's turned in a cobwebbed old banger that hasn't been out of the garage since the 70s. She's kitted out in tight jeans, bare ankles and black stilettos – is that what those things are called? Tight, armless black t-shirt with the silver word *squeeze* on it, little tattoo on one milky white shoulder. She's with that other bloody harlot, tough-looking older lady in a miniskirt and fishnet stockings. Her brown face is over-ripe with experience. Hard, axe-like eyes. Don't know her name, but you think of her as Maud. Seems like a good name for her.

They stop outside a bar a few doors down the street and take out a cigarette each from their little handbags. Brandy plus the sight of a fresh packet of cigarettes is too much to take. You stand up, your back stiff from waiting. You gather your bag on your shoulder and start shuffling towards them and you don't know what you're going to say or do. It's Maud who breaks the ice though.

'What do you want, you grubby old loser? If you've just stopped to chat we'd prefer that you didn't.' She looks at you like you're a boil.

You ask: 'Got a match? Got no matches to light my smokes with.' It seems like a reason to talk. Brandy reaches into her shiny red handbag and searches. She hands over a cardboard book of matches with the name of some hotel on it, and you feel the thrill as your fingers touch hers ever so briefly. Difficult little pause – Christ, got to keep this going, can't just walk away now. So you say, 'Got any smokes? Got no smokes to light with these matches.' She reaches into her bag and there's a whole packet, a whole glorious packet, and she pulls one out and gives it to you.

'That's all,' she says, 'I need the rest.' And Maud says, 'Why don't you get a job, then you can have all the smokes you want?' You shrug.

And now they're both looking at the street. A couple of cars slow down and Maud waves them on. You say, to break the silence and make conversation, 'Got any money?'

'Righto, mister,' says Maud, 'that's it, go away over there,' and she points down the street. But you look into Brandy's eyes and there's that look that's both innocent and knowing at the same time. You drink her in as long as you can without Maud going crazy at you, and then take your leave with 'Okay ladies, good evening,' like a right old charmer. You shuffle off down the street feeling quite pleased with yourself.

You feel so good that you let your feet walk, with no sense of direction, no thought for eating or finding a place to sleep. Before you know it, you're in Lambton Quay, which is a fair old hike. She's emptied out now, she's all quiet, only the occasional trolley bus going past. The false world has shut up shop for the night, but all the office buildings will hum again in the morning with Mr Pretenders and phony transactions. You carry on past parliament. There's a light on in the top level of the Beehive, watching over the city.

Heading up Mulgrave Street, you quite unexpectedly find a crowd of people outside Old St Paul's church. They're mostly grey haired, all dressed up, ladies in coats and gloves and perfume, fellas in collared shirts and jackets. They're talking fast, sounding excited. Some silly bastard getting married? Not at this hour of evening, surely. And the mood ain't sombre enough for a funeral. It's a funny sort of crowd, this. They let you get close. You can even mingle in amongst this lot and they don't seem to mind. Some sort of do-gooder convention? No – you look around and you don't see Robbie anywhere. And then you see that there is a guy giving out pamphlets, so you go over and take one. It turns out to be familiar. *Thorndon Bible Society Autumn*

Lecture Series #3. Late Antiquity – The End of Classical Civilisation and the Triumph of Christianity. The doors are opened and you move with the crowd through the door, under the bell tower. The surroundings are all brass and dark wood, clean and polished. There are sprays of flowers either side of a lectern that's been put at the front. You take a pew a few rows back from everybody else.

A tall bloke with neatly sculpted black hair and a puppyish face walks to the microphone and taps it three times. He smiles nervously as the buzz of conversation dies down and people begin to fix their attention on him.

'It's my pleasure to introduce one of our leading authorities on early Christianity.'

Man, you need a smoke, and you start fingering Brandy's durrie that's in your pocket while this speaker starts adding a lot of unnecessary points of his own. Pretty soon you feel like you want to say something, you want to yell at him to sit down and let the main act come on. You can feel that the whole audience is also getting restless and that they are relieved when he finally wraps it up.

'Ladies and gentlemen, Professor Hugh Dannett.'

He creeps back to his seat and the main speaker steps forward.

Dannett takes a couple of seconds to shuffle papers. He's got a shiny bald head and thick glasses. He's wearing a brown jacket over a white shirt and polka-dot bow tie. He begins to talk. What is he, Scottish? Or some kind of Pommy? Lovely speaking voice, deep and effortless, flows like whiskey through the room.

'Late Antiquity,' he says, 'was the period between the fourth and sixth centuries AD.'

A lot of what he says sails over a man's head. But you get the picture: the once great Classical civilisation becoming weak and corrupt and cruel, ripe to be thrown down by God. The late antique sun shone on Constantine's triumphal procession through Rome – a triumph for the spirit over the flesh, a defeat for the false world. Except that the victorious Christians soon started fighting each other. What was Jesus? This was the dispute, according to Dannett. What was he made of: earthly or spiritual DNA? Was he human – purely flesh and blood? Or was he spirit, made of the same stuff as his divine father? There was a small hill in Palestine where iron nails were hammered in, ripping wrist sinew and splitting ankle bone. Roman soldiers, the best in the business when it came to professional cruelty, smiled at his misfortune and drew lots for his belongings. The flesh and pain and humiliation were all real and human. And yet he must have been spirit too, because he knew something beyond the normal. He predicted the end of the false world, and foresaw its towers and parliaments toppling and Mr Pretender burning up like cardboard.

Dannett finishes to enthusiastic applause. One of the ladies comes up, gives him a kiss and presents him with a pounamu. He seems a bit unsure what to do with it – is it a garland or some kind of lucky charm that you carry around like a fob watch? Eventually the lady shows him, to polite laughter, that he should wear it around his neck. He looks a bit sheepish – bloke in jewellery and all that.

The puppy-faced man steps back up, gives his three taps on the microphone and invites everyone to move a couple of doors down the road for drinks and nibbles. Sounds pretty top hole. So you follow the crowd to the next venue.

Someone says grace over the fancy cheeses and pastries and fruit tray. Then you're into it, trying not to appear too enthusiastic. You're offered wine – red or white? You take one of each. Soon the young girl with the wine tray is being taken aside and being told not to offer any more to that old bum over there. You can feel the tolerant mood shifting. There are sideways glances and whispers, perhaps even discussions about having a man escorted from the premises. So you make your move first. You fill your pockets with the catering and walk for the door, into the fresh night. Must be – what – nine-thirty? You walk down to parliament buildings and ease yourself onto the neatly cut and sloping lawn, where you can turn out your pockets and start on the feast. You've got filled rolls, some fried fishy things, pastries filled with fruit and a couple of bananas. When this is done, you brush the crumbs from your beard, wander over and water one of the ornamental trees, and then return to lie your old bones down on the grass and enjoy the feeling of a full stomach.

Now is the right time to have the cigarette. This good mood won't last and you've got to ride it while it's here. You hold the ciggie in front of you and turn it over in your fingers for a few seconds of contemplation, then you light her up with a fizz of one of Brandy's cardboard matches. You imagine that maybe Brandy's lips have touched this cigarette, perhaps she took this one out, put it in her mouth and then decided to put it back for some reason, chose another one. Now you lie back and look up. You inhale and exhale, loving the smokiness in your nostrils and the sense of wellbeing that starts to flow through your bloodstream. You blow smoke up towards the stars, watch it swirl for a couple of seconds and then disperse in the gentle breeze. The starry sky here is not like in Fiji, where a man went with

Late Antiquity

the army, where you can see millions of the bloody things. Here in the city all the faint ones can't compete with the streetlights. What's that big fat bright star up there? Jupiter or Saturn or something? Sergeant Collins used to know the names of them all. You know that one is not your lucky star, anyway. It's too much of a bright show-off. So you pick a nice inconspicuous one. There, that one seems to be roaming loose, not really attached to any constellation, struggling to shine out against the city lights. That one will do nicely. You make a wish on it, for the kids, wherever they are, and for their happiness, not your own. You hope you can find it again next fine night.

You puff away on the cigarette, and all too soon she's all over, you've smoked her right to the filter. But you can lie back and the ecstasy will remain for a time. You can let your thoughts go, you can feel the ghosts moving around you – not the white man's ghosts, though they are here as well – but you think of the old people working at their nets and hauling canoes up onto the pebbly beach that is now paved over with the streets of the city.

Hello, the wind has changed. It's picked up ever so slightly. Your skin feels somehow more sensitive after smoking that fag, and you can feel the breeze breathing cooler against your cheek. It brings some fluffy high cloud and a faint smell of the sea.

'Late Antiquity,' you mumble smokily. You go to sleep wondering whether you'll ever wake up.

Trust

MARK SWEET

As soon as their eyes fixed on me I feared I might be stopped, so I put my head down and walked quickly, but they blocked my way.

'Stop right there,' the older one said.

I froze.

'Where've you been?'

'Drinking ... and ... dancing,' I said.

'Whereabouts?'

'Bennets.'

'Look at me,' he said.

And he sneered when I looked at him, and he muttered, 'Paki queer.'

The younger one said, 'Against the wall, arms, legs, spread 'em out.'

I backed into a glass door reinforced with wire mesh and spread my arms out. The older one grabbed my wrist and, pulling hard, he spun me around. With his other hand he pushed my head against the glass, and as he kicked my legs apart said, 'I don't want to see your ugly Paki mug no more.'

I raised my head and was able to say, 'Not Pakistani,' before he paralysed me by twisting my arm up my back. I nearly fainted with the sudden rush of pain.

He slackened his grip enough for me to say, 'I'm Māori.'

'From New Zealand?' he said, as he let me go.

'Yeah.' I rubbed the back of my neck where his grip left me aching.

'My sister lives in Wellington.'

'Nice place,' I said. 'I'm from Napier.'

'That near Hastings?'

'Yeah, you know it?'

'Had a mate went there.'

The young cop's radio murmured and he walked away a few paces while he answered. He looked me up and down, and when he saw I'd wet my pants, he grimaced. We were about the same age.

The old one said, 'Sorry about that. Thought you was someone else.'

'You thought I was ...' and I stopped short because the younger cop was shaking his head indicating I should not say, '... a Paki queer.'

Instead, I said, 'Yeah, well. Can I get on?'

'Sure. You take care now,' the older cop said.

I didn't acknowledge him, but to the young cop, I gave the chin up salute. He smiled and flicked his head in reply.

A month later I double-parked outside Organic Supplies. I left my pick-up running and rushed in to collect an order. Mere seconds passed, but when I returned, my truck was gone.

Back in the shop, Annie asked, 'Forgotten something?'

'Yeah,' I said. 'I forgot I'm in Glasgow. My truck's been stolen.'

'Ring the Police, quickly,' she said. 'They might find it before it's chopped.'

'Chopped?'

'Aye. They strip them down and sell the bits as parts.'

The controller was very sure. Police would come within minutes.

I heard the crackle of his radio before I saw his face.

'It's you,' I said.

'We meet again.' He took off his cap and released a crop of ginger curls.

'My truck's been stolen. Just minutes ago,' I said.

'Come show me,' he said.

'It was there.' I pointed to a spot beyond a Fiesta parked on the curb.

'Double-parked?'

'Yeah.'

'You got the keys?'

'Nah. I left it running.'

'You must be joking.'

'No, I'm not. I was only seconds.'

He called in to make the report, asking me the details of my brand-new Peugeot pick-up – diesel, white body, black trim – and he relayed them on.

'G something, I think,' I replied to his question about the registration number.

He relayed my answer down the radio with a chuckle.

'What happens now?' I asked.

'You get a taxi,' he replied with a grin.

'Jeez, insurance probably won't pay, will they?'

'No way,' he said, 'and I can't believe anyone would be so stupid.'

'Just habit, mate. It's what I do back home. Never lock cars, or the house.'

'You don't lock your house?'

'Nah. Where I was brought up we never locked the house. We'd go away for weeks and leave the house unlocked.'

'Is your house like a shack on the beach?'

'No. A proper house. Four bedrooms. Full of stuff. It's all about trust, man.'

'Well, you're in Glasgow now,' and he hesitated before saying, 'And be careful walking alone at night.'

'What? Because you cops think I look like a Pakistani?'

'You know what I mean,' he said.

'No, I don't know what you mean. You wouldn't have stopped me if I was white.'

'I'm not like that,' he said.

'So you just go along with it?'

'I've got no choice when I'm out with the Sergeant.'

'You could always change jobs,' I said.

The following day I rang him. Constable Peacock was his name. If my truck wasn't found within three days, chances were I'd never see it again, he told me.

I was cleaning mussels when he came into the kitchen, and by the look on his face, I knew my truck had been found. A week had passed since the theft.

'Car park in Maryhill. I can take you now. You got a spare key? It's locked,' Constable Peacock said.

Trust

The keys were resting on a folded piece of paper on the passenger seat. Written in tight script, the message read:

> *Sorry for trouble*
> *to you*
> *my Ma was sick*
> *in Aberdeen*
> *nice motor by*
> *the way*
> *ps. I gave her*
> *the cheese.*
> *Ma loves cheese*
> *Many Thanks*

I unpeeled the cover from the deck, and the box of groceries from Fazzi's was intact, except for the round of Camembert.

'I can't believe this.' Constable Peacock was reading the note.

'Not all bad, eh? He only took the cheese. There's fifty quid of olive oil here.'

Constable Peacock was putting the note in his pocket.

'I'd like to keep that if you don't mind,' I said.

'It's evidence,' he replied.

'Come on. There's no harm done here. Whoever stole my truck was a decent person.'

'How can you say that? He stole your motor.'

'The guy loves his mother. Read the note. And he only took the cheese.'

'Stealing's stealing.'

'Black and white, eh. That how you see things?'

'That's my job.'

'What, no room for compassion?'

He shook his head and took off his hat and he passed me the note.

The next time I met Constable Peacock he told me I was 'stupid beyond belief', and he was right.

I could see the French sticks bagged up sitting on the counter of Ma Brown's bakery. There were no parks outside. I was in a hurry. So I double-parked and ran into the shop, and when I got back to the pavement, I saw my pick-up turning into a side road. But I knew the street was a dead end, so I ran after it, and as I turned the corner there he was, sitting at the wheel. The window was wound down and he waved me over.

'It's not about trust,' Constable Peacock said.

'No, it's stupid, I know.'

'Some junked-out kid could steal this motor as easy as me, and crash, and who knows what.'

'Yeah, yeah, I see that now. I'm sorry. Look, can I make you a coffee? My restaurant's just around the corner.'

'I'd like that,' he said, playing with the gear lever. 'I like the column shift,' he said.

'I'll get in. You drive.'

'Great motor for getting away,' he said.

'Yeah. I go up to the Highlands a lot.'

'Tramping?'

'And drinking and staying in old pubs overnight.'

'Must be nice.'

'Yeah, it's great. Maybe you could come with me sometime,' I said casually, looking out the window.

'You mean that?'

I looked at him to make sure his expression matched the sincerity of his tone.

'Yeah, I mean it. I like you, and it'd be good to get to know you out of uniform.'

The last time I saw Constable Peacock was late one night when he tapped on the restaurant door after everyone else had gone home. As he'd done many times before, he took off his cap and slung it over a coat hook.

'I got the job in London,' he said. 'I start next week.'

'The one working with young offenders?'

'Aye.'

'This is what you want?'

'Aye.'

'Well, I think this calls for a toast.'

I poured generous measures of Lagavulin, Alan's favourite whisky.

'Slangiva, my friend.' I raised my glass.

'Thank you,' he said, 'for giving me … what did you call it? Kia kaha?'

I cupped his head in my hands and said, 'Courage'.

'Aye.'

And we soon found our way to the floor.

Morningslide for Life

TERENCE RISSETTO

The sun threw slender tentacles of Taser de-light at the dark semi-dreaded head disarrayed on a Slumberhead pillow perched precariously on the leading edge of a mismatched Sleepyhead mattress.

No response.

Outside the house, a tattered and chortling white van billowing strident white smoke careered sideways on two wheels around the corner lamppost, swerving wildly in pursuit of a black cat running across its path. The cat hurriedly scrambled under a nearby black pimped-up Holden and the van barrelled straight up and over the front nostrils of the car into the back passenger seat with a huge roar and crash loud enough to frighten the Republican Party.

No response.

A moment or five later, the same fugitive fugee scratched insistently at the bedroom door of the slumber-pillowed dead, the sound flickering a heavily bloodshot eye briefly into zombie killer life then out again.

The cat meowed imploringly, the thin sound cutting through the air like nails screeching on a hot tin roof. A second semi-detached suburban head, waka-blonde, tousled and ten drilled, extracted itself from the first head and dreams of a third and fourth, opening a sleep-slurred mouth.

'Hon? Hon, can you feed the cat?'

No response.

'Hon, please feed the cat,' the waka prow squeaked in a voice as plaintive as the cat's.

'Fuckoff!'

'Honey, please. The poor thing's hungry.'

'So's Africa. Fuckoff.'

'Look, feed the fucken cat, Manu. It's your turn. I can't sleep, I fed it last week.'

Blam! A freshly bedraggled half-clothed male figure lurched Quasimondo-like out of the bed and rummaged noisily in the nearby wardrobe, haphazardly tossing out assorted items of organic and inorganic apparel.

'Hon? What are you looking for?'

'Cat food. Gonna feed that mongrel what it deserves.'

'Hon, the cat food's in the kitchen. You're in the wardrobe.'

'I know where I aren't and I know what I don't know. What's the brand?'

'ONE of course.'

'Sweet. I want to give him one and when I find my shottie I'm going to give him TWO.'

'Your shottie? Manu! You can't shoot the cat! It's against the law.'

'Missy, if those Nesian neighbours can do home kills for church, I can shoot a cat for peace. Morningslide for life!'

'Der. This is Māngere, not Morningslide. Besides, you can't go outside with your turkey gizzards hanging out. You'll kill the old ladies coming back from Mass.'

'Nah. My turkey grew up in this neck of the woods! Not like your ficking pussy. Besides, it's Thanksgiving.'

'Sure, but that's no reason to shoot the poor thing, it's never done you any harm!'

'I'm not going to shoot it, I'm going to feed it. Ah, here it is! Boo-yah!'

Manu grabbed a pistol-grip sawn-off side-by-side shotgun from the bottom of the wardrobe and, breaking it open, loaded it with cartridges dragged from a box strewn under the bed.

'Honey, don't be stupid.'

'Too late now! It's not as if I wasn't born this way. Yeehaa! Rock and roll! Noise control! How can a man sleep with all that fucken racket going on?'

'I think there's been some sort of car accident outside.'

'Not that! I mean the fucken cat meowing all over the place. Sirens are normal. This is Mangree remember, not Ponce fucking Zombie.'

'Honey, please don't do it, you'll wake the kids.'

'Bugger the bloody kids. What've they ever done for me? I don't even know if they're mine.'

'Don't be silly, Hon, of course they're yours. I've had an onioni twice with you and got hapū each time. You know I make everyone else use protection. You're so big and strong you don't need to use any.'

'Blah blah blah blah. So how come there's three kids out there then, Missy pantsonfire brainbox?'

'No there's not! You can't count for shit!'

'Yes I can. Rua and Toru and then that cocobum kid that looks like that Sione prick next door.'

'Yeah, that's his kid. Fa. He's very close to our two boys and stays over a lot.'

'So how come Sione and his wife only have girls then?'

'Dunno. The boy must be an accident. Come on, Manu, put the gun away and come back to bed and smoke a pipe or two with me.'

'Nah. I'd rather smoke the fucken cat, then Sione. One for the money and two for the 'ho. Shit! Who's that knocking at the door at this time in the morning?'

'It's the afternoon, Reizenstein.'

Manu takes a quick look out the window and hurriedly moves back against the wall.

'Bugger bum! It's the cops. What the hell do they want?'

'Probably heard the cat meowing. Better put the gun and your turkey buzzard away and answer the door before they knock it down.'

'You answer it. There's warrants out for me.'

'Ummm. That's traffic fines and the odd vehicular homicide from when you ran over the neighbour's cat.'

'That was a dog and it was a bloody mongrel. Pissed on my wheels. Wasn't my fault it fell asleep in the middle of the road.'

'You were the one who fell asleep. The dog was on the neighbour's front lawn behind the fence. Sione loved that dog more than his own son, I can tell you that for sure.'

'Exactly. It was an ugly fence. Anyway how do we know these guys are real cops? Remember on the news that guy that posed as a cop and raped that chick in the next street? They gave out warnings, he's still around. Tell you what – you answer the door. See if you get any response, you're not bad-looking when we're all drunk. I'll back you up.'

'No way. I'm not taking any chances with cops. I watched this thing about police group sex and videos on the old education channel, doing it with female bodybuilders and filming it and stuff. Real.'

'Real? Bodybuilders? Well Missy, that leaves you out, unless you've got a spare body kit lying around!'

Manu sits down on the edge of the bed and uses the business end of the sawn-off to scratch the back of his head.

'Actually, come to think of it, I remember reading about a cop who used his police iPhone to video a young chick having a shower at his house. Jeez these guys are perverts, why can't they watch revenge porn with the rest of us no-brainers? Bet they sell their stuff to the local video store.'

'Hon, speaking of showers, I can't go out, it's almost my time of the month.'

'It's always your bloody time of the month. Even when it isn't. Okay fuck it! I'll go. If I'm raped and they video it, it'll be your fault.'

Dressed in denim cut-off shorts with sawn-off inserted at the back, cut-off shirt showing heavily tattooed arms, tied-back dreads, with a couple of strategically placed puffs of Dolce and Gabbana's 'The One', Manu opens the front door cautiously. Two uniformed police in stab vests, one tall, the other short, both with iridescent crimson-dyed hair and thick horn-rimmed glasses, looking like an Asian Peter Cook and Dudley Moore on non-synthetic $5-shop magic mushrooms and peyote buttons, stare quizzically back at him.

'What up dog?' the shorter one asks, politely but enthusiastically.

Manu looks around for camera lights or anything resembling women wrestlers, and, finding none, turns his attention to the two men, his right hand holding the grip of the sawn-off firmly behind his back and his prison glove held up like a traffic stop sign.

'Fuck me dead with a shovel and call me a taxi. Great disguise hombres – undercover detectives? East Auckland's the other way round. If you're really lost, try Chinatown next to the Aurora cathouse by the Federal Street Deli and the Casino. Say hello to the barmaid at the Glass Goose for me, would you?'

'Sir, we're actually from Auckland Central Police, Community Relations, and Asian Task Force. We were just coming from the Bader Drive market when we got a call. Are you Manu Iti by any chance?'

'Maybe. Who told you I was, if I am, which I'm not if I was?'

'A little bird did, sir, like the one in the cage behind you.'

'Well actually, I'm Manunui. Big bird. Big Pecker, big flapper. Who are you little peckers? Never seen an Asian cop before. Round here cops are usually Pākehā dickheads. White on the outside and yellow on the inside.'

The shorter cop nodded vigorously. The movements, accompanied by the pixilating sun reflecting off large overbite gleaming white teeth, momentarily caused Manu to hallucinate that he was at a beaver conference.

'Yes sir, you know how you coconut guys are brown on the outside and white on the inside? Look on us as bananas. Yellow on the outside and white on the inside. You and us are both tattooed with the same airbrush underneath.'

Manu is not impressed.

'Dog, easy on the coconut icing desiccating. Do I look like OMC? Or got up in the last Dawn Raids? I'm Māori bro, better believe it. Sieg Heil!'

'You're Mouldy?'

'Hard! Tangata whenua. Aotearoa bread and butchered!'

'Tongue in the manure? Excuse please, what sort of fruit is that?'

'Easy bro, don't push it. There's no way I'm a fruit. What you do in prison is what you do in prison.'

'No excuses please, for me to understand. What fruit if not a coconut?'

'Kūmara bro – brown outside, off-white inside.'

'But I no understand, kūmara a vegetable. Purple on outside like gay colour, orange on inside like prison jumpsuit.'

'Sir,' the tall Peter Cook intervened politely, 'do you own a black Holden – rego number S U P D O G?'

'Aw for Christ's sake! It's not about that fucken mongrel is it? Look, the bloody thing pissed on my car. I had to fucken knock it. Dog eat dog round here. What am I supposed to do? I got a fucken rep to uphold.'

'Sir, do you mind with the language please?'

'No I don't fucken mind. It's my fucken language. I fucken speak it better than you fucken canaries do. Where's your IDs? I don't trust you. I heard some weird sex stories about kinky kops and threesomes on the job at Harlech House. Show me the fucken IDs!'

The taller cop smiled winningly and in a placating tone, with matching multiple morpho-butterfly blinks, tried again.

'Look, sir, we don't want to cause any trouble on Thanksgiving Day. Do you own a –'

Manu had had enough. He grabbed the shotgun from the back of his shorts and pointed it at the two men, holding it in both hands and cocking back the hammers, spreading his legs a little to stop his shorts from falling down.

'Listen candy flossies, show me your bloody IDs now or I'll clip your tickets for the last train home to Clarksville! They'd better not be from the Asian copyshop up the road where I got my driver's licence and passport.'

'Sir, put the gun down please. We don't want accident here.'

The shorter cop held up his hand in warning, a Taser held in place by his thumb.

'Let me put it this way, ossifer. I've killed a dog, I was going to kill my cat, I've got a bird locked up behind me, a wife who's bleeding upstairs and now there's two pigs at my door. Get the connection? This ain't Animal Farm, cuz, and we ain't playing Sesame Street.'

'Sir, I'll have to use my Taser on you.'

No response.

'Sir, put the gun down!'

'Fuck off.'

Zzzsst! A flash like the afternoon sun ignited and shot languid tentative tentacles of elasticated livewire clawing into Manu's chest. His eyes dilated: zombie killer. He fell backwards, Richard Harris Sundance style. The shotgun ignited and shot both barrels at the large birdcage standing in the lounge behind Manu. The cage and the bird inside it exploded and the heavy cage bottom fell onto the hopeful cat sitting underneath, feathers and fur flying. The cat's short sharp death scream was followed by a shrill bellow from the bedroom as, after a moment or five, Missy came running out, naked skin trembling inside a short silk dressing gown.

'You little bastard! What have you done to him?'

The shorter cop looked uncomfortably at the blonde haired, brown skinned, semi-naked banshee apparition that had appeared before him from nowhere, and quickly moved the Taser to recharge with a trembling thumb and forefinger.

'Madam, we're from Community Relations. We had to Taser him, there was no other way,' he began to stammer. Missy looked at him disdainfully.

'Not you, Columbo. Fuck-head here. He's just killed my cat.'

Missy started to kick Manu in the face with her bare feet, making his nose bleed and right eye close, the movements jiggling her full breasts out of her dressing gown and into the hallway. The cop's eyes dilated in Taser-like illumination, flickering zombie killer before dousing.

'Madam! Do you mind covering, um, yourself up please? Take a couple of deep breasts and relax. We're trained in this sort of thing. He'll have to be taken to Central and processed. We'll be gone for a while.'

Missy looked closer at Dudley and faltered mid-kick, clinging to him and breathing heavily, hastily covered breasts stabbing sharp nipples repeatedly into his protective vest with each breath. She pushed her hair back from her face, which coincidentally pushed her pelvis into the cop's growing groin area.

'Sorry, Hon. I'm a bit overwrought. Are you boys trained in deep massage by any chance? I've just undergone deep trauma and need some counselling. You don't look anything like the cops on the education channel; in fact you both look quite cute and sexy!'

Manu started to stir groggily on the floor in front of them.

'You bastard Manu! You killed Precious and Fluffy!'

'What the fuck? I killed your slippers?'

'No, you prick! You shot my cat and the bird! They're both splattered all over the lounge thanks to you.'

'Sir, we are arresting you for the possession and presentation of an illegal firearm without lawful excuse and also discharging it with reckless disregard.'

'Look, guys, we're all men here, some more than others, I'll admit, but it's all a little misunderstanding, a storm in a titty cup. I was just going to feed the bloody cat to shut it up. You've met my wife. Doesn't every man have a right to silence?'

'Oh, sorry. Yes you have the right to remain silent, however anything you say can and will be used in evidence against you in a court of law. Peter, take him out to the wagon please, and stick him in with the other one.'

Missy and the shorter cop stand and watch in silence as Manu is led out, wrists trussed with blue plastic, the sawn-off shotgun bundled into an evidence bag.

'Madam, do you know the owner of a white van? The driver was intoxicated and crashed into your friend's car. There's a funny smell like dead bodies inside the van and signs of attempts to clean blood and flesh up from the interior. The driver had this boy in the van with him who said you're his mother – is he yours? He's the spitting image of this Sione guy we're holding on suspicion. Couldn't get any sense out of the guy, he just kept saying, "How bizarre, how bizarre."'

'Sione? Please call me Missy, it's a bit more friendly, like. Unfortunately I can neither confirm nor deny that the boy belongs to his father. Go to your room and see Toru, fa please,' she says to the boy sweetly.

Hustling him off down the hallway into the bedroom and locking the door behind him, she returns to the cop, folding her arms under her breasts so that they appear even bigger and the short robe shorter. Her smile is as inviting as a cat looking at a caged bird.

'Can I borrow you boys for the next hour or so before you go? I'd love a kid with red hair like yours. I've always had good community relationships with the Police. Nothing on video or anything like that, but I don't mind rehearsing. I'm traumatised and very horny. Feathers and fur and blood and violence does that to me. We can de-brief together and negotiate price later if you like.'

Sione is slumped in a stupor in the corner of the paddy wagon. He rouses himself as Manu climbs in and kicks and swears at the door as it is slammed closed on them and locked. Sione curses to himself and then puts on a broad pastor-accepting-donation smile.

'Manu! Hey bro. What've they got you for? Going by your nose and the bruises on your face you put up a mighty big fight.'

'Yeah, cuz. Tough country. Would you believe I was just ganking after this cat who'd been giving me a lot of grief and wouldn't shut up his whining? I got so fed up with the prick, I gave him a short sharp and long one with the shottie and ended up killing him and this bird who was sitting on top of him at the time. Both barrels. Boo-yah! Blood and guts everywhere, what a mess!'

'Wow, bro. Hard! Poor guy musta thought he was in heaven between the pearly gates getting his end away, but just got his end! How'd the cops jack you so quick?'

'Pure bad luck, wrong place at the wrong time. Apparently they saw it all going down. I was so out of it at the time I don't remember anything til the wife gave me a nudge. She was pretty pissed, I can tell you. Boots and all. What'd they get you for, cuz?'

'You wouldn't believe it, bro. Drunk in charge and killing a couple of pigs in the back of the van. Thought I'd cleaned it all up.'

'Pigs? Really? Shot, cuz! Don't blame you for killing the fuckers. You see the calibre of cops they got around here nowadays? Nothing like the old days. These two look like a pair of comedians. Don't know what the world's coming to. Seems everything comes from China these days, even dim sums and wontons. We'd make better cops than these guys. Think they musta been recruited from the market gardens by the airport. The short one said they came from there. Not sure where they got their ginger hair from, though.'

'True brew.'

Sione crossed his arms and settled back against the window to doze. Manu looked at him and then past him out through the window.

'Shit, bro! Who smashed into my car? There's a fucken white van climbed all over it like a bulldog caught rooting his old lady's fur coat. Hey, wait a minute, looks like your fucken church piece of shit. That your fucken van, Sione? I'll fucken kill you for this! You prick! It took me years to steal the parts for that car! Where's the fucken cops when you want them?'

Sione leant back from the window and squinted blearily out against the glare.

'Nah, Manu, wasn't me, dog. That's not my piece of shit. God's honour. I've just got back from church. Took your son. Even if that shit black cat of yours ran in front of me, I wouldn't take the risk. I know how much you love that cat, just like that dog of mine someone did a hit and run on.'

'Church? Cat? Oh. Sorry about your fucken dog. It was an accident. I was pissed as a mute and the stupid thing was asleep in the middle of the road. I had no choice. Besides, it was a fucken ugly little mutt anyway. Missy's pussy had more growl than that shit thing.'

'Yeah. That's okay, bro. No harm done. Sorry for fucking your ugly mutt missus as well. I had the same problem.'

'What'd you say Sione? You taking the piss, bro? You want me to fuck you over?'

'Nah, nah, bro. It's all cool. I said, sorry for flipping your nut biscuits.'

'That's what I thought you said. Okay, sorry. Must be cause I'm hungry. I feel like a feed now. Never got a chance to have anything this morning before Bill and Ben turned up. Hope these two clowns get us to the big huey in time for dinner cuz, long as it's not Chinese. I've gone off Asian food at the moment.'

'Amen to that, bro. What are you looking at?'

'Ah, nothing. Just wonder what's keeping the gingerbred boys so long? They should have finished with Missy by now and got out of there. Hope they're not giving her a hard time.'

Manu sat and thought for a while. His nose hurt.

'Hey, Sione? You didn't notice if those fools were carrying a video camera, did you?'

'Nah, bro, just the usual Police issue iPhone pluses, got a good camera on them apparently. Just point and shoot, same with video. Everything's digital nowadays.'

The Authors

PIRIPI EVANS

Piripi Evans was born in 1971 in Ōtautahi, and grew up in Te Whanganui-a-Tara, where he lives with his wife and three children. He is of Ngāti Mutunga and Kāi Tahu descent. He came across the phrase 'late antiquity' while gaining a post-graduate degree in Classical Studies from Victoria University. He balances writing with a full-time job and whānau, and regards himself as a young writer with potential, given that fifty is the new forty. His stories have previously been published in *Huia Short Stories* 8, 9 and 10.

ANN FRENCH

I believe neither age nor gender should be a barrier to doing anything in life.

I began to write at fifty when I wrote a column in a small rural paper for and about women. My husband was almost banned from the local pub and told he should beat me more often, but he only snorted and said, 'You're willing to try.' Which is why we've been married fifty-two years. After six months they stopped printing my column, saying it courted controversy, so I took that as a nod I had accomplished something. It showed me the power of the written word and how it can polarise people and opinions.

Taking my writing seriously, I wrote horror stories.

Entering writing competitions, I had minor successes, but then turned to science fiction. There is a lot of scope with sci-fi and I wrote about the Apocalypse, the world running out of water, flying cockroaches and giant spiders who secretly ruled the world. I also solved the mystery of JFK's assassination but no one was interested.

Endeavouring to be more scholarly, I went to night school and took a class in creative writing, shortly afterwards winning US$1,000 in Saudi Arabia and then first and second place in an Australian short story competition. They changed the rules after that, making it more difficult for New Zealanders to enter.

I completed an on-line course through Whitireia that took two years. I was the first person to receive a diploma for writing from the polytechnic, and I discovered I wasn't half as smart as I thought I was.

Huia Publishers came along and, thanks to them, I have managed to achieve high standards and goals. They have published many of my stories and have solidified my belief that at seventy-two, you are never too old.

The Authors

JAMES GEORGE

James George is a novelist and short story writer of Ngāpuhi, English and Irish descent. He is author of *Wooden Horses* (Hazard Press, 2000), *Hummingbird* (Huia, 2003) and *Ocean Roads* (Huia, 2006). *Zeta Orionis* (an excerpt from *Hummingbird*) won the premiere award in the 2001 Māori Literature Awards, judged by Keri Hulme. James's short fiction has appeared in anthologies such as: *Second Violins* (Vintage, 2008); *The Best New Zealand Fiction* (twice) (Vintage), and *Get on the Waka – Best Recent Māori Fiction* (Raupo Publishing, 2007). Writing in the NZ Herald, Margie Thomson described *Hummingbird* as 'demanding and ambitious … [and] above all incredibly moving'. Writing also in the NZ Herald of James George's short story 'Walking to Laetoli' in *The Best New Zealand Fiction* Volume 1, reviewer Siobhan Harvey said: 'George's stunning Walking To Laetoli lovingly explores the dysfunctions of father and son relationships. Like all of George's offerings, it's wonderful reading.'

Amongst his awards and prizes, his second novel *Hummingbird* was a finalist in the Montana New Zealand Book Awards 2004 and the Tasmania Pacific Fiction Prize 2005. *Ocean Roads* appeared on the 2007 Commonwealth Writers' Prize shortlist as one of the best books in the South East Asia and South Pacific region, and was shortlisted in the fiction category of the Montana New Zealand Book Awards 2007. James was also a recipient of the Buddle Findlay Sargeson Fellowship in 2007.

James is completing his fourth novel, *Sleepwalkers' Songs*, to be published by Huia. He teaches creative writing at AUT in Auckland, on both the BA and MCW programmes.

PATRICIA GRACE

Patricia Grace (Ngāti Toa Rangatira, Ngāti Raukawa, Te Ātiawa) is the author of many well-loved and award-winning novels, short stories and children's books. She has won numerous awards, including the Kiriyama Pacific Rim Book Prize for Fiction for her book *Dogside Story* and the Nielsen BookData New Zealand Bookseller's Choice Award for her novel *Tu*, and was the 2008 laureate of the Neustadt International Prize for Literature. *Tu* won the Montana New Zealand Book Awards for best book of fiction for 2005 as well as the Deutz Medal for fiction or poetry 2005. Patricia has also been long-listed for the Booker Prize.

Patricia received a Distinguished Companion of the New Zealand Order of Merit for her services to literature in 2007 and was the Honoured New Zealand Writer at the Auckland Writers Festival in 2014.

Patricia's most recent work is a children's book retelling the origins of the Ngāti Toa haka 'Ka Mate', *Haka*, and the Māori language version, *Whiti te Rā!*

BRIAR GRACE-SMITH

Briar is of Ngāpuhi descent and is an award-winning writer of plays, feature film screenplays, short fiction and radio and television scripts. She was an inaugural recipient of the Arts Foundation Award and was the Writer in Residence at Victoria University in 2003. Her short fiction has been published in various anthologies, and her plays include *Purapurawhetū, Ngā Pou Wāhine, When Sun and Moon Collide* and *Paniora!* Briar's first feature film, *The Strength of Water*, premiered at the Rotterdam and Berlin Film Festivals in 2009, and the comedy horror *Fresh Meat* played in the Midnight section of the Tribeca Film Festival in 2013. Briar's television credits include *Fishskin*

Suit, Kaitangata Twitch and *This is Piki* (2016). She has worked as a development executive for the New Zealand Film Commission, and taught Writing for Theatre at the International Institute of Modern Letters, Victoria University. Briar lives in Paekākāriki on the Kāpiti Coast with her whānau, including two cats and one dog.

K-T HARRISON

Kia ora, I'm not gonna write broken arse any more, and if I do, it's not gonna be my arse that's broke.

> But, hey ehoa, my treaty partner
> Take my hand
> I'll show you how to poi – ay?
> Watch me, see me spiral away,
> From a con-structed narrative centre
> To a thematically, culturally safe one
> I watch; learn, know, perfect
> See – I make myself my own.
> *Nemesis in mimesis.*

(from 'Theoretical Fringe Benefits', by K-t Harrison, *Mayhem*, spring 2015)

ERU J HART

Eru J Hart (Ngāti Kahungunu, Ngāi Te Whatuiapiti) is a 36-year-old writer, born in Hawke's Bay, who chooses to live in Wellington. He currently teaches English at Wellington High School. Several of his short stories have been published by Huia and appear in their *Huia Short Stories* anthologies. In 2005 he won Best Short Story in English at the Māori Writers Awards, for a piece called 'Who Bore the Force', which subsequently aired as a play on Radio New Zealand.

Eru studied creative writing at the International Institute of Modern Letters at Victoria University, but is ambivalent about the value of such experiences. He grew up in a home with no books, apart from the Scriptures and commentaries on Scriptures, which no one was reading anyway. He sees books as magical devices, capable of lifting children out of poverty. He spends much of his working week trying to divert teenagers' attention away from bright flashing screens that make a lot of noise.

His first novel, *The Clockwork of gods*, is due for release by Huia Publishers in 2016.

TINA MAKERETI

Tina Makereti writes novels, essays and short stories. Her newest short story, 'Black Milk', recently won the Pacific Regional Commonwealth Short Story Prize (2016). Her first novel, *Where the Rēkohu Bone Sings* (Vintage, 2014) has been described as 'a remarkable [book that] spans generations of Moriori, Māori and Pākehā descendants as they grapple with a legacy of pacifism, violent domination and cross-cultural dilemmas.' It has been longlisted for the Dublin Literary Award and won the 2014 Ngā Kupu Ora Aotearoa Māori Book Award for Fiction, also won by her short story collection, *Once Upon a Time in Aotearoa* (Huia, 2010). In 2009 Tina was the recipient of the Royal Society of New Zealand Manhire Prize for Creative Science Writing (Non-fiction) and the Pikihuia Award for Best Short Story Written in English. She has been writer in residence at Randell Cottage, Wellington, and the Weltkulturen Museum, Frankfurt. 'Frau Amsel's Cupboard' was written during that residency, and originally published in *Sport 42*.

Tina is also a teacher and curator, convening the Māori and Pasifika Creative Writing Workshop at Victoria University. She is of Ngāti Tūwharetoa, Te Ati Awa, Ngāti Rangatahi, Pākehā and, according to family stories, Moriori descent.

JACQUIE MCRAE

Jacquie McRae (Tainui) lives in Te Arai with her husband, and has three young adult children. A late starter to writing, she has twice been a Pikihuia Awards finalist and received a place on the inaugural Te Papa Tupu scheme that mentors emerging writers. Her first novel, *The Scent of Apples*, won a gold medal in the 2012 Independent Publisher Book Awards (the 'IPPYs') in New York. The same year it was selected by the International Youth Library in Munich and received a White Ravens label.

Last year Jacquie completed a Masters in Creative Writing with first class honours. She is currently working on a draft of the novel she produced for her Masters. Her ultimate goal is to be in a position that encourages more people to write.

'Writing is how I make sense of the world. It's like therapy, except it's free.'

PAULA MORRIS

Paula Morris (Ngāti Wai, Ngāti Whātua) was born in Auckland, and has spent much of her adult life in the UK or the US. She is the author of the story collection *Forbidden Cities* (2008) and seven novels, including *Queen of Beauty* (2002), *Hibiscus Coast* (2005), and *Rangatira* (2011), fiction winner at both the 2012 New Zealand Post Book Awards and

Ngā Kupu Ora Māori Book Awards. Her most recent publications include a children's book, *Hene and the Burning Harbour* (2013), and a long-form essay, *On Coming Home* (2015). The founder of the Academy of New Zealand Literature (www.anzliterature.com), she teaches creative writing at the University of Auckland.

ANYA NGAWHARE

Anya Ngawhare lives in the Bay of Plenty, where she spends most of her time chasing after her three-year-old niece and her growing collection of costly, oddball animals. When she was nineteen, her strong-willed parents forced her to pursue her dream of becoming an author. She completed her NZIBS Creative Writing Diploma one day before finding out she had been selected for the 2012 Te Papa Tupu Programme, and in 2015 she received a highly commended award in the novel extract category of the Pikihuia Awards. The short story she entered was also chosen for publication.

TONI PIVAC

Toni Pivac (Ngāti Whātua, Te Rarawa, Ngāpuhi) wants to live in a world where kindness reigns supreme, books come bundled with her favourite snacks and keyboards have force fields that repel spilled coffee and sticky fingers. With the support and encouragement of Huia Publishers, she has finally embraced the notion that she is, in fact, a writer, and as a writer, is a two-time winner of the Pikihuia Awards best short story written in English and has been published in *Huia Short Stories* 10 and 11. She holds a Bachelor of Communication Studies from AUT University, a qualification she aspired to obtain having always enjoyed the strange and wonderful world of storytelling in all its forms. Fiction is and always will be her passion, though.

She lives in her hometown of Whangārei, where she leads a full and happy life with her partner, Wiremu, and two children, Mila and Matija. She currently works part-time as a self-employed typist and communications consultant, and full-time as a mother to her beautiful tamariki. She somehow manages to squeeze in writing between family, work and life in general.

From a young age, Toni fell in love with stories under the guidance of her storyteller father and would often be found hidden behind the pages of a novel. She understands that storytelling is an extremely powerful instrument that humans have to communicate and motivate and knows that stories can entertain, teach and move us. Toni doesn't often follow the advice to write what she knows and instead writes stories to explore ideas and emotions and to experience things from someone else's perspective. She writes to make sense of the world and figure things out.

When she's not working, writing or playing hockey, Toni can normally be found exploring with her family, or making and unmaking messes with her kids. Toni is a dreamer who believes in the enormous power of storytelling and is convinced that it can change the world.

RENÉE

Renée is a playwright, fiction and nonfiction writer, mentor and teacher and has published many novels, plays and one short story collection. In 2013 she was awarded the Kingi Ihaka Award in recognition of a lifetime contribution to Ngā Toi Māori, and in 2015 received the New Zealand Screenwriters Guild Mentorship Award for her teaching and mentoring of both aspiring and experienced writers.

Renée is writing her life story as a piece of crazy patchwork, and each Wednesday a new patch is published on her blog, WednesdayBusk.

TERENCE RISSETTO

Terence Rissetto is of Ngāti Pāoa, Kāi Tahu, Ngāti Māmoe, Waitaha and European descent. Besides a seven-year stint as a psychiatric nurse in Melbourne, he is a long-time resident of South Auckland. Currently a public servant, he has several degrees from the University of Auckland and several from the school of life.

Terence's stories are about the dispossessed and possessed, the displaced and misplaced, the affluent and the effluent, the outsiders and the absurd; ordinary people living ordinary lives, told with an underlying humour and irony. For him, writing creates an order on the chaos of the world, and in turn creates the possibility of a new chaos.

Terence has had work published in *Landfall*, *Huia Short Stories*, *Takahē*, *Café Reader*, *Penduline Press*, *Blackmail Online* and *Bold Monkey Online*, and was chosen for the 2014 Te Papa Tupu Incubator Programme. His resulting collection of short stories, *Theatres of the Absurd*, awaits publication by a generous publisher. Terence can be contacted at terraroxa52@gmail.com.

The Authors

MARK SWEET

Hawke's Bay–born Mark Sweet, of Titahi hapū – Ngā Māhanga descent, took up writing after selling Pacifica restaurant (Napier) in 2007. Previously he had established the Two Fat Ladies restaurant in Glasgow (1988) after working as a property valuer in Hong Kong. His first novel, *Zhu Mao* (Huia), was published in 2011 after Mark was mentored in the Te Papa Tupu writing incubator programme. His next, *Going Down of the Sun*, set in Hawke's Bay in the 1960s, is due to be published in 2017. As well as fiction writing, Mark is a regular contributor to *Baybuzz* magazine, focusing on environmental and social justice issues.

ALICE TAWHAI

Alice Tawhai is the author of three short story collections: *Festival of Miracles*, *Luminous* and *Dark Jelly*, all published by Huia. She was inspired to start writing when she read Keri Hulme's *The Bone People* as a teenager, and loved it big-time.

Alice thinks of writing stories as being like painting with words. The colours and the shades have to be exactly right. She doesn't start each story at the beginning and finish at the end, she just writes random paragraphs until she knows that they're all there, and then she strings them together in an order that makes some sort of sense. Alice is a happy, sunny person who likes to laugh. She hopes that her stories might be for people whose voices aren't often heard.

HELEN WAAKA

Helen Margaret Waaka (Ngāti Whātua, Ngāti Torehina) completed a Graduate Diploma in Creative Writing at Whitireia in 2011. In the same year she won the Pikihuia Award for best English-language short story, with 'Hineraumati'.

Her stories have appeared in Huia's short story collections 9, 10 and 11. Her first book, *Waitapu*, a collection of interconnected short stories, was published by Escalator Press in October 2015 and was listed twice, by Albert Wendt and Paora Tibble, in the Booknotes Unbound 2015 list of favourite books. Reina Whaitiri, Pikihuia judge for 2011 and 2013, described the stories in *Waitapu* as 'real, authentic and close to the bone.'

Some of the characters from Helen's debut collection appear in 'The Apology', which explores an event referred to in *Waitapu* in more depth. There is a slight change to the original storyline, however, to bring Rowena's sister, Ruby, into the story. 'The Apology' will appear in some form in Helen's second book, a novel, which she is currently working on.

Helen works part-time as a nurse in Hawke's Bay. She thanks her family for their ongoing support of her writing, which she finds incredibly hard, but rewarding work. She especially thanks her readers. Ngā mihi nui ki a koutou katoa.

MAUALAIVAO ALBERT WENDT

Albert Wendt is one of the Pacific's and New Zealand's most renowned authors and has been influential in the development of New Zealand and Pacific literature. He has an extensive list of works and has received many literary prizes, including the Prime Minister's Award for Literary Achievement in Fiction 2012. In the 2013 Queen's Birthday Honours he was appointed a member of the Order of New Zealand. His most recent novel, *Breaking Connections*, was published by Huia in 2015. The two stories in this collection are from his short story collection *Ancestry* (Huia 2012).